WINGED LOVE

Torn by love, torn by war...

Maurice Dupont, the young French pilot attached to Neil Richardson's squadron as a liaison officer, talked of nothing but his fiancée, Julie – a girl as warm and beautiful as his homeland, Provence. He wanted so badly for his friend to meet her. The problem was that when they did meet, the Englishman fell in love with the adorable Julie and she with him. Now, out of loyalty to Maurice, Neil and Julie must strive to extinguish their passionate love – and meanwhile the merciless German war machine sweeps across France, shattering the hopes of nations and individuals alike.

WINGED LOVE

WINGED LOVE

by

Denise Robins

Dales Large Print Books
Long Preston, North Yorkshire,
BD23 4ND, England.

British Library Cataloguing in Publication Data.

Robins, Denise
    Winged love.

A catalogue record of this book is
available from the British Library

ISBN   978-1-84262-813-3 pbk

First published in Great Britain
by Hutchinson & Co. (Publishers) Ltd., 1978

Cover illustration © Ellie Belcher by arrangement with
Arcangel Images

The moral right of the author has been asserted

Published in Large Print 2011 by arrangement with
Patricia Clark for Executors of Denise Robins' Estate

Dales Large Print is an imprint of Library Magna Books Ltd.

Printed and bound in Great Britain by
T.J. (International) Ltd., Cornwall, PL28 8RW

1

It was Maurice Dupont himself who suggested to Neil Richardson that he should spend his sick leave in Provence.

The young French aviator had for the last six months been attached as liaison officer to the R.A.F. Reconnaissance Unit in which Neil had recently been promoted to flight-lieutenant.

In the last week of May, Neil had just escaped by the skin of his teeth from being shot down whilst flying over the Siegfried Line with a pilot-officer who was taking photographs. With a German bullet in his left shoulder, Neil had managed to bring his machine back to the French lines, and now for the last three weeks he had been in hospital.

It was on a perfect day of June that he was discharged from the hospital, and returned to collect his belongings from the Château de la Marche, in La Chaume, where his unit was stationed ninety miles behind the Maginot Line.

Maurice Dupont, *lieutenant d'avion,* had shared a bedroom with the English airman ever since his attachment, and they had become great friends. Maurice had missed Neil while he was in hospital.

Maurice sat on the edge of the bed smoking, whilst Neil packed his suitcases.

'I am getting quite adept at doing everything with one hand,' Neil said with a smile, as he paused to light a cigarette for himself, and inspect his labours.

'*Mon Dieu,* but you are lucky, to get away from this place and have some peace and some amusement,' said Maurice Dupont with a sigh.

'I'd rather not have had the bullet through my shoulder all the same,' said Neil Richardson. 'Don't much care for being an invalid.'

'But, *mon brave,* you will now not be an invalid any more, you will have an arm in a sling and all the pretty women will look at you, and what a time you will have!' exclaimed the young French officer.

'I'm not particularly interested in pretty women.'

'Ah! That is because you have not met one like my Julie.'

'Maybe...' admitted Neil, and his gaze turned to the photograph which stood on Dupont's dressing-table.

It was a photograph with which he was now very familiar. He had lived with it for the last six months. He knew every feature of it by heart. It was the only photograph in the room because Neil, himself, had brought none out here. His mother was dead and he was neither engaged to nor sufficiently interested in any girl to carry her likeness about with him.

But he had become accustomed to the portrait of Julie de Vallois who was Maurice Dupont's fiancée. Accustomed also to Maurice's perpetual stories about her. Had they been uninteresting stories, Neil might have been bored. But it seemed that this Julie was a very unusual girl, and, in Neil's opinion, the young Frenchman's perpetual rhapsodies were justified by the remarkable beauty of the girl's face.

Neil looked at it thoughtfully while Maurice made the suggestion that he should go for his sick leave to the fishing village of La Marita, where Julie lived.

Julie's eyes looked back at Neil. Large soft eyes with sweeping lashes which, Maurice said, were raven-black like the delicate crescent brows. But that cloud of hair, looped back from her forehead and fastened with a bow at the nape of the neck, was of silver fairness. She was a true blonde, Maurice said, and had that exquisite skin which goes with it, but her face was a golden tan because she lived in the sun. She was a child of the sun. When she was not working at the hospital-supplies depot in Aix, she was out on the sea in her boat. A motor boat which she ran herself. They had an island in

La Marita. Julie's special island on which she spent long hours bathing, fishing, lying in the sun.

She adored music and she sang. Maurice had repeated for Neil the words of some of her songs. Little French sentimental songs which sounded delightful in her sweet crooning voice.

Parlez moi d'amour ... that was one of her favourites. Maurice was always humming it. It was a tune which Neil now associated with the young French officer. And he associated it also with Julie de Vallois.

So many details had he heard about Julie that he felt that he knew her. The name of her favourite scent. The way she loved to take the stalk of a cherry between her lips and then with a little quick movement jerk the ripe fruit into her mouth and laugh as the small teeth crushed it. Her amazing knowledge of flowers and the very names of the flowers which grew in profusion on the island of La Marita.

Maurice was talking about those flowers now.

'You couldn't find a lovelier place for a rest cure, *mon cher ami*. The fuchsias, the zinnias of every exotic colour, the golden broom, like a sheet of gold over the rocks. Your arm is wounded, but your two legs are sound and you can climb to the top of Julie's island, as high as the crucifix which stands upon it, and you can look down on the blue sea and on the mountains behind the village. Ah! You do not know the beauty, the wonder of our Provence in June!'

Neil Richardson listened as he had listened a hundred times to Maurice. The young French aviator was a little too theatrical, too exaggerated at times for the Englishman, who had the reserve of his race and felt a slight embarrassment at any undue display of emotion. Yet he could not listen to Maurice without his attention being caught and held; without some envy of him, too.

It must be pretty good to come from a place like Provence and to dream of La Marita and of Julie with her dark eyes, her silvery hair, her cherry-loving lips, her songs of love, waiting for you to come home on leave. Waiting for you to marry her. They were going to be married in the autumn, Maurice said. They had been betrothed for two years now, since Julie's eighteenth birthday. They had known each other since they were children, when both their families had lived at Aix. They had always known, according to Maurice, that one day they would be husband and wife.

Julie was not wholly French. She had had an Irish mother. Gaston de Vallois, her father, who was once a prosperous wine merchant of Aix (since retired), had spent a fishing holiday in Ireland and had met his

11

wife there. From her Julie had inherited that dazzling complexion … the cleft in her chin … her varying moods. Maurice had told Neil how moody she could be … up and down like a thermometer … but it was fascinating … it made her an enchanting mixture, he said … the Irish and the French.

Neil was sure of it. Funnily enough he had always told himself that when he married it would be either to an Irish girl or a French one. Women of both countries appealed to him, and here was Julie de Vallois with the blood of both in her veins. Doubtless Maurice did not exaggerate her charms. There were moments when Neil had an uneasy peculiar longing to see this girl. He had thought about her while he was in hospital. He had grown so used to hearing news of her. Every other day or so, Maurice read him bits from the thin, closely written sheets of note-paper … letters from La Marita. Yet he had never dreamed until today of actually going to see Julie herself.

'There is a hotel in La Marita in which you can stay. I myself will wire to Madame Huillard who runs it. And you will receive every attention, *mon brave*,' said Maurice at this moment. 'Yes, you tell me that you have nowhere to go, and no family waiting to welcome you in England, so why not spend your few weeks of convalescence there in Julie's village? And you shall write to me and tell me how she looks and take photographs of her to send to me. *Hein?* Is it not a good idea?'

Neil Richardson hesitated, but only for a moment. What Maurice said was true. He had nobody in particular waiting for him in England. Only an aunt at whose house he was always welcome. But as for women ... Neil liked beautiful women just as he liked everything that was beautiful. He had light passing affairs like any other man of his age. But there was never anybody in particular. In the mess it was a bit of a joke because Flight-Lieutenant Richardson was hard to please and not as ready as some of them to take out any little 'painted piece' who made eyes at the Air Force uniform.

No, his main interest in life was in his job, in his flying; and in helping to win this war. Now that this wound had taken that away from him temporarily he had to concentrate on getting well. Why not get well in this place which Maurice Dupont made out to be a paradise? A Provençal paradise! That sounded good. And he would have an introduction to Julie and her people.

He decided that he would go, and once having taken that decision began to look forward to it. A sunlit island, a profusion of flowers, warm starry nights, and the company of people whom he almost felt that he knew because he had heard so much about them ... that sounded attractive after the shock of his wound and the weary weeks of pain and discomfort in hospital. It had taken two operations to get that shoulder right.

Dupont was already writing out a telegram for Madame Huillard. He would send one of the troops down to the post office with it. His good friend Richardson would stay under the patronage of Madame at the Auberge du Clos Marita. It was right on the quayside and faced Julie's island. The fish that Madame cooked there... *Mon Dieu*, it was good, Maurice said enthusiastically. The *bouillabaisse* ... and the *gallette* of Madame's own baking... Richardson would never wish to leave La Marita once he had tasted it.

Maurice talked incessantly. There were so many things to tell Neil. He must give him a letter and a present to Julie. He must ask how her pigeons were faring. She had two tame pigeons which she had trained and which sat one on each shoulder. Their names were Co-co and Ton-ton (yes, Neil had heard about Co-co and Ton-ton before). He would be greeting the pigeons like old friends, he told himself with some amusement. And he would ask her to sing all the songs which he had heard Maurice trying to sing (but Maurice had no ear for music). Neil loved it. Music had been his hobby before he entered the Air Force. The only thing to which he looked forward on leave was going to a good concert or opera.

14

But on this leave he must content himself, apparently, with Julie's singing.

He finished his packing, taking in all that Maurice was telling him. He paused in front of the glass to straighten a lock of hair which had fallen across his eye. Maurice looked at him and laughed.

'*Voilà!* You see something worth while to regard, is it not so? I told Julie in my last letter that my English friend, Flight-Lieutenant Richardson, was of a great handsomeness. Julie likes tall men. I am, perhaps, too short; but I shall try not to be jealous of you, my friend...'

'You certainly need not be,' said Neil, echoing the laugh.

The two men were a complete contrast. Both aged about twenty-six or -seven the Frenchman was built broadly, fair-haired, blue-eyed, and of ruddy complexion. Neil had always found him a good officer and good-humoured, but without a great deal of personality. To Maurice Dupont, on the other hand, the English aviator was an outstanding person. He had a wit, a rapier quality of mind which Dupont admired enormously. Nothing went by Neil. He was alert and more sensitive, in the Frenchman's opinion, than the average Englishman he had met in this unit or elsewhere. He was also an unknown quantity, which made him all the more interesting. Maurice was never

15

quite sure what lay behind those keen grey eyes. He could be charming … he could be cold … withdraw suddenly into himself. He was without the Frenchman's gaiety, yet Maurice had never found a better companion than Neil. When Neil chose to be gay, he was the one in the mess who kept them all laughing. And as for looks, he was, of course, superb. Six foot one, broad-shouldered, slim-hipped. Not an ounce of superfluous fat on Neil's body. Face brown, a little thin. Hair of a dark chestnut brown with a slight wave which no amount of brushing or oiling could smooth out. A thoughtful face, but he had a sudden and very sweet smile, which showed white teeth, and in a flash made him look years younger.

He was utterly without conceit, which was one of the things that Maurice liked about him, and he was without fear. 'Devil Richardson' they called him in the Squadron, and it had been hinted last night that he would be recommended for the D.F.C. for the way he had brought his machine back with those invaluable photographs of the German fortifications.

Dupont was genuinely sorry to see his English friend go off on leave that afternoon, and definitely envious.

'I'm not due for leave for another four months. It breaks my heart to think of you tomorrow at La Marita, seeing my Julie,' he said, when he saw Neil off to Lille where he would get a train for Aix-en-Provence.

'It's very good of you, Maurice, to have given me all those introductions and settled my holiday for me,' said Neil. 'I'll drop you a line tomorrow night and tell you all about everything.'

As the train steamed out, Maurice ran alongside the train, his red plump face grinning at Neil.

'Don't forget to ask after Co-co and Tonton ... don't forget to take photographs of Julie ... and to kees her for me ... one little kees ... like a brother, *hein*...?' he shouted laughingly.

Neil Richardson leaned out of the window of the carriage, waved his cap at Maurice and shouted back:

'I won't forget anything...'

2

In the walled-in fruit garden of the Villa Vertige, Julie lay on the grass, smoked glasses protecting her eyes from the sun, reading again the telegram which Pierre, Madame Huillard's son, had just brought her. Pierre was in the post office.

It was a telegram from her fiancé, telling

her at length that the English aviator, Flight-Lieutenant Richardson, was on his way to La Marita. And Pierre said that his *maman* had also had one, asking her to reserve a bedroom for the English lieutenant. *Maman* was in a great excitement. The whole village was excited. They had not had an English flying officer here before. And as he was a friend of Maurice Dupont's, it made the event all the more momentous.

Julie stretched her arms out on either side of her and, with Maurice's telegram crushed in slim brown fingers, contemplated the news which she had just received.

The June sun was hot upon her face. She wore only a thin pink linen dress with no sleeves. Her throat and slight childish arms were tanned like her face to a golden brown. Her hair looked bleached against the green grass on which she was lying. Grass of which Julie was very proud because it resembled an English lawn. Ever since her family had moved her from Aix-en-Provence, they had concentrated on that piece of grass to please her mother. Everything green had pleased her dear Irish mother. Alas, she was dead now! There were few people in La Marita to whom Julie could speak the English she had been taught from birth, and which she spoke perfectly. And although she adored her native Provence, and in particular her beloved island, where she spent so many leisured hours, she had a great hunger for everything English.

Upstairs in her bedroom, there were rows of English books on the shelf. There was a big painting of the Lake of Killarney where her mother's people lived ... a landscape softened by a silver mist of rain ... it often rained in Ireland, Julie had learned. And it seldom rained here in La Marita where the sun shone nearly all the year round. But sometimes she would like to have felt that soft Irish rain upon her face, and to have seen London where her mother had been educated.

It was an excitement for Julie that an English officer was coming to stay at the Auberge de Clos Marita. She knew quite well what he looked like, because Maurice had described him in many letters. Richardson *le diable* he was called in the Squadron. He must be very brave, Julie reflected, and now he had been wounded by those vile Germans. Poor man! But here in La Marita he would soon get well again.

Julie pondered a few moments longer upon the thought of the Englishman's arrival and then sprang to her feet. She must go down to the quay and see old Jean Taupin about cleaning and oiling the machine of her motor boat. Neil Richardson would want to use it and go out to the island. It must be in good working order.

'Give him every hospitality and kindness...' Maurice had said in the wire. Well, of course, she would do so. She would tell everybody else to look after him, too. Was he not their English ally and Maurice's friend? She, Julie, could not always keep an eye on him, because she had her mornings at the depot. She went by bus very early to Aix. For hours at a time she sat making bandages and splints. She would have been a nurse but her father refused to permit it because three years ago she had had an accident riding and had hurt her spine a little. It was well now, but *Papa*, who adored her, would not allow her to do the strenuous work of a nurse. So she did what she could.

Today was Sunday and she did not go to the hospital. But she had been to church, and had just had her afternoon 'siesta' when Maurice's wire was brought to her.

Taking off her glasses, she took a swift look around the garden. Already the fruit was ripening against the wall. Through the gate she could see the silver-green of olive trees and the swelling yellow globules of the *pamplemousse,* the grapefruit which grows so luxuriantly in Provence.

Close to the veranda of the villa there were rose trees which had been her Irish mother's delight. Already they were scarlet and pink with blooms. And in front, the beds were purple with stocks and spiced carnations.

The English officer would like this garden, without doubt, Julie thought, as it would remind him of home.

Julie, her brown slim legs bare, bare feet wearing the *espadrilles* (Provençal sandals), walked swiftly away down the hill to the little village. She walked gracefully... Maurice called her *petite gazelle*. Dear Maurice! She had missed him since the war commenced and he had been called up. At least he could speak some English with her. And she loved him. She was going to marry him. It had all been arranged between their families, and when war broke out, and he had appeared for the first time in his uniform with his fair hair shining and his jolly red face serious with love for her, she had given the assent to their engagement which she had for so long withheld. For she was not sure that she was in love with Maurice ... in love as writers and poets meant when they wrote those words. Not in love, for instance, as her Irish mother must have been when she left her country and came to Provence to her Gaston. Julie had read some of the letters her mother had written when she was still Mary O'Connor. They had burned with a young girl's ardent longing to join the man of her heart.

Sometimes Julie wondered whether she would ever really 'burn with longing' for Maurice. His kisses were sweet and his caresses soothed her, and they laughed together, but she could never quite imagine herself leaving the whole world for him. Still she liked him better than any man she had ever met and it was all arranged that she should be his wife. He had loved her for years and she would reward him by marrying him when he returned from this terrible war. He wished it to be in the autumn. Julie was not quite sure about that. To become a wife would mean perhaps having to say goodbye to her youth ... to running about bare-legged, bare-headed like a child ... dancing on the feast days ... spending hours alone in her boat and on her island. She would have to become more dignified ... a suitable housewife ... and assume the decorum which would be necessary for Madame Maurice Dupont.

However, why worry about that? And what did her personal feelings matter so long as her dear *lieutenant d'avion* was rewarded for his bravery and his devotion?

Julie de Vallois, so well known in the village, was greeted by everybody as she walked down the narrow cobbled street towards the quay. The shops were all closed. But the good people of La Marita were out in their Sunday clothes enjoying the sun. The little café in the market-square was packed with customers. There was a smell of roasting coffee, the sound of popping corks, of wine being poured into glasses, of voices raised in discussion.

There were only two topics of discussion nowadays, Julie thought. *La guerre,* or the amount of fish that had been caught during the week.

Down on the quay, she found old Jean Taupin sitting on his boat mending a net, with his clay pipe in his mouth. There he was always to be found. He was part of the scenery to Julie. She was as used to the sight of him sitting there as to all the loveliness of the fishing village and the surrounding landscape. Used to it, yet never bored by it. She was of Provence and it was in her blood. She adored it all; the little white cottages, the tall cypresses, the chestnuts and plane trees, the striped awnings of the cafés, the tiny shops, the whole perfect village nestling in a hollow behind which the hills towered. High, purple-blue hills.

In the little quay, the fishing fleet was moored today. It did not go out on a Sunday. But tomorrow the red sails would make splashes of crimson on the blue waters of the Mediterranean.

Shading her eyes with one hand, Julie looked at the sea contentedly. It was like crinkled silk, faintly ruffled by the faintest breeze. And there stood her island, dim in the haze but ever beckoning. Her lovely lonely island which took her a quarter of an hour to reach in her motor boat. (On that island, after poor Maurice had first gone to join his squadron, she had lain and wept a little, wondering if he would ever come back.)

Old Taupin greeted Julie. She spoke to him about the engine of her boat. He assured her that it would be oiled well that afternoon. He would do it himself although it was the day of rest.

'We cannot do enough for our officers, and if the English *lieutenant* wishes to use your boat it must be ready,' said old Taupin placidly.

'He's coming today,' said Julie.

'Ma'moiselle de Vallois will, *sans doubte*, show him the island,' said Taupin.

'*Sans doubte*,' said Julie.

She only showed it to her friends. Others who wished to go there might do so, but they must take themselves out and she would not go with them. It was *her* island, and she resented it being used by others, particularly tourists. But since the war there had been no tourists, for which she was thankful.

She did not know what time Neil Richardson would reach La Marita. He would go to Aix by train and then hire a car. Possibly it would be about five o'clock.

She had meant to put on her new blue silk dress and pin her hair up into a discreet little bunch of curls on top of her head, put on Maurice's diamond ring, and become M'moiselle de Vallois as she was 'at home' when there were guests. Become very English and *propre* and *convenable*. But she was so busy assisting Jean to oil and grease the engine of the motor boat that she forgot the time and it was five o'clock before she returned to the villa. She hurried through the wrought-iron gateway up the drive past the two tall cypresses which were like black sentinels pointing to the sky, just in time to see a tall man in the pale blue uniform of the Royal Air Force stepping out of a car.

The Englishman had arrived.

Julie, thrilled and pleased, hailed him, proudly airing her English.

'Hello! Flight-Lieutenant Richardson ... welcome to La Marita!'

Neil turned in the direction whence came that clear sweet voice. As soon as he saw Julie he knew her. He was conscious of two sensations. Of pleasure because that tanned oval face with the enormous dark eyes and the silvery hair was so familiar ... and of surprise because she looked so young. She was pointing out the smear of oil on her pink linen dress, the oil on her small brown hands, her general untidiness.

'I do apologise. I meant to be changed to greet you. I've been so busy with my boat.'

He saluted and held out a hand.

'I'm delighted to meet you, Mademoiselle,

and please don't apologise for your appearance. It's quite unnecessary, I assure you.'

His fingers closed over hers. She, too, was conscious of a variety of sensations. Mainly of admiration for the sheer physical good looks of the Englishman. So tall he was, and brown, and what frighteningly strong hands he had! Thin fingers, yet hard; and such a resolute chin. Just a little frightening until he smiled, and then he was charming.

She smiled up at him. Her bleached hair barely reached his shoulder.

'We are all so pleased to welcome you here,' she said, 'and I, especially! I shall be able to talk English to you, which is so wonderful for me because you see...'

'Your mother was Irish, I know,' Neil broke in, smiling down at the vivid young face, 'and you speak English perfectly and with just a delicious accent.'

'And how do you speak French, Flight-Lieutenant Richardson?'

'Look here, we can't have that long name each time. Please call me Neil, as Maurice does, and in answer to your question, I speak French imperfectly and with an atrocious accent.'

They both laughed. Julie led the way into the villa. Neil explained that he had been down to the *auberge*, left his luggage and came straight up here to see her. She took him into a small room, where it was cool

26

and dark, because green jalousies shut out the sunlight. A typically French room. A little too ornate for Neil's liking. But so far he had been enchanted with what he had seen of the village and he knew that he was going to enjoy his convalescence.

Monsieur de Vallois was away in Aix for the day but would be back this evening, Julie explained ... of course, Neil ... she pronounced it with a stress on the vowels – 'Neel' – must dine with them. Had he had tea? No, then Hortense would bring him some. Real English tea. Her mother had taught Hortense to make it. And there were English cigarettes in the cedar-wood box which had been specially bought for him, she said as she handed it to him.

Neil sat on the arm of a chair, lit one of the cigarettes with relish, and was conscious of a real welcome. It was very gratifying. And queer how much at home he felt here. He even knew this room ... the striped red and grey silk of the chair covers ... that gilt clock on the mantelpiece with its delicate bell-like chime ... the snow-leopard rug before the fireplace. He had heard about them from Maurice. And most of all, he had heard about Julie, and she was just as Maurice had described her. Like her photograph, Neil thought, only more beautiful. Really quite disturbing the way those velvety dark eyes scrutinised him, the way she ordered tea for him, fussed over him; she was an enchanting mixture of woman and child.

He gave her Maurice's present and letter. She put the letter in her pocket and opened the present. It was a cigarette case with the R.A.F. badge on it.

'Ah, it's your squadron,' she said delightedly. 'I'm only just beginning to smoke. I shall use it and feel very English with this badge.'

She asked him how Maurice was. He gave her every little bit of news that he thought might interest her.

'I hope the poor dear will soon get leave,' said Julie.

'You're expecting to be married on his next leave, I believe.'

She shrugged slender, graceful shoulders.

'Maybe. Nothing is settled.'

He watched her thoughtfully. It struck him in an instant that this beautiful young girl was not as deeply in love with her fiancé as he was with her. She was casual. She spoke of Maurice with great affection, but more as a woman would speak of her brother than her lover. Neil, remembering Maurice's *grande passion,* was vaguely disturbed by this thought.

Then he started to question her, telling her that he had promised to send the answers back to La Chume.

'How is your island?'

She sat in a chair, bare legs crossed, cigarette in one hand, eyes shining.

'My island is glorious. I shall take you there tomorrow. It's the perfect month. All the wild flowers are out. You have never seen such lavender as we have this year ... and the veronica is lovely. And the fish ... you must see the shoals of little fish of every colour, so clear is the water between the rocks.'

'You don't know how enticing that sounds after La Chaume.'

At once she had to know about La Chaume. And when he described the dull village, the mud-caked roadways, the constant stream of khaki-clad men, the rumble of lorries and tanks going up the line, the incessant roar of engines ... the planes circling overhead, she shivered.

'Oh, it is terrible, this bloodshed ... this slaughter. One human being seeking to destroy another, yet each one, perhaps, a lover of beauty and peace. Here, in La Marita, one hardly thinks of war. It is all so peaceful, so beautiful.'

'That's why I've come here,' he said.

'You must be so tired of the war.'

'It's hardly begun,' he said with a short laugh, 'but I am tired of it. Not of my flying, though. I love that.'

'Ah, and you are called "Devil Richardson!" ... I know,' she laughed back, *le diable,* isn't it so?'

His brown face flushed with some embarrassment.

'Who told you that?'

'Maurice.'

'Maurice has told us a lot about each other. I know many things about you, Julie. How are Co-co and Ton-ton?'

She clapped her hands delightedly.

'To think that you know my darling pigeons by their names. You shall see them. They are fine, and perhaps if Co-co is good and sits on her nest there will be little Co-cos and Ton-tons quite shortly. It's very late for nesting, but perhaps Co-co thinks better late than never for love.'

Neil sipped his tea, his eyes watching her over the rim of the cup. She was delicious, he thought. There was an infectious gaiety about her. Yet he could imagine her in a serious moment. And what a mouth the child had! The way it pouted! Made for kisses. He could see her playing 'cherrybob'. He found himself saying:

'Do you still love cherries?'

'I adore them. You know *that*, too?'

'Yes, and your music ... you're going to sing to me?'

'Are you fond of music ... but of course I remember now ... in one of Maurice's letters he said you played the piano. You are a musician.'

'Hardly that. Very amateur.'

'Like my singing.'

'I shall be a judge of that.'

His grey eyes laughed at her and under his breath he whistled a tune.

She bit her lip.

'*Mon Dieu.* What do you not know about me? That is *"Parlez moi d'amour"*, my favourite song.'

'I expect there is quite a lot I don't know,' he said.

Her enormous eyes gleamed with fun.

'You will have time to find out.'

'From what I have seen so far, it is going to be such a perfect holiday for me, I shall not have time to do half that I want.'

'It is right that you should have a perfect holiday,' said Julie, 'and I want to help.'

'You're being very charming to me,' he said.

He raised his cup to his lips again. She found herself looking at his hand, fascinated. Those hard, brown fingers with the short, dark hairs on the wrist. How very masculine they were. Maurice had plump, rather soft hands. Somehow, Maurice seemed a long way away, but it did not matter. It was thrilling and wonderful to have his English friend here … to see that long, graceful body in the armchair in which Maurice often sat talking to her.

After tea she showed Neil the garden. The more he saw of it, the more he liked Villa

Vertige and its young mistress. Her total lack of affectation was so refreshing. He had never met a girl like Julie. He could not blame Maurice for talking about her all the time.

He dined that night with Julie and her father. It was years since Neil had enjoyed a meal more. Gaston de Vallois was a typical Frenchman, voluble, gay, a shrewd business man, a warm patriot. At one time he had obviously been handsome, but now he was growing fat. Thick curly hair and beard were grey, and his nose had grown fleshy and purple-veined. He was a man who liked his food and drink enormously. He was an excellent host.

The table was laden with good things. There was no sign of rationing here, Neil thought. Julie had chosen the meal and the wine was the best from Gaston de Vallois' cellar.

The dining-room was Julie's especial joy because *Papa* had given it a British atmosphere with the Irish hunting prints against the white walls; good solid Chippendale table and chairs, and the green velvet curtains that had been up in her mother's lifetime.

Julie spoke little during dinner. The conversation was almost entirely in French between old Gaston and the English officer on the subject of war and of flying.

But Neil's gaze wandered continually to the girl at the foot of the table. This grave, courteous hostess was a new Julie who had burst upon his vision, not at all like the bare-legged child in the oil-stained dress... This was a chic young woman with all her French blood in evidence. She looked taller and older in the long dark blue silk dress, which had touches of soft Mechlin lace at the throat fastened with a little jewelled brooch in the shape of a cross. The silvery hair was piled high on her head, and against one curl she had pinned a red rose. That full, pouting mouth of hers was stained a deeper red. The brilliant eyes under their sweeping lashes continually wandered to Neil. She seemed to hang on his words.

Neil, watching her, sipping the excellent wine and smoking the cigar which his host had given him, felt far removed from the war, his work, and everything that was going on in the outside world. This was a little world of its own ... this was sheer contentment here, dining with Julie and her father. He was profoundly glad that Maurice Dupont had made him come.

But later, when he strolled in the garden with Julie whilst her father settled down to read the evening paper as was his habit, Neil became conscious of something more than contentment ... of that same uneasy longing which used to seize him when he looked at Julie de Vallois' photograph in the room shared with Maurice.

It was altogether too alluring here, he thought … and Julie was the incarnation of allure itself, walking beside him in the velvet darkness cleft by a moonlight so brilliant that the shadows were knife-edged. Through the space between the two cypress trees at the bottom of the garden they could see across the village to the sea. Shimmering and milky lay that water in opalescent light. And a little way out from the shore stood the dark, hazy shape of Julie's island.

She pointed it out to him.

'I am going to take you there tomorrow, Neel, in the afternoon when I come back from my work at Aix.'

'I shall look forward to it,' he said.

She looked up at his clear-cut profile. He really was very handsome, she thought, in that blue uniform with the wings over the tunic pocket. The injured arm in the black silk sling … made him all the more interesting.

'Does your arm hurt you at all?' she asked him.

'No. Not unless I play tricks with it.'

'How long leave will you have?'

'A few weeks until the arm is healed enough for me to be able to use it. I shall have to get a doctor's report.'

'Do you think you are going to be bored at La Marita?'

He looked down at her, took the cigar from

his lips, then looked down at the moonlit island again.

'I could not possibly be bored.'

She followed his gaze.

'I look forward to showing you *that*.'

'And I ... to seeing the beach, the little rocks on the hillside. Rosemary and thyme grow in the crevices, don't they? And there's a crucifix on the summit of the island.'

'You know. But it is astonishing what you know!'

'Yes, nothing here is strange to me.'

'It's queer,' she said in a hushed voice, 'I don't feel you are a stranger, either. I know you very well.'

For a moment he looked down into her eyes, then with a sense of shock flung the stump of his cigar into the bushes and moved away from her. His pulses were quickening. A man could not stand in the moonlight in this warm Provençal night so near to Julie and not feel a queer vibration of his whole being. He suddenly remembered that there was one thing that he had not done which Maurice had asked him to do ... to give her one little kiss ... (like a 'brother', Maurice had said).

Neil did not give Julie de Vallois that kiss. Pleading fatigue, he wrenched himself abruptly away from the beauty of the night and of Julie's presence, paid his respects to his host, left Villa Vertige, and walked down to the *auberge*.

Long after he had gone, Julie stood in that same spot in the garden where they had talked together. She stared at her island. There was a half-bewildered look in her large eyes. An excitement stirring in her blood. And with that excitement came a sudden fear.

Julie was a good Catholic. In her room there was a little statue of the Madonna on a ledge. Julie always kept a bowl of fresh flowers before her Madonna.

Tonight she lit a candle and placed it on the ledge. She went down on her knees, and with a rosary in her sun-browned fingers bent her fair young head in prayer. She prayed as usual for the safety of Maurice, her fiancé. But between the thought of Maurice and herself there kept coming another face; a strong, brown, English face, with grey, far-seeing eyes. A mouth that was stern till it broke into a smile.

Tightly Julie shut her eyes and tried to shut out the remembrance of Neil Richardson.

'Blessed Virgin, Mother of God, pray for me...' said her lips.

But her whole being was thrilling with the anticipation of showing the Englishman her island tomorrow.

3

Two weeks later, on a Sunday morning, Neil Richardson was wakened from his sleep by the sound of a clear, flute-like whistle outside the widow. In a moment he was awake. It was so easy to wake, he thought, on these sunny Provençal mornings when one had had plenty of fresh air and exercise the day before, and he was feeling fitter than he had felt since his accident. Even the arm was no longer in a sling, although he had not recovered the full use of it. He thrust aside the mosquito net, opened the jalousies wide, and stepped on to the veranda.

Down below in the courtyard he saw Julie. She wore a striped, yellow, cotton dress with a tight little bodice and a full skirt, and there was a huge Mexican straw hat on her head. In the one hand she carried a basket, and in the other a towel and a bathing suit.

Her vivid face laughed up at him.

'*Bon jour,* Neel. Are you ready for our picnic?'

He rubbed his eyes and ran his hands through his thick tousled hair.

'Good heavens! It can't be very late. Are you dragging me out at this unearthly hour?'

She pointed to the sea.

'It is past sunrise, and is it not the perfect time for us to go? I have hot coffee here and hot rolls and plenty of fruit for your breakfast.'

He was wide awake and enthusiastic now. The morning was superb. The blue sea looked like a millpond. The sky was still flushed with the rose and gold of the sunrise. Little gilt-edged clouds were drifting away into infinity. Julie's island looked tranquil and mysterious in the summer haze. It was going to be another hot day.

'I'll be with you as soon as I can,' Neil called down to Julie.

It took him only a few minutes to shave, wash, and get into a pair of grey flannel trousers and silk tennis shirt. He whistled while he brushed his hair. Automatically he whistled one of Julie's tunes. He knew them all by heart. He had known them all before he came to La Marita, and now she had sung them all to him. He loved that sweet husky little voice of hers. On one or two evenings he had accompanied her on the old piano in Villa Vertige which her mother used to play, and which nobody else ever used nowadays.

Last night they had decided to make this early rise and spend a whole day on the island. An island that was no longer a mystery to Neil. He had explored every inch of it and learned to love it almost as much as Julie did.

What a fortnight it had been, he thought, as he completed his toilet, and, making sure that he had cigarettes and matches, went downstairs to join the girl.

A fortnight that seemed now like a dream. So sweet, so packed with exquisite experience, it had little relation to the stern realities of today; in fact, he only remembered that there was a war when he bothered to look at a paper or saw an aeroplane flying high over La Marita.

He had forgotten his old life ... everything connected with it. *'Devil Richardson'* was a man of the past. This was a man who led an ideal existence in ideal surroundings, and Julie was the ideal companion.

Greatly though Neil had grown to like La Marita ... although he was under the spell of Provence now and for ever ... he could not blind himself to the fact that it was Julie's companionship which had done much to make his leave a perfect one.

They had spent every afternoon and evening together. Her father did not seem to object to their friendship. Maurice wrote continually to them both, urging Neil to amuse Julie while he could, and Julie to entertain his friend. And Neil had written a note every other day to Maurice, describing the life he was leading. He had taken countless photographs of Julie, and sent prints of them to her fiancé. He had never allowed himself to forget that Julie was Maurice Dupont's affianced wife. But he was only human and he knew that there had been times when he wanted to forget that fact. Wanted it with all his soul.

What chance had he, he asked himself cynically, to remain cold and impervious to all this enchantment? What hadn't they done together? Spent hours in her motor boat, chugging through the sea, round the promontory, exploring the coast almost as far as La Ciota. Sunbathed on her island, lunched there, picking masses of wild flowers, or fishing off the rocks. (What fun it had been that day when Julie slipped off the rocks and he had dived in after her, regardless of his arm. They had lain on the warm sand, panting and laughing, neither of them hurt.)

Once or twice they had driven to Aix together, dined there in the Café Vendôme by the Casino, sitting on the terrace in the soft, warm night, looking at the floodlit fountain in the market square before them. They had looked at the famous historic tapestries together, shopped in the town, walked along the cliffs at La Marita by moonlight. Danced in Madame Huillard's dining-room to gramophone records. And Neil had learned a great deal about the beauty of the girl's mind, her honesty of purpose, her joyous love of life. Experienced, too, those moods which

Maurice had told him about. Julie was not always joyous. She was sometimes sad and remote, would hardly speak to him. And he understood. That was the artistic strain, the Irish blood warring with the French, but generally the gay French strain conquered and she was happy.

Every morning before she went off to her war depot he watched her feed Co-co and Ton-ton. He had photographed her standing by the dovecote with the pigeons on either shoulder. He thought he had never seen a more enchanting sight than those grey birds fluttering from her slender wrists to her shoulders; kissing her brown cheeks with their red beaks ... cooing as she spoke to them, calling them by little endearing French names.

He had found himself talking to her as he had never talked to any other girl who had been his companion. Yes, he had even told her about his boyhood, which had been an unhappy one. His mother had died when he was a baby, and his father had been a difficult man with an irascible temper and a profound contempt for his son's talents as a musician. He had brought Neil up sternly, and the boy had had little fun in life until he was old enough to break away and make a life of his own.

Always Julie was a sympathetic listener and, for all her childish ways, had an understanding of life and of men.

Oh, they knew each other very well now. Too well, thought Neil moodily as he joined Julie this morning. It was not going to be easy to leave her and La Marita, perhaps never to see either again.

If he was depressed he did not show it to Julie, however. He smiled and greeted her gaily, took the picnic basket, and walked with her down to the quay. Nobody was about. The village was deserted except for old Jean Taupin, who was always to be found after daybreak, looking at his nets.

When Neil hailed the fisherman and remarked on the beauty of the morning, the old man was not too optimistic.

The *lieutenant* and Mademoiselle should be careful today, he said. There would be a storm. Jean Taupin had seen signs of it. He let forth a flood of explanations about the crows flying down to the valley, which always meant that there would come the *orage*. But Julie laughed as she and Neil climbed into the boat.

'Jean always thinks there will be a storm when he sees a crow. We need not worry.'

'It doesn't look like anything but a perfect day at the moment,' said Neil.

'Shall I take her across or will you?'

'I like to see you do it,' he smiled.

A few minutes later Julie was steering them over the tranquil blue water towards the island. Neil lay full length in the boat with his head near her sandalled feet, a cigarette between his lips, and the mounting sun growing ever warmer upon his face.

He said:

'Julie, my child, this is the perfect life.'

'I know it,' she said. 'I never want to do anything else, but when I marry Maurice...'

Neil frowned.

'What then?'

'It may have to be different. Maurice is not a regular officer. He is in private life a wine merchant, like my father. His father's business is now in Nice, and maybe I shall have to live there.'

'Nice,' repeated Neil, and grimaced. 'A town ... a promenade ... casinos ... crowds ... ugh!'

'That's what I say,' Julie nodded.

'You ought never to be taken away from La Marita,' said Neil. 'I would like to see you settled here, where you could always have your boat and your island.'

She sighed.

'I pray every night that I may stay, but if I marry Maurice ... it will be Nice.'

Neil made no answer. He smoked in silence. The thought of Maurice Dupont made him feel guilty. But the thought of Julie married to a wine merchant and having to live in a town like Nice made him profoundly sad. It would be like gathering one of the lovely wild flowers from her island and putting it in a hot-house where it would wilt and die, he thought.

They reached the shore. Now the mists were clearing and the island rose clear and green before them. High up on the top stood the iron crucifix, to which they had so often climbed.

Neil moored the boat and they walked together to a sandy bay. The rocks above them were orange coloured, and from the crevices sprang the multi-coloured flowering herbs which were Julie's delight. By the waters edge the dark cypress trees looked splendid and stark against the blood-red cliffs.

'We will leave our picnic basket under the lavender bushes here,' said Julie, choosing a place, 'then we will go and bathe before we have our breakfast.'

'Yes,' he agreed.

They swam together in the cold, clear water. Neil could move his left arm sufficiently now to enable him to bathe, and the doctor in the hospital at Aix had said that the sea water would be good for it.

After the bathe they returned to the place chosen for the picnic and were both exhilarated and hungry. Neil, drying his hair briskly with a towel, a cigarette between his lips, thought how lovely Julie looked. Her long fair hair had not got wet under the close-fitting rubber cap which she wore, and it was like a cloud of silver against her brown shoulders, on which there glistened drops of salt water. Her small slim figure was perfect in that white swim suit. At first she had a towel about her, but she soon flung it off as the sun dried her. She gave him hot coffee, buttered rolls which were still warm, and hard-boiled eggs.

He thought it was the most perfect breakfast he had ever eaten. He felt glad to be alive. They had the rest of the day before them. He tried not to think of tomorrow when he must leave Julie and La Marita and return to duty. Yes, he must go back to the château, where he would see only her photograph, and hear only second-hand news of her through the lips of the man who was going to marry her.

The worst part of it to Neil was that he knew now that she did not love Maurice Dupont. Without actually telling him so, she had hinted it. The hints had not been deliberate, but he had guessed it from the casual way in which she always spoke about her fiancé, and the 'moods' which came upon her after they had discussed him. It seemed to Neil iniquitous that this marriage should have to take place just because it had all been 'arranged' between Maurice's father and hers years ago.

Yet, deliberately, when he spoke of Maurice he spoke with admiration and praise and told her that she was lucky to be engaged to Maurice. It was his duty to do so.

This morning he had not the slightest inclination to mention Maurice's name, let alone to praise him.

They spent the morning fishing. At lunch time Julie lit a little fire of dead wood. She had a small, iron cauldron here and, after the manner of the Provençal fish-wives, she cooked a kind of *bouillabaisse*. It was the first time she had done this and Neil vowed that he had never tasted anything better than the dish of mixed fish. Afterwards they had green salad, and a sweet cream cheese which she had brought with her. The repast ended with figs and fat white cherries.

Neil remembered how Maurice had described the way in which Julie ate the cherries. He put the stalk of one between her lips. Immediately she jerked it upwards, and it fell into her mouth and she laughed at him.

'Oh, how did you *know* I could do that?'

'I knew,' he said.

She ate the cherry, then her laughter sped while she looked at him.

'*Mon cher Neel* ... I believe that you know more about me even than my fiancé?'

He moved uneasily.

I doubt that. It is Maurice who told me these things.'

'Perhaps. But I still feel *you* understand

me. You would not take me to Nice!'

'No. I would keep you in La Marita, or build you a little house on this island.'

'How lovely, Neel! What would we call it?'

'Oh … Villa Belle Ile … but no, that's too ordinary…' he bent nearer her and caught the fragrance of her hair… 'Villa Baiser, after your scent.'

Her enormous eyes sparkled at hm. She put another cherry in her mouth.

'Even the name of my scent you know?'

'Yes.'

She gave an amused little laugh.

'But we could hardly call it "The Villa of Kisses". That would not be at all *propre.*'

'Not at all. But as I can never build you a villa on this island it doesn't much matter.'

'It's nice to pretend sometimes,' she said wistfully.

He pretended not to notice the wistfulness. He dared not. Neither dared he tell her how entrancing her pouting lips looked with the cherries between them. He rose and glanced round the island. It was very hot now, and there was a shimmer of haze over the water which made the shore and the fishing village seem a long way away. He wished to God that it was hundreds of miles away, and that this was a desert island; and that no ship would ever pass it and that nothing could take Julie from him again in this life. It flashed across him in that instant that he was crazily in love with her.

'God forgive me,' he thought. 'I must control myself. Maurice Dupont is my friend ... a brother-officer... Julie can never be anything to me ... *never!*'

She was smiling up at him and beginning to hum under her breath the old favourite, *Parlez moi d'amour.*

'Don't do that,' said Neil harshly.

Her cheeks went hot and pink, and she looked like a hurt child.

'Neel ... you are *angry* ... but why?'

With a conflict of spirit which he had never thought possible he answered with the same harshness.

'There's too much sung about love ... too much said about it ... let's do some more fishing.'

For a moment she stared at him in astonishment. He saw her colour fade. He was so sorry that he had hurt her that he longed to throw himself at her feet, put his arms about her knees and kiss the brown satin smoothness of them. Instead he turned and began to unravel some fishing tackle.

Julie was unhappy for the rest of that afternoon and the man was in torment, facing hard bitter facts. And most bitter of all was the knowledge that, for the first and only time in his life, he loved a woman, and that woman belonged to his friend.

The fishing was not a success. Neither of

them enjoyed it. At four o'clock, Neil gave it up.

'I'm tired,' he said abruptly, 'and my shoulder is aching.'

He had wounded her by his harshness and his inexplicable change of mood, but because she thought his injured arm hurt him she was at once soft and sympathetic.

'Poor Neel! You would like to go back home, yes?'

There was nothing he wanted to do less, for he knew that once he left this island today he must never come back or otherwise he would be lost, and this girl would be lost with him. Tomorrow he had better take the first train back to La Chaume whether his arm was properly well or not.

At this hour, when the shadows were lengthening, it was as beautiful on the island as it had been at sunrise. He could not bear to leave it yet.

'Let's rest a bit first,' he said abruptly.

On other days they had taken what Julie called a 'siesta', and had a special place for it. It was up on the summit of the hill. There stood a dark green umbrella pine and under it the grass was dry and soft. They could lie down upon it with comfort. Lacing his hands behind his head, Neil Richardson looked at the crucifix which was opposite. The body of the Christ was roughly sculptured, but had a tragic beauty. Neil suddenly said:

'I suppose you believe in praying, Julie?'

'Yes,' she said, 'I'm a Catholic.'

'I used to pray as a small boy, but I haven't done much lately,' he said, 'yet when I look at that cross, I feel that there are many things I would like to ask. And what would be the use! There are circumstances which even *prayer* cannot alter...'

She looked at him. He looked back at her. She had taken off the swim suit and was wearing her little yellow dress again. Her face was sad. He felt that all the joy of life had gone, that an intense sadness was enveloping them both. Julie did not quite understand what was wrong with the Englishman, but she, too, was conscious of depression.

'Go on praying, Neel,' she said, 'don't be afraid to pray. Who knows that your prayer may not be granted.'

'It couldn't be,' he said hoarsely, and thought of Maurice Dupont.

'Why were you cross with me when I started to sing to you a little time back?' she suddenly asked him.

'I am sorry I was cross.'

'You upset me.'

He felt contrite and enormously tender towards her. So near to him she was lying there in the warm dry grass under the shade of the pine, he could see the rise and fall of her breast as she breathed. He said:

'Forgive me. Sing to me now.'

Her pouting lips smiled.

'No. *You* shall sing to me. You promised that you would. You said that you knew some old French songs.'

'I know only one,' he said. 'The words are by Guillem de Cabestanh.'

'Oh, but he is one of my favourite French poets. Please, *please*, Neel, sing it to me. He is a poet of Provence.'

'I don't sing,' said Neil, 'I merely hum. But I will hum it to you, Julie.'

She sat up and looked down at him eagerly with her great eyes. He did not look at her now, but the words came clearly in that low baritone voice which he was shy of using, but which had quality.

He sang in French because he dared not speak those words aloud in English. In another language they sounded more impersonal. But he knew the translation by heart, and it was all too appropriate to the hour.

'That pleasant fever
The love doth often bring,
Lady, doth ever
Attune the songs I sing
Where I endeavour
To catch again your chaste
Sweet body's savour
I crave but may not taste.'

When he'd finished, she drew a long breath.

'*Merci* … that was so wonderful, Neel.'

'Just a song…' he said, but he thought of those two lines about the *'sweet body's savour… I crave but may not taste.'*

Julie remembered them as they were written in her book of Provençal poems:

'Vostre cors car e gen
Cui eu desire
E cui non fasz perven.'

The old French spelling, which so many times she had read and barely understood, leapt at her now from the page of memory, white-hot with poignant meaning. And she looked a little wildly at the brown, fine face of the man beside her whose deep voice had sung the words. Now she understood the full significance of every poem of love, every tale of love which she had ever read.

She knew, too, that what she felt for Maurice was what a sister feels for a beloved brother. She understood why sometimes she had been restive, passive in his embrace … reluctant when he grew over-passionate.

But for Neil Richardson, her whole body trembled with love, she ached for the touch of those strong, fascinating hands.

A little wildly she gazed at the crucifix before them and she sent up a voiceless prayer … as she had done upon her knees, before the Virgin in her room.

'*Jesu* ... help me...'

And suddenly she flung herself down on the warm sun-baked grassy earth and burst into a flood of tears.

Immediately Neil sat up and stared at her, dismayed.

'Julie ... dear Julie ... my *dear* ... what is it? Have I upset you again? Did my song offend you? Julie ... please ... speak to me ... *please...*'

She sobbed:

'No, no ... it is nothing. No ... I am not offended. Oh, *Neel.*'

He understood then. He could not do otherwise. He knew that this girl was racked with the same torment of love ... the same despair that had settled itself in his own soul. He was aghast. With all his heart he wanted to do the 'right thing'; to remember Maurice Dupont ... honour ... propriety ... everything that stood between Julie de Vallois and himself.

He spoke more harshly than he intended.

'Don't cry, Julie. This is my last day. To-morrow I shall be gone. For God's sake, let us have laughter to remember and ... not weeping.'

She rolled over and faced him ... big brown eyes distraught ... brown face wet with tears ... cherry-lips piteously twisted. A cold hand seemed to clutch her heart.

'You are going ... *tomorrow?*'

'Yes.'

Her tears had ceased to flow. She seemed stupefied by what he had said.

'I didn't know. You didn't tell me.'

'I had to go sometime, Julie.'

'I know,' she whispered, 'but not so soon...'

'The sooner the better,' he said bitterly.

'Oh, no,' she whispered. 'Oh, *no*. You... I...' she broke off helplessly, her big eyes swimming.

And suddenly she turned over on her face again and he saw that the slim young body was shaken with a tempest of grief. It broke him. It broke down his resistance, his control, everything that was making him fight for Maurice Dupont. And he suddenly flung himself down beside her. His right arm went about her waist. His voice was close to her ear:

'Julie, Julie, my darling ... my *darling* ... don't cry. For God's sake, don't! I can stand anything but that.'

She moaned his name.

'Neel.'

Her face, distorted with tears, had never looked lovelier to him. The sunlit sky was blotted out. He could see nothing but that brown, beautiful face, and suddenly his lips were upon her mouth where they had so longed to be. A mouth that tasted of cherries and sea water and the salt of her tears.

Immediately he small hands went round his neck drawing him closer. It was a kiss that drained him of all further resistance, a kiss that to her was a revelation of all the love which the world contained.

A little lizard slipped out of the warm rocks, blinked at them and hopped away again into the wild thyme at their feet. The Figure on the crucifix hung motionless, pitying.

To the north the perfect blue of the sky was gradually being blotted out by great clouds which would shortly drift across the face of the sun. In a moment it would be colder. A little wind was already rustling the pines and the cypress trees on the shore. The storm which old Jean Taupin had predicted was coming.

But the man and the girl on the hill lay locked in each other's arms, mouth pressed to mouth in a wild ecstasy of love, and of loving which knew no law save the law of love itself.

4

When for a moment Neil drew his lips away from the girl's mouth and buried his face against her smooth shoulder, she became suddenly aware of the fact that the sun was no longer shining and that great drops of rain were spattering against her hot face.

She drew a deep breath. Her arms fell away from him and she stretched them on either side of her against the grass, languidly, trying to think … to think sanely … to realise what she was doing … what she had done… But her brain would not register more than the poignant fact that she loved this man in whose arms she was lying. Loved him wholly and absolutely with a love that seemed to have no beginning and could have no end.

She was no longer little Julie, half-awakened child who in lukewarm fashion had betrothed herself to Maurice Dupont. She was all woman now, fully roused, fully aware of the potentialities in herself for love and loving. Those wild kisses pressed upon her eager mouth by Neil Richardson had taught her that love was not just a friendly affection, a thrill, an exchange of compliments, a diffident acceptance of an embrace. But a mighty torrent of feeling that can rush over a woman's body and heart like a great relentless tide wakening every impulse, raising her to the pinnacle of a rapture almost too great to be borne. But now, when that tide receded, it left her gasping … blind, deaf, and dumb … mentally groping for some explanation of the miracle and for some enlightenment in the darkness of her problems.

She loved Neil. She loved him madly and

with all the fire and force of her newly found womanhood. And she was engaged to be married to Maurice. And he was Maurice's friend.

What greater catastrophe could have befallen her, she asked herself dazedly.

And in that daze, she became still further aware of the approaching storm. The rain was falling more thickly, drenching her cheeks and her hair. Neil's warm strong body lay motionless against her. He did not seem aware of anything. He was like one stupefied.

Then she stirred and spoke to him, touching his head.

'Darleeng ... Neel ... look, *bien aimé*, the storm is coming here.'

He roused himself, drew his arm away from her, rolled over on his back and looked up at skies which were darkening with every passing minute. Now he could feel the rain against his own face. He blinked and rubbed his eyes.

'God!'

'Jean was right,' she said. 'We had better go down and make sure our boat is there.'

She gained her feet as she spoke. Mechanically she brushed the grass and little fronds of fern which were clinging to her skirt. Neil sat up and looked at her. He thought how beautiful she was with the raindrops glittering on her fair tumbled hair. He, too, stood up. Catching both her hands, he crushed them to his lips.

'Julie … my darling, darling little love! Tell me that you're not sorry.'

'Sorry for what?'

'For this…' he whispered, and caught her blindly to his heart, putting his cheek against her rain-wet face.

She sighed:

'I don't know yet… I can't think properly. It's all so wonderful … and so awful, too.'

'I know. It's wrong. I had no right to make love to you. You belong to Maurice. And yet I couldn't help myself. I went mad with love for you, Julie … and I'm still mad!'

'I, also! And I don't feel that I belong to Maurice. I feel only that I am yours, my Neel! I didn't know what love was until today.'

'I've been fighting against it ever since I first saw you. I think I loved the thought of you first of all. I knew you so well before we ever met. I had heard so much about you … seeing your photograph. Hearing your letters. It was almost as though I shared with Maurice his thoughts of you, his dreams.'

Julie held Neil closer to her. Her voice was a little sob against his ear.

'Oh … dar … leeng.'

The storm rapidly increased in violence. Around them there was a sighing, as of a thousand rustling trees. Only the crucifix still stood calm, isolated, immovable. Came the first zig-zag of lightning, brilliantly

58

illuminating the whole island, followed by a deep rumble of thunder which echoed back from the hills across the water.

Neil pulled himself together.

'Look here, sweet, we'll talk this out some other time. We must do something now about taking shelter. I'm rather worried about that boat. Let's go down the hill and make sure that it's all right.'

She gave him her hand and they began to run on their rope-soled sandals down the pathway, through the trees to the little cove where only a short while ago they had bathed and lunched.

There was an unbelievable change in the whole landscape. The blue of the sea had darkened to the hue of gun-metal, and whereas a little while ago the water had been so calm, it moved now in angry waves, foaming and churning about the rocks. It was one of those storms which break with such violence and rapidity on this coast, and which the fishermen dread. The peace of the golden day had given place to all the noises of the angry elements ... a demoniac wind which swept the sea into a fury and tossed the branches of the trees until they creaked and groaned, swaying like black human shapes, writhing in agony.

Neil and Julie were drenched to the skin by the time they reached the shore. The storm was right overhead now and Julie put her hands to her ears and shut her eyes as the lightning shot across the heavens, followed at once by deafening peals of thunder.

Neil cursed himself for a fool for not tying the motor boat up more securely. But he had not thought the storm would come, nor gain this pitch with such rapidity. The motor boat was no longer where they had left it. It had broken from its moorings. They could see a white shape bobbing on the metallic water far out from the shore.

'Damn,' he said. 'She's gone! And it's too far for me to swim.'

Julie caught his arm.

'Of course you cannot swim so far. With your bad shoulder, too.'

He looked down at her with a wry smile.

'Sorry, sweet, I've landed you in for this.'

'No, it isn't your fault any more than mine.'

'Well, there's nothing to be done for it but to try to find some cover. Is there a hut of any kind on this island?'

'Nothing.'

She had to shout at him now because the sound of the wind and the thunder drowned her voice. He thought that she looked like some fairy being, standing there with her silver hair blowing about her head … an all-silver, radiant figure every time the lightning illuminated her. He shouted back:

'Scared of the storm?'

She shook her head.

'Not with you…'

'Run then,' he said.

They turned their backs on the sea and hand in hand began to race up the pathway again. They made for the umbrella tree which would afford the most protection from the heavy rain. Not that it mattered much because they were both soaking wet long before they reached it. Now Neil pulled her down on to the grass under the tree. It gave them some kind of protection, and Julie was able to find a handkerchief and wipe the raindrops from her face. With a gasping sigh, she looked at Neil. He, too, wiped his streaming face and ruffled hair. It was dark and eerie under this little tree with the storm raging on around them. Every now and then the lightning lit up the figure of the Christ on the cross, investing it with an unearthly splendour.

Neil looked back at the girl. The thought of the storm and the lost motor boat faded from his mind. He could think of nothing but Julie. He was filled with a queer kind of exultation at being marooned here on this island with her. All the electric currents of earth and sky and sea seemed to be sparking about them. They fired his blood, like the beauty and sweetness of this girl upon whose lips he had tasted such supreme delight.

'You won't be afraid with me here?' he whispered.

Her heart rocketed.

'Never afraid with you, my Neel, I love you,' she said, and with a little breathless sigh surrendered herself again to his embrace.

Their lips clung and clung again. The storm raged on and they were oblivious of it. Until at last passion spent itself, and they lay together quietly, cheek to cheek, whispering of their love.

Gradually the storm subsided. The wind dropped and the cypress trees on the shore were still again as though exhausted. It no longer rained. But the sky remained grey and lowering and a deathly silence followed the storm ... a silence almost as sinister as the howling wind itself. It was as though the whole of nature on this island was in a state of exhaustion. And the lovers under the tree became at last aware of the world outside themselves ... no longer hurled into each other's arms by the storm of their own emotions, but still and thoughtful, face to face at last with tragic realities.

Julie's face was grave and pinched. Those great eyes of hers looked down at the Englishman mournfully. He sat with his head on his bowed arms, pondering deeply. At last he said:

'What in God's name are we going to do?'

'Jean will fetch us. He will remember that we are here and send out for us if we do not get back.'

'I didn't mean that,' he said gloomily. 'I meant, what are we going to do about *us?*'

'Ah!' She made an expressive gesture of the hand, typically French and indicative of complete despair.

He fixed a brooding gaze upon her.

'Julie,' he said. 'This has been a mad day. An unforgettable day. But there is one thing that you and I have *got* to remember now and that is that you are engaged to Maurice ... that he is my brother officer, and that I've been an unspeakable cad to let my feelings get the better of me.'

She felt very cold now. In his arms a few moments ago she had been warm and pulsating with life and love. Able to laugh at the storm, at danger, at anything and everything. Laugh with the sheer joy of being in Neil Richardson's embrace. But now, like the rest of the island, she was deadly calm, aware that something sinister and terrible had swept like a blight across the beauty, the magic of everything. The wild hour of love had passed and the reckoning must be faced. It was as Neil said. She must remember *Maurice*.

Neil added:

'I have no excuses except that I love you.'

'Please, please don't apologise. That would hurt me so very much,' she said. 'Let us face simple facts. I love you and you love me, and it was too much for us. We had to tell each other of our love. We must neither of us apologise for such honesty.'

He fumbled in his coat pocket, found a packet of cigarettes, lit one and began to smoke it, feeling that he had never needed the solace of tobacco so much. Every nerve in his body was jangling. He had faced unbelievable dangers in the air. He was ready to face more. German guns ... anti-aircraft fire spattering about his fighter-plane ... such things were things of war which a man knows how to face and tackle. But this emotional problem, Neil could not so easily withstand. And he knew he was afraid ... afraid for Julie and for himself and for poor old Maurice. It was just the old story, the eternal triangle, perhaps the most hackneyed of all human stories. And each time that it happened it was a fresh tale that must inevitably bring fresh suffering in its wake.

Here were the salient facts. He, Neil Richardson, had fallen in love with another man's promised wife. And she loved him and never really had loved the man whom she was going to marry. There were only two solutions to such a problem. Either they must tell Maurice the truth and ask him to give Julie her freedom or he, Neil, must go out of Julie's life for ever.

5

Almost as soon as the two solutions presented themselves, Neil Richardson knew which one he must take. And about that he must be no coward, and there must be no vacillation. He must leave La Marita tomorrow, as previously planned, and he must never see Julie again.

He began to tell her so with a determination which grew with every word he spoke. She protested a little ... just a little, poor child ... and his heart ached for her even more than for himself when she put up a pitiful barrage against his decisions.

She wished to be loyal; yet why, she asked, must she carry out a contract which had really been made for her by her parents and Maurice's, without giving her a chance to meet other men in the world. Why must she marry a man whom she did not love? Why must he, Neil, turn his back on her, the first woman whom he had ever loved? Why couldn't they tell Maurice the truth?

To each protest, Neil answered:

'I know, darling, I *know*. You're so right. And I want more than anything on earth to stay with you. You must realise what hell it will be to me to leave you. How much easier if I could ask Maurice to let you go. But I can't. He is my friend and we have fought together. Friends and allies, Julie. We couldn't let each other down. I have done wrong enough by holding you in my arms today, but as you asked me not to be sorry for that, I won't be, I'll be glad. It will be a memory that will never die. But there it must end. I can no more take you away from Maurice, than he would take you away from me, were our positions reversed.'

Very still sat Julie, her arms locked about her knees, her body shivering in the damp clothes that clung to her slender limbs. Her heart was sinking like lead in her breast. She felt as though a great weight was crushing her down. Yet she knew in her heart that Neil was right and, although every word that he said was a nail in the coffin of her joy, her love, she was proud of him. She adored him for his loyalty and for his honour. She told herself that she, too, must be loyal and share in that honour. Nothing now would have induced her to make a further appeal to Neil. She was well aware that she could exert her feminine wiles, her powers, if she chose. She knew that he was vulnerable, that if she flung herself into his arms now and said that she would die without him, he might capitulate. But she would not want to love him, or be loved by him in dishonor. She rated their love too highly for that.

At last she turned and looked at him.

'You're right,' she said in a low voice. 'We must say goodbye.'

He looked at the point of his cigarette, not trusting himself to give more than a fleeting glance into those large beautiful eyes. They were so desolate. They wrung his heart. The ecstasy of their mutual passion had died down to an intolerable pain which, like stolen happiness, must be shared. It seemed such a long price to pay for that brief heaven which they had known together.

'Darling,' he said abruptly, 'I think we had better go down to the shore again to look out for Jean.'

She nodded. They moved out from beneath the sheltering trees. It was still grey and ominously still. But they could see now across the leaden sky towards the west. The clouds were rolling behind the mountains. Raindrops spattered from the soaked trees on to the grass. Everything was wet ... drenching wet. Neil became aware of his own dampness and of a chill in his limbs. Of a sudden throb of pain, too, in the old wound. He touched it apprehensively.

Julie saw that gesture and quickly questioned him.

'Your wound? Is it all right?'

'I think so. Just a sudden stab.'

'It isn't quite right. We must get you home

quickly before you catch cold.'

'And what about you? You're shivering.'

She put her arms about herself, hugging her trembling young body, and tried to smile.

'I'm all right.'

His hungry gaze swept over her, looking at every dear and lovely curve of her. It was as though it was for the last time he took in the details of that beauty. It seemed to him so tragic and so cruel that they should love each other and be destined to part. He would so willingly have laid down his life for her. To have her for his wife would have meant ultimate happiness. And he could have made her happy, too. He knew it. He understood her. It might have all been so ideal.

'Oh, Julie, my dear,' he said. 'Life's played a rotten trick on us. On all three of us. You and I are not the only ones to suffer. Maurice will suffer unless we are careful… You must forget me quickly, Julie, and give Maurice the love he deserves.'

She turned her eyes to the sea, her face strained. It struck him that she had changed in one short afternoon. It caused him great pain to see that change. The young, laughing Julie had been happy in her way before he came. He hated himself for having hurt her, and brought her unhappiness. It was the last thing he had intended to do.

'I shall never forget you,' she said. 'But I will try to do my best for Maurice.'

He took her hand and pressed it, longing with all his soul to draw her into his arms, but denying himself that privilege.

'You're a brave sweet thing, Julie,' he said.

Then she tore her hand away and looked at him with wild eyes that were bright with tears and a twisted young mouth.

'I'm not brave! I'm miserable. I can't *bear* the thought of losing you. I can't bear it... Oh, it isn't fair... I wish that the storm had killed me this afternoon ... that the lightning had struck me ... that a bomb would drop on my island and wipe me out of existence, since it is an existence which I cannot share with you!'

To know that she cared as much as that was sweet and bitter to him. But still he did not touch her. He could not comfort her. He was sorely in need of comfort himself, well aware that his life would be solitary and meaningless without her. He felt now a passionate longing to get back to his squadron. He must put love out of his life and devote himself utterly to the war.

'I shall love you all my life, Neel,' added Julie in a strangled voice. 'Remember that, please...'

Then she turned and ran from him. She ran, not down to the shore, but up to the summit of the hill. To the iron crucifix. She flung herself down on the wet grass and knelt in an abandonment of grief at the foot of the Cross.

'Holy Mary, Mother of God, pray for me, help me,' she moaned.

Neil Richardson stood irresolute for a moment, torn between his longing to go to her and his resolution to be strong.

Bitterly he looked at the young figure crouching before the crucifix, and measured the extent of her pain by his own.

'So this is love…' he thought ironically. 'That is what love can do to a man and to a woman. My God! It's annihilation!'

His attention was caught suddenly by an object moving on the metallic waters below. He heard a long cry echoing across to the island. It was the cry of Jean Taupin, who had come in search of them. Glancing at his watch, Neil was astonished to realise how long they had been on the island. Several hours had elapsed since the storm. Soon it would be dusk. Julie's father must be growing anxious and had possibly sent the old fisherman out to search for them.

He cupped his lips with both hands and sent an answering call down to the sea. Then he went to Julie. For a moment he knelt beside her, putting one arm about her shoulders.

'Yes, pray, my sweet,' he whispered. 'Prayer is the only thing left for us. Pray for strength and for courage. And God help us both.'

She turned a mute, tear-stained young

face to him. He dared not kiss her. But he put his lips against one of her hands. It was so cold, poor little hand! Poor little Julie, he thought, to whom love had come as such a blinding revelation of joy and sorrow.

Gently he raised her to her feet and led her down to the shore. Just before Taupin's boat reached him he looked back to the island, registering a silent goodbye to it. Goodbye to La Marita and to love. When he left here tomorrow his heart would remain, it would be buried here where he had known such wild happiness and pain, he thought.

A few minutes later they were in Taupin's boat, speeding back to the mainland. The fisherman was discussing the storm in his voluble fashion. Julie and Neil answered mechanically. It was as Neil had thought. Monsieur de Vallois had grown anxious. They could see him there on the quay, waiting for them.

Julie was like one in a stupor when she stepped out of that boat and mechanically embraced her father. And Neil had never felt more exhausted both in body and mind. Every now and then that shoulder of his gave a nasty jab of pain. It was beginning to worry him. He had thought the wound quite healed. Whatever happened, he must get back now to the Front. There must be no more sick leave with Julie here, in Provence.

Julie and her father left him at the inn.

'We shall see you for dinner, yes?' Monsieur de Vallois asked Neil jovially.

Neil started to make an excuse, but Julie's father would have none of it. Of course the *lieutenant* must dine at the Villa Vertige. He was expected. So Neil gave in, having no real excuse to do otherwise. He bade father and daughter *au revoir.* For a moment Julie's eyes looked into his. They were so large, so full of pain, that he could not bear to look into them. Hastily he turned away and walked into the inn.

Like one in a strange, dark dream, Julie walked home with her father.

Dinner that night was not at all one of those gay, friendly affairs which had made life so pleasant for Neil Richardson since his arrival at La Marita. He enjoyed neither the good food nor the wine. He could barely bring himself to listen to what his genial host had to say. And Julie, in her black dress with a little jewelled cross on her breast, sat opposite him in silence, her lashes downcast. Only once or twice did she raise those large eyes to him or address him, and then he became aware of her pain and of his own acute depression at the thought of leaving her tomorrow.

The emotional tension was, in a way, relieved by the news to which they listened on the radio afterwards. Here was fresh national disaster. Leopold of the Belgians had surrendered to the enemy. The B.E.F. was forced into a grave position, and the Germans were pouring through the gap towards the coast.

Monsieur de Vallois left nothing unsaid about the traitor king. Julie spoke of her fiancé with deliberation.

'Maurice won't be at the château any longer, he will be in the midst of this new attack.'

'That is so,' said Neil gloomily, 'and I wish to God I were with him.'

She stared down at her plate, biting hard at her lips, for she knew what had prompted these words. She felt wretched, stunned with a sense of impending loss ... the loss of her heart's love as soon as she had gained it, and she had been wondering the whole evening how best to face the calamity. She had even begun to feel that it might be easier once Neil had left La Marita. It was more than she could bear to see him ... that beloved figure ... that lean brown face ... everything about him which had become so thrilling and dear to her.

For some time the two men discussed the war. And as the moments slipped by, Neil became more acutely aware of the pain in his old wound. It had been growing steadily worse since he left the island. His temples were throbbing and he felt hot. Every limb was aching. After his experience in hospital, he thought he recognised the signs of rising fever, and it worried him. Once or twice he put out a hand instinctively to touch the shoulder. And then, Julie, quick to notice it, questioned him.

'You are in pain again. Are you sure that wound is all right?'

'Not altogether sure,' he answered abruptly.

Julie's father suggested that Neil should see Monsieur Poiret, the local practitioner. But Neil rejected the idea.

'I shall be all right,' he said. 'I must go to Aix tomorrow as early as possible to catch a train to the north. I must find out where my Squadron is, and rejoin it.'

Monsieur de Vallois suggested that his daughter should sing.

'It is pleasant to forget the war in such a manner. Is it not, *mon cher lieutenant?*' he smiled at the young English airman.

Neil forced his gaze to Julie. She sat like a little nun, he thought, so quiet and pale and demure with her hands folded in her lap and her downcast lashes. But no; 'nun' was the wrong word, and when he looked at that full, red mouth with its provocative upper lip ... when he thought how he had pressed cherries between those lips and then kissed them in wildest passion ... when he remembered the sunburnt grass, the sea, the glorious fusion of their senses, he was filled with a fresh longing for her which he savagely resisted.

He had to pull himself back to earth with a jerk and to speak to the old man.

'I always like to hear Julie sing,' he said.

'I'm tired. I would rather not sing tonight,' she said.

And he knew that she was remembering how they had sung to each other on the island and how they had laughed and that laughter had ended in the passionate stillness of their embrace.

He resented bitterly the fact that she belonged to Maurice Dupont. He tried to hate Maurice and could not, for the young French airman was his friend and they had flown together, drunk together, shared each other's lives. And Maurice had sent him here to La Marita to see Julie. That was the tragic irony of it!

God! How his arm ached! His head was swimming. Undoubtedly he had a temperature, but to the devil with that. He would not give way to it. He would leave this beautiful, damnable spot tomorrow, somehow ... he would put as many miles as possible between Julie de Vallois and himself.

When he rose to take his leave he was a little unsteady on his feet, and he felt a sick man. Julie saw him to the door and walked a little way into the garden with him.

After this afternoon's storm, it was fine

and clear again. The earth, still wet from the torrential rain, gave up a strong rich fragrance. Through the darkness the fireflies were glimmering and above them a million stars shed their cold, pure light. So still was the night that they could hear the soft hiss of the sea down upon the shore.

Neil's eyes were burning. They turned in the direction of the island on which he and Julie had found their heaven and their hell. He said in a harsh, queer voice:

'I'm going now. Good night, Julie. Goodbye.'

Now all her terror at losing him was concentrated into one flame of misery. Her hands clutched the cross which was suspended from her neck by a thin, fine chain, clutched it so fiercely that the chain snapped and the cross came away in her hand. She said:

'Oh … must it be…?'

'Answer that question for yourself.'

She swallowed hard.

'Yes … yes… I know it. Goodbye, Neel, goodbye.'

Through the dusk of the night he searched for her face and saw it, pale, anguished, with the great eyes uplifted to his.

'I must be able to face Maurice without feeling ashamed,' he said hoarsely. 'Understand that, and try to forgive me. I love you. I'll love you all my life, but I must leave you.'

'Oh, *mon très cher!*' she said. 'I, too, will love you all my life.'

He turned from her and began to stumble like a drunken man along the path. His arm was on fire and his head was spinning. Those were shooting stars now, he thought ... none of them still ... all jazzing across the heavens crazily. And he was crazy with pain and misery and the fever against which he had been fighting a losing battle since he left the island.

Julie, with a little indrawn breath, saw his peculiar gait and ran after him.

'Neel ... oh, *mon coeur* ... *mon amour* ... you are ill.'

He put a hand up to his eyes.

'I shall be all right,' he muttered.

'But I know you are ill. You have looked it all the evening. I cannot leave you like this.'

He staggered, caught her fingers a moment and pressed them with lips which burned her flesh like fire.

'Julie ... adorable darling... I must go...'

His voice faded, and his body sagged suddenly, lurched against her, and fell on to the grass at her feet.

Aghast, she looked down at him and saw that he had fainted.

She called out frantically.

'Papa! Papa! *Venez ici* ... quickly! Come quickly. Neel is ill!'

And while she stood there, waiting for her father and the servants to come out, she realised that fate had intervened ... either for them or against them, she knew not which, just at the moment. She only knew that Neil Richardson would not leave La Marita tomorrow morning and join his Squadron as he had intended to do. With a conflict of wildest emotion, she watched her father and one of the men-servants carry the English-man's unconscious body into Villa Vertige.

6

When Neil Richardson came back to consciousness he found himself lying in a strange bed and in a strange room. For a few moments his eyes did not focus clearly, and then he saw two people in the room. One he knew. The figure of Julie. She was no longer in her black dinner-dress, but in a long housecoat of some soft wool and of a Madonna blue shade which he had not seen her wear before. Her long fair hair was tied back with a blue bow. In one hand she held a bowl from which came the clink of ice. In the other a pad of lint and cotton-wool. She soaked the pad in the iced water and laid it across his forehead.

The other person was a small, bearded man with glasses. Presumably the doctor whom Monsieur de Vallois had recommended during dinner.

The doctor, speaking in French, bent over Neil and said:

'So you are awake, my friend! That is better. But you must be reprimanded for doing nothing about this shoulder of yours before. You must have suffered great pain and said nothing. The consequence is that you have done harm to yourself.'

Neil was fully awake now, with all his senses alert. He grimaced as he tried to move his left arm.

'God, that hurts!'

'*Certainement*, it hurts,' said the little doctor briskly, and he removed his pince-nez and tapped them on his fingers.

'While you were still insensible, *mon cher lieutenant*, I made examination, and the wound is suppurating. The skin has healed, but trouble has started up underneath, in the old spot. Possibly I shall manage by opening and draining it. Or if it is worse than I think, you may have to go into the hospital in Aix.'

Neil cursed under his breath. The last thing he had wanted was to be detained in Provence, and just when he had been on the verge of returning to his duties at the Front. As for remaining here, in Julie's villa ... that was unthinkable.

He told Doctor Poiret at once that he could not remain here and inconvenience the de Vallois family.

Then Julie intervened:

'You need not go to the hospital. I can look after you. I've studied nursing even though I'm not allowed to be a nurse, and I know enough to poultice your shoulder and help dress the wound if Doctor Poiret opens it.'

He avoided her gaze. She was altogether too lovely in that blue gown and with the childish blue bow confining her silver curls. He said:

'I wouldn't dream of causing you trouble. I must go tomorrow to the hospital.'

'We will not argue about that tonight, *mon lieutenant,*' said the little doctor. 'While you have this fever there is no question of your being moved from this bed. The point under consideration now, is whether I shall open the wound tonight or tomorrow. The sooner it is drained the better, and the more relief you will have from your pain.'

Neil, all too conscious of that red-hot agony in his left shoulder and of his feverish limbs, ceased to protest. He lay back on the pillow and closed his eyes.

'Do as you think best,' he muttered.

Outside the room the little doctor had a discussion with Julie and her father. It was a discussion which ended in preparations being made for that small operation.

Monsieur Poiret had in his day been a surgeon with a big practice in Paris. He had retired through ill-health and become a general practitioner in this small fishing village. But he was an able man and Julie knew this, and had no fears for Neil. And when it came to the question of her assisting, she offered her services without hesitation. She had a courage and a determination inherited from her Irish mother. She was not afraid of the sight of blood. And to do a service for this beloved man was an inestimable pleasure to her.

Neil now saw a new Julie in a white overall and with a white handkerchief bearing the red cross, which she wore at her depot, covering her hair; Julie preparing the room for the operation. The doctor had gone down to his house to fetch some medicaments. Monsieur de Vallois had sent a servant to the *auberge* for Neil's things.

Neil was astonished and more than a little touched as he watched Julie going about her job with such method and precision. The little *amoureuse* of the island had changed her personality entirely and become an efficient nurse. She cleared the spare bedroom of all unnecessary articles. She brought in rubber sheeting, towels, cotton-wool, everything that the doctor would require. Just before Doctor Poiret came back she stood by Neil's bed and took his temperature, slender fingers on his pulse, eyes fixed on her watch.

But suddenly all her pretence of being the cool practical nurse flew to the wind. She caught the look in the handsome eyes of the man whose wrist she was holding, a wrist that burned to her touch. He whispered her name.

'Julie.'

'Ah, do not,' she said under her breath. *'Do not!'*

His feverish fingers caught her hand and pulled it against his lips, which were like fire. In a broken voice he said:

'You're too damnably sweet. I love you and you love me and it's all *much* too difficult.'

She laid the thermometer on the bed, and knelt beside him, no longer the nurse, but all woman now, her eyes brilliant with passion.

'I love you, Neel, *mon amour.* You know that, but we cannot tell each other so. It is forbidden.'

He ran one hand over the white-veiled little head, and groaned.

'It's madness for me to stay here. Let me go to a hospital, Julie. Let me go.'

'Oh, *darleeng,* you heard what the doctor said. You must not be moved while you have this fever.'

For a moment he did not reply. She watched him with those luminous eyes of hers and saw his teeth bite into his lower lip and his features contort.

In an agony of pity for him, she took his hand between both of hers and held it against her breast.

'*Mon amour* ... my beloved Neel ... you are in pain.'

'It's pretty bad,' he admitted.

'Soon we will put you to sleep, and when you wake up again it will be easier.'

He opened his eyes and gave her a grim smile.

'Nothing can be easier while we love each other hopelessly like this. Julie, darling child, for the Lord's sake go away or give me an anaesthetic quickly. I feel as though I'm in hell.'

She bent and pressed a passionate kiss on the hand she was holding, then stood up, her young face pale and set.

'It will come right for us one day some-how... It must!...' she said desperately.

Doctor Poiret returned with his young as-sistant, a youthful doctor who had only just gained his degree and whom Poiret was training, for he wished soon to give up his practice altogether and retire to a house in the mountains which he had built for him-self.

The young doctor acted as Poiret's anaes-thetist. Julie knew him well. He had had an incurable passion for her ever since he came to La Marita, and stammered and blushed whenever she spoke to him. Sometimes she teased him. Tonight he found her very serious and could not even get a look from her. She was concentrating on the wounded

English airman and her job as a nurse.

Neil Richardson knew nothing more for many long hours. When he opened his eyes again another beautiful day had dawned over La Marita. Outside was a miracle of blue sky, lilac sea, and an amber haze of sunshine. But in Neil's room it was still dim and dark behind the closed jalousies.

He opened his eyes, struggling against the mists of the dope which had been given him. He felt utterly weak and nerveless. But the violent pain in his shoulder had gone.

For a moment he could focus his gaze upon nothing in particular. Then he saw Julie (once more in her blue woollen gown) curled in an arm-chair beside his bed. She was sleeping.

Through a haze he saw that young face, pale, and bearing traces of exhaustion. He could not remember why she was here in his room or what had happened to him. The one thing clear in his mind was the knowledge of his intense and overwhelming love for her.

He spoke her name aloud:

'Julie.'

At once she was awake and bending over him.

'Dearest one ... do you want anything?'

His lashes flickered. His arms went round her with a slow, weak movement.

'Thank you for everything,' he muttered.

'Stay with me, darling. Stay with me – always.'

She could tell that he was not fully conscious … that he spoke and acted like one in a dream. Her whole heart went out to him in response. She surrendered to his embrace and laid her cheek beside his on the pillow. With passionate tenderness she smoothed the tumbled brown hair back from his forehead.

'I'll stay,' she whispered.

'I can't live without you,' he murmured.

'I'll stay,' she repeated, and the tears welled into her eyes.

She had been through a difficult night. Helping Poiret with that operation had been a considerable strain on her nerves. Now that it was all over, she broke a little. She was trembling and her lashes were wet as she lay there in Neil's arms. She kept saying:

'*Tout pour toi,* my darleeng Neel, *tout pour toi … toujours.*'

He did not answer. Just for the fraction of an instant his lips brushed hers and his arms drew her closer. Then they relaxed. The dream was over. Julie saw that he was asleep again. Gently she drew away from him and returned to her chair, huddled up in it, and wept in silence and secrecy for the love that she knew must pass, as dreams pass … into nothingness.

Later that morning when he was conscious

again and well enough to be propped up with pillows and take some food, he remembered nothing of that moment in the dawn when he had held her against his heart. Julie did not remind him of it. She was his nurse again, doing her job efficiently, seeking to avoid any undue display of the real sentiments that were within her heart.

There were even moments when they could laugh together. When he thanked her for all she had done for him last night, she said with an attempted gaiety:

'You can thank me best by getting quickly well, and by promising that you will not try to rush away from Villa Vertige to some hospital where they will not look after you as well as I shall do.'

'Ought I to stay?'

'Yes … if we are good.'

'*Can* we be good?' His lips, dry with fever, took a humorous curve.

She answered with a throb in her voice:

'Yes, *mon cher.* We will remember Maurice.'

'Yes, we will remember Maurice,' he repeated. Then added: 'Did I say anything when I was going under the dope?'

He saw a bright carnation pink stain the golden tan of her soft face and throat.

'Many things.'

'Tell me.'

She shook her head.

'Nurses and doctors never repeat what

their patients say when they are under an anaesthetic.'

'Did I speak of you?'

She laughed and bit her lip.

'It was an enormous embarrassment. I don't know what Doctor Poiret thought. But he will keep his thoughts to himself.'

'Julie, tell me what I said,' he begged.

'You called my name many times. You said: *"Je t'adore..."* and you sang just a bar of two of that Provençal song ... do you remember?'

'I remember,' he whispered... *'"Where I endeavour to catch your chaste sweet body's savour I crave but may not taste..."'*

Her face now was a deep scarlet and her heart clamouring.

For a moment they held each other's eyes, hungrily. Then Julie picked up one of his hands, kissed it passionately, and fled from the room.

He lay still and thought:

'We must remember Maurice ... my God ... how hard it is!'

And it was indeed one of the hardest things he had done in his life. Hard for Julie de Vallois as well as for the English airman who had become her patient in her sun-drenched Provençal home.

Time and time again Neil tried to be strong-minded and to insist upon leaving La Marita for the hospital at Aix. Yet that seemed so weak. To run away from temptation was to admit weakness. So he stayed, and under the care of the good little doctor, Poiret, and with the tender and unceasing devotion of his nurse, Neil rapidly recovered from the breakdown. The time approached when the wound gave every evidence of closing, so that he could make arrangements for returning to the war zone.

God alone knew what his next destination would be. A major military disaster had befallen the Allies during Neil's sick leave at La Marita. A miracle had been performed by the British Navy and Air Force who helped to take the war-scarred heroes back to England in that memorable retreat. But where Neil's Squadron was at the moment, he did not know. He intended to return to Lille to his old headquarters, from whence he would get in touch with his commodore.

During those days spent at Villa Vertige, Neil Richardson's love for Julie and for Provence grew more profound, more difficult to eradicate.

He knew that he must pay for the pleasure of staying here and being nursed by Julie; pay for it by the pain of the final parting when it came.

Old Monsieur de Vallois had insisted upon him moving his things from the *auberge*, and remaining at the Villa as an honoured guest until he was passed fit again. Eventually he would attend a military board.

Neil spent most of those long golden days of convalescence lying in a *chaise-longue* under the trees in the sunny garden of the villa. And once he grew stronger, he was able to go down to the seashore, or out in the boat with old Taupin. But never once did he go near the island alone with Julie. He could not face it. Dared not spend another hour in that fatal, lovely, lonely place, with her for whom his very blood clamoured, and whom he would love until he died. There were limitations to loyalties and to strength, and they were both only human.

7

Still there was no news of Maurice.

The Duponts came over to La Marita for lunch one day. They were anxious, harassed parents, pathetic in their pleasure at meeting a friend of their son's. Neither of them spoke English, so the conversation while they were at Villa Vertige was held in French.

Neil was thankful that he had some command of the language.

'Maurice is a good boy and writes regularly, so something must be very wrong,' Madame Dupont observed, sadly shaking her head.

'When I last saw him at Château de la Marche he was well and in fine spirits,' said Neil, 'but since then, of course, Madame, much has happened. During the retreat of the allies and the evacuation from Dunkirk, Maurice may well have been slightly wounded and conveyed to some hospital.'

'If he were in hospital in France, we would have heard,' said Maurice's father gloomily.

Neil drank some of Gaston de Vallois' excellent red wine … *Château Neuf du Pape* … the *vin du pays,* and sought for an answer … for some way of alleviating the undisguised fear and misery of these two. He looked at them with pity and concern. A typical French couple of middle age and of middle class. The father short, rotund, with Maurice's twinkling blue eyes, a bushy grey beard, and a rather violent taste in clothes … broad check suit … butterfly collar, and satin cravat. Madame Dupont small, thin, dressed in black (these French women were always in black, Neil thought … perpetually mourning some relative), a heavy gold chain and cross on her bosom. Aquiline features and dead-white face. A certain charm of manner, a gesture of pretty fingers, a hint of coquetry in once-lovely eyes, and that was Maurice's mother. Neil was sorry for them both and a little ashamed as he sat there at this family lunch party. He felt himself to be an interloper.

Once or twice he caught Julie's gaze and was all the more uncomfortable. What would the Duponts say if they knew that their son's affianced wife was no longer in love with him, and that his, Neil's, convalescence in this village had been remarkable for one great passion of his life – and, perhaps, of hers!

Julie said little during that meal. She sat with lashes downcast, eating and drinking without appetite. The Duponts both spoke to her with great affection and sympathy.

'Ah, *mon Dieu!* My heart bleeds for you, poor little Julie,' Madame Dupont sighed. 'How terrible it is for you to be without news of Maurice.'

'Yes, yes, the poor little one,' seconded Monsieur Dupont, in his booming voice. 'It is hard on the young, this war.'

Julie's cheeks burned. Her feelings were similar to those of the young English flying officer opposite her, and she hated the whole luncheon; hated being made to feel guilty because she loved Neil. She wished that Maurice's parents had not come. And most of all, she wished that they would not keep sympathizing with her.

It was true that she was anxious for Maurice. She still cared for Maurice as a brother. But how could she simulate that same ravening fear and despair which would have been hers were it Neil in Maurice's position?

She was thankful when Madame Dupont

turned to recollections of 1914. She had been married for ten years, she told Neil, when the last great war broke out. No children had blessed her union with André Dupont during those years, and then in 1914 when André, who was a reservist, had been called up to fight for his country, a beautiful little boy had been born. Their Maurice, their one and only son upon whom all their hopes were centred and for whom they had built up their business in Aix.

'I remember,' she said, 'when he was four, and his father came home on leave, our great joy, and Maurice clinging to his father with his little arms, saying: *"Papa, Maurice will be a soldier one day, too."* ... Alas ... those words have come true!'

Madame Dupont sighed and delicately wiped the tears from her eyes with a lace-edged handkerchief.

Monsieur Dupont cleared his throat.

'Come, come, Thérèse, calm yourself. Our boy is not yet lost to us.'

'Some more wine for Monsieur and Madame, Hortense,' put in Monsieur de Vallois, with an attempt at being jovial. 'We must not be too morbid in our imagination. I am sure that our dear Maurice will return safely, and that we shall soon see my little Julie entering the church of Sainte-Michele on her old father's arm – her face as radiant as the flowers.' And he chuckled and cast a sly look at his daughter.

'Ah! What an exquisite bride she will make,' murmured Madame Dupont, fondly.

Julie stared at her plate, a sick little feeling in her heart. Her slender fingers nervously crumbled her roll. She dare not look at Neil. She knew what he must be going through because of her own lacerated feelings, but in that moment it rushed across her with strange finality, that never, never, could she enter the little church in La Marita for her marriage with Maurice. Never could she lie in Maurice's arms as his bride. Not while she felt like this about Neil. It would kill her.

Unfortunately, for her, the Duponts once more focused their attention upon her and her future with their son. He must eventually live in Nice and manage the main branch of their wine business, they said. As they ate Hortense's delicious lunch and drank more wine, the couple became more cheerful and expansive. They enlarged on the excellent prospects which awaited Maurice when he left the Air Force. This setback of the Army was only temporary, announced Monsieur Dupont. The retreat from Mons had been as bad if not worse, and then had come triumph. And once again there would be triumph for France, and peace and plenty in the land. The children of Maurice and Julie would live to see prosperous days.

When it came to talking about hers and

Maurice's children, Julie could bear no more. She cast an agonised glance at Neil. He looked grim and there was a dark flush under his tan.

Julie rose from the table. Her own face was as white as death. In a suffocated voice she said:

'I beg you to pardon me … the room is a little close: I feel faint… I will go to my room for a moment.'

Neil turned his gaze upon her. His sensations were varied and unpleasant. The others at the table were commenting upon Julie's pallor, her father open a window, Madame Dupont offered to go upstairs with her, which Julie declined. And he, Neil, alone knew what was really wrong with her. He was wretched for her and for himself. But what could he do?

Had he never come to La Marita, never loved Julie in return, it might have been better for all of them, he thought. She had been a happy child when he first met her. She had not known the real meaning of love, but in her fashion she had been content with poor Maurice. God! thought Neil, what a lot of harm he had done without meaning to do it. Himself, he could face a rather barren and loveless future, but he could not bear that Julie should suffer. Could not bear the torment that lay in her eyes when she looked at him.

After she had gone out of the room, the conversation was mainly about her. But Neil did not join in until Monsieur Dupont addressed him:

'She's very beautiful and good, our dear Julie, as you must see, *mon cher lieutenant*. It is a great grief for her that there is no word from Maurice.'

Neil forced himself to answer:

'Naturally, Monsieur.'

'We are so pleased to meet our boy's English friend,' put in Madame Dupont, smiling at him, 'in all Maurice's letters from Château de la Marche, he mentioned you and your great friendship.'

Neil set his teeth. These good people were unconsciously heaping coals of fire on his head by every kind word that they said. What sort of a friend had he been to Maurice ... making love to his promised wife? He felt almost that he had betrayed these simple, honest people who were offering him hospitality because of their son. Asking him to go and stay with them in Aix and make use of their car, their house, all that they had to offer.

'I'm afraid it will not be possible for me to stay with you,' was his reply. 'I thank you deeply, but I am hoping that this arm of mine will heal within a few days and then I must return to my Squadron. I cannot continue to stay here, enjoying peace and comfort, while my brother-officers are in action. I only wish to God I had been with them when the balloon went up … when I think what months we spent being bored, doing nothing but make a few reconnaissance flights.'

'Do not be in too much of a hurry, *mon brave*,' said Julie's father, 'your turn will come.'

'The sooner the better,' muttered Neil.

Madame Dupont looked at him wistfully. In her imaginative fashion she pictured the dangers that would attend this young English aviator once he was back on active service. She thought how handsome he was, what a splendid type of English manhood. Timidly she asked:

'Would it be impertinent of me, *mon lieutenant,* to inquire if you have a fiancée in England?'

Neil set his teeth.

'No, Madame, I am not engaged.'

'Oh, but that is tragic!' she said, playfully. 'What are they doing, your lovely English girls, letting such a prize slip through their fingers?'

'Thank you, Madame,' said Neil dryly. 'I'm no prize. I'm sure I should make a very poor husband. I like my independence.'

'Ah! Maurice said that until he met Julie,' said Madame.

Neil wished heartily that he could follow Julie out of the room. He had never had a more uncomfortable lunch and he felt a hypocrite as well as a traitor. Were he sincere, he would tell these people that independence meant nothing to him now that *he* had met Julie, and that he could not tolerate the thought of Maurice returning to claim her. He would like to see Maurice married to any woman in the world *except* Julie.

At last the long-drawn-out meal ended. In the cool little *salon* which never got the sun, coffee was served, but Neil excused himself. He had an appointment, he said, at the doctor's house, and he must walk to the village.

He bade goodbye to the Duponts and went upstairs to find his dark glasses which he had left on his dressing-table.

Passing Julie's door, which was ajar, he paused a moment, and saw her kneeling on her prie-dieu with her head on her folded arms. She might have been praying, or weeping, or both.

His heart constricted at the sight. He had seen her many times before, kneeling before her little altar. An immense depression seized him. Poor sweet Julie ... poor child. God must indeed help her for he, the human being who loved her most, could not do so.

As though she sensed him being there, Julie turned her head and saw the tall figure outside in the passage. Slowly she rose from her knees and came towards him. Her face was wet with tears, her eyelids red. She looked piteously young, he thought, without make-up, without vanity. Just a weeping child.

'Oh, my dear,' he said, 'you mustn't cry, you mustn't be so unhappy. It hurts me terribly to feel that I have done this to you.'

With both hands pressed to her breast, she looked up at him with those large fevered eyes which had such power to twist his heartstrings. 'You have done nothing. You cannot blame yourself, it was just fate.'

He gave an unsteady laugh, longing to snatch her in his arms, and kiss away her tears.

'They are very worried about you downstairs. They think you're ill.'

'*They* worry *me!* They make me ashamed because they think it is the thought of Maurice which is killing me.'

'It upset me, too.'

'That is the cruellest part. We should be able to be proud, oh, so proud, dearest Neel, of a love like ours.'

'Well, we can't be, darling,' he said, with another laugh.

'Why have you come up?'

'To fetch my glasses. I've made an excuse to go to the village. I need fresh air and some exercise.'

She nodded. Her gaze never left his face. He said:

'For God's sake, don't look at me like that,

child. Go back to your prayers.'

'Are you angry with me because I'm unhappy?'

'No, no, why should I be angry with you? With myself, yes, perhaps, for ever having allowed things to come to this pitch.'

'We couldn't help it, Neel.'

'Go and pray for me as well as for yourself, my sweet.'

'Do you ever pray, Neel?'

'Not in the way that you do, my dear, but I envy you your faith.'

'But you *must* have faith,' she said, in a shocked little voice which he found delicious because of the reproach which lay behind it. 'Without faith we are lost. There is so much pain and sorrow in the world, you must believe there is Someone who understands and guides us... Someone who can comfort us when everything else fails.'

He looked over her fair young head at the little shrine before which she had been kneeling. At the ledge bearing the small blue figure of the Madonna with the Child, a half-burnt candle, and a pot of roses. He found that shrine and this faith of hers immensely touching. Before it, he mentally bowed his head. He said:

'I wish I could believe, as you do, in the efficacy of prayer. But no matter how long we were to pray for things to straighten themselves out for us, I don't see how they could, without bringing pain and grief to someone, which is what we most wish to avoid.'

Her brows knit.

'Oh, I know it all seems difficult – especially for you. You are not a Catholic. But I have been brought up to believe in prayer.'

'And have yours always been granted, my darling?'

'Mostly,' she said with gravity, 'and I believe that, when they are not, it means that what I pray for is not good for me.'

He gave an imperceptible shrug of the shoulders. It seemed to him this love which existed between Julie and himself would certainly not be acceptable in the eyes of God. Therefore Julie's tears and prayers were futile. But nothing would have induced him to be openly cynical about it. 'I hope you'll keep your faith, Julie,' he said.

'I pray for you … always…' she whispered.

He made a quick move towards her and for a moment drew her into his arms and kissed her lips and throat with desperate tenderness. Then, gently, he pushed her back into the room and went his way.

8

Time went on and still that wound in Neil's shoulder refused to heal completely, and no matter how much he chafed and worried, the medical Board would not pass him fit to return to his Squadron. An airman must be one hundred per cent fit to do his job properly, and Neil knew it only too well.

Julie's state of mind was curious during that period. She felt almost as though she was living in some kind of trance ... an unnatural calm between two storms. One emotional storm had already broken over her ... all but annihilated her by its force and all but broken her heart. Yet having steeled herself to bid him farewell, he was still here, her tall, strong, handsome Neil. She could still listen to his voice. Still look after him. Still know all the delights of his companionship – but with reservations! And she, too, lived under a strain, endeavouring to the best of her ability to think of him only in terms of friendship, and of herself as the affianced wife of Maurice Dupont.

When the news came through of the first German air raid upon Marseilles, La Marita was profoundly shocked. The war was coming nearer to them. It was the first real echo of it.

But worse was to follow. On the third of June came the horrifying news that Paris had been bombed and only a few days later that Italy had stabbed her old friend and ally in the back and entered the war on the side of Germany.

Almost before old Gaston de Vallois had finished saying what he thought of the Italians, the Germans entered Paris.

They heard that news in Aix that memorable evening when old Gaston took his daughter and the young Englishman out to dinner, after which he wished to spend an hour or two at the casino.

He was not an inveterate gambler, but enjoyed an occasional game of *chemin de fer*. In the days when Julie's mother was alive, he had been seen often at the little provincial casino with the lovely Irish woman at his side, but for years after her death he could not bring himself to enter the Salon de Baccarat. Once Julie was old enough, however, to be taken to the casino, de Vallois occasionally revisited his old haunts.

All through today he had been ill at ease, worried by the sinister news which was coming over the radio. With an attempt to throw off the clouds of depression, he arranged the little party *à trois*.

They drove into Aix through the tranquil

starlit night and dined at the Café Vendôme, where the food was still so perfect and the wine so good.

Julie, like her father, tried also to be gay, to forget the sorrows with which life had so recently burdened her, and Neil was determined to enjoy the evening.

'One can't go on being unhappy, one must keep one's sense of humour,' he had told Julie before they left La Marita.

So by mutual consent the three of them kept off the subject of the war, and laughed and talked during their meal and toasted each other and the future.

But sometimes the laughter died on the lips of both Julie and Neil. Eyes looked into eyes and found little gaiety, only dark apprehension.

Never had Neil seen Julie look so lovely; in a rose-coloured evening dress, and a little rosy coat of feathers, which one of her relatives had sent from Paris. There was a small diamond star gleaming in her curls, and the starlight in her eyes. His heart ached with love, with longing for her. And for Julie there was not another man on that terrace … in Aix … or in the world. Just the tall, grave, handsome young man in his blue uniform, and with his arm in a sling, and a joke on his lips which the look in his eyes belied.

There was dancing at the casino. Gaston de Vallois, his pockets bulging with plaques for which he had just exchanged some crisp mille notes, and with a cigar in his mouth, went off to the Salon de Baccarat to try his luck. Neither Julie nor Neil was particularly interested in gambling. Dancing was much more to their taste.

It was the height of bliss to Julie to move round the floor in the circle of Neil's good arm, to the lilt of a dance band, feeling that, for a few hours, she was his again and nothing else mattered in the world except the two of them. She had danced so many times in the casino ... in this same room ... with Maurice ... with other young men in Aix whom she knew, and who were now away in the Services. She had been happy here in a purely childish, carefree way. But this ... this dance with Neil was different. It was sheer intoxication, and she surrendered herself to it, dancing with head slightly tilted back and eyes half-shut.

He looked down at the rapturous young face, and felt untold bitterness at the thought that so soon he must leave her and never see her again. It was maddening to see love, such love as this, within his grasp, and yet to know that he must not take it.

In all his life he had never felt for any woman what he felt for Julie and he knew himself well enough to realise that such a love could never be repeated in his life.

If only she was not the promised wife of

his friend! If only Maurice would come back so that they could see him and talk to him and be honest about it. If … *if* … that futile, maddening word!

The orchestra was playing *Tristesse*. The plaintive, haunting melody seemed fitting to the hour. Julie gave a long sigh and lifted those heavy lashes which seemed to weigh down her lids.

'I'm so happy,' she whispered, 'and so unhappy!'

'You promised you wouldn't be unhappy tonight, my darling.'

She smiled.

'I try not to be. But I love you so much. If I didn't love you like this, it wouldn't be so hard.'

He gave a bitter sigh.

'I know! But let's make the best of it, darling little Julie. It's heaven dancing with you.'

'It's heaven for me.'

He looked dreamily around the room. Possibly he was the only English person here. They were all French. Very few in evening dress. Most of the younger men, on leave, in uniform. Middle-aged couples in sober black. Several heavily made-up women of the *demi-monde*. There were always one or two of them haunting every casino in Europe, thought Neil, and always one or two sleek, pallid gigolos, who, somehow or other, had evaded being called up.

He thought of the news which he had listened to over the wireless before leaving Villa Vertige. News that the Germans were drawing nearer Paris. He thought:

'The whole world's mad. We're all dancing with the enemy at our gates.'

Then ... the news that shook this little town of Provence just as it shook every town in France, and in the countries across the frontier. The news that was at first a whispered rumour, passed from mouth to mouth, then became a solid, staggering fact. 'THE GERMANS HAVE ENTERED PARIS.'

The orchestra ceased to play, and the people to dance. Huddled in groups, in pairs, the thing was discussed. Horrifying and unbelievable. Making an end of music and laughter and light-heartedness.

The enemy was in the capital. It couldn't be true. There wasn't a Frenchman who could credit such a thing. It had happened once before, yes, but not in the lifetime of any of these people who were gathered here tonight. They had not been born when the Germans entered Paris that other time, and these young people of today had been brought up to believe that such an occurrence was not only improbable, but impossible. The Prime Minister had said that he had believed in miracles and that a miracle would save France. But even now there were Germans goose-stepping down the steps of Paris, along the boulevards, up the Champs Elysées. *No, no,* it wasn't true. The next thing they would be told was that the swastika was flying from the Eiffel Tower.

Julie and Neil walked out of the dance-room and into the vestibule. They held hands tightly. Their faces were pale under the tan.

Julie said:

'Do you believe it? Isn't it just a wild rumour?'

Grimly Neil answered:

'I think it's true enough.'

'Then it's the end,' said Julie under her breath.

Gaston de Vallois came hurrying out of the baccarat rooms followed by a crowd of people who had hastily gathered up their belongings and changed their chips back into money. They could carry on with the game in the face of a minor defeat, or harrassment and suspense, but not in the face of such a national calamity as this. The Germans had entered Paris!

Old Gaston, his rubicund face a greyish colour, looked at Julie and Neil with shocked eyes.

'*Mon Dieu!* You have heard?'

'Yes, sir,' said Neil, 'it isn't too good.'

'That is putting it mildly, my boy. It is the end.'

'Oh, Papa!' exclaimed Julie, taking his

arm, 'that is what I said. Now we are lost.'

Gaston stuffed his wallet into his breast-pocket and shook his head.

'I feared the worst when I listened to the news this afternoon, but I didn't know it was as bad as this.'

'Those vile Germans in Paris,' wailed Julie.

Gaston rolled his eyes heavenwards.

'*Incroyable!* Let us go home.'

They moved out of the casino followed by a shocked, deeply worried crowd. Over Aix there hung a veritable pall of horror.

Driving home, Gaston repeated various remarks made to him by business friends and acquaintances whom he had met in the baccarat *salon*.

Useless to revile the Government … to protest that France should have fought to the last ounce of blood before letting a single German set foot in the capital … it was too late. It meant capitulation now or the total destruction of France. That was what Monsieur Boulanger said. Gaston did not agree with him. France must never surrender. Even now, with the capital in the hands of the enemy, there was still time to fight. Pierre Benoit, the banker, had said that France had been let down by the English. That, too he could not agree with.

Julie held on to Neil's hand.

'Of course the English haven't let us down,' he protested.

'No,' said Neil slowly, 'I don't think it can be laid at our door, sir. I think you'll find it's more complicated than that. The whole show is the result of inside corruption among your ministers, if you'll allow me to say so.'

'God knows you're right,' said the Frenchman with great bitterness, 'but I did not think I should live to hear news such as I've heard tonight.'

Julie was in tears. The joy of the evening had faded. That short-lived joy of dancing with her Neil. Things were happening in her beloved country that she could not begin to understand. She had never worried her young head about politics. She only knew that something very terrible had taken France in its grip and the repercussions of the fall of Paris would be far-reaching.

She let the two men talk, and looked with tear-dimmed eyes at her beloved island as it came within sight. Set like a dark jewel in the moonlit sea. It seemed cruel and futile that such beauty, such peace, should exist only to be broken by the savagery of the wars which men made upon each other.

With a heavy heart she said good night to Neil and left him to continue his political discussions late into the night with her father, and she, tired though she was, fell back on that great consolation – her prayers. She was praying not for herself and her love tonight, but for France.

9

The wild alarm which surged through the once peaceful Provençal country found a serious echo in Neil Richardson's heart. That next morning he came to the conclusion that, whether that arm of his was healed or not, he knew that it was time for him to make a move. And it seemed to him that now not only was France in mortal danger, as her Prime Minister had already announced, but that La Marita itself might soon be no longer safe. And that meant that *Julie* would not be safe.

On a tranquil golden morning – a day when it seemed impossible to believe that France was threatened with such dire destruction – Neil left Villa Vertige and drove into Aix.

When he returned, it was with grim news for old de Vallois and Julie.

He sat with them in the garden, drinking the tea which Hortense had brought them, and announced that this was the last tea which he would share with them in their Provençal paradise.

'We must leave France immediately, all of us,' he said with a grim face. 'It must be in

England that we three drink together again.'

Julie and her father stared at him. They began to question him, both at once. Quickly he answered their questions.

In Aix he had waited a long time but he had managed to get a call through to the base hospital 'somewhere in France' run by a British Colonel, a doctor who was a friend of his from home. This man was in process of evacuating the wounded. He advised Neil to make no effort to rejoin his unit in France, but to go at once by any means possible to England.

'That reason being,' said Neil slowly, 'that there is every reason to believe that France is about to surrender to the enemy, and all ports and frontiers will shortly be closed.'

Gaston de Vallois went ghastly white. He sprang up, knocking his teacup over. Julie sat paralysed, her large eyes staring at Neil.

'It is impossible!' exclaimed de Vallois in heated French. 'Never, *never* could such a thing happen.'

'It is happening,' said Neil grimly. 'Already Reynaud has resigned and I have it on the best authority that Marshal Pétain, as the new premier, will ask for peace terms tomorrow. The English who are fighting here will be caught like rats in a trap. I will be of more use to my country back in England, and want you two to come with me.'

Julie gasped.

'It can't be *true*.'

There followed a difficult half-hour for Neil. The old Frenchman, a loyal patriot and a friend of Britain's, could not reconcile himself to the truth. It appeared too shameful. But almost before that violent discussion between them ended, a telephone call for M. de Vallois from influential friends in Bordeaux confirmed Neil's gravest suspicions.

Julie's father was a broken man when he returned from that call and spoke to the young English airman again.

'*Mon Dieu, Mon Dieu!*' he said tragically. 'You are right, my boy. All I can say to you is … go to Marseilles. Go at once. Get the first possible boat and take Julie with you.'

'You, too, sir,' said Neil.

'No,' said the old man bitterly. 'I stay here where I have lived all my life. I will die. But they will do nothing to me, those *sales Boches*. I am too old. There is more danger for the young. Julie's mother belonged to Great Britain. She must go to her mother's country and let it protect her.'

'I can never leave you, Papa,' said Julie frantically.

'My dear, you must. It will be better for your father to know that you are in safety. Believe me, you will not be safe here very much longer. Your very island will, perhaps, be under the heel of those damned Germans.'

'But there's Maurice!' said Julie in a tone of

112

despair. 'What shall we do about Maurice?'

'I'll make every effort to get in touch with him,' said Neil. 'We will leave messages with his family and at every source which might find him. We will tell him to follow us to England at once. He is loyal to my country. I know that from all the talks we have had together. Maurice will never agree to capitulation.'

'Never!' repeated Julie.

'It may be difficult to trace him now, with the whole of France in chaos,' added Neil. 'But there is no official news as yet that he is wounded or missing. It is even on the cards that we shall find him in England when we get to the other side.'

Julie looked wildly around her. She could scarcely think straight. To leave her father, her home, her beloved island ... to know that Provence might soon be under a German dictatorship, seemed too fantastic to be true.

Never had the gardens of Villa Vertige looked lovelier. The cypress trees were pencilled black against the radiant blue of the sky. The chestnut trees were heavy with pink and white blossom. The flowers of the Mediterranean heath dropped in a cascade of snow over the balustrade, intermingled with another creeper which had star-shaped flowers of purest blue. All so lovely, so utterly tranquil.

And her thoughts leapt away from this garden down there to her island ... the sweet, wild, lonely little island where she had known the heaven of Neil's love.

She looked at him, frantic trouble in her gaze. She realised that he, manlike, would not be giving way to sentiment in this hour. He would be thinking of sterner things ... his mind would mainly be concentrated upon getting back to his own country before the Germans could dominate France and take him prisoner.

She was filled with sudden, nameless terrors for him.

'You must go, *at once*, Neel,' she said.

'And you,' he said. 'You, Julie, will come with me, won't you?'

10

Old de Vallois answered for his daughter.

'Mais oui, mais oui, you must go, Julie. I shall trust you with our English friend who will, I know, *ma petite,* convey you to safety.'

Trembling, she looked from her father to Neil. Hands in his pockets, he was pacing up and down on the lawn in front of them, brows contracted, eyes deep with thought.

'I must get out of uniform,' he muttered,

'borrow some clothes, and some glasses, get through France as a civilian. It would never do for me to wear my uniform. We might be stopped by Germans, and I should be taken prisoner at once. I cannot be taken prisoner, I should go mad. I must get back to England and fly for my country.'

Julie's mind was in chaos. She put two small hands up to her cheeks in anguished doubt and bewilderment. Her father drew her into his embrace and kissed her tenderly.

'Courage, my child. There will be an end to this one day as our dear Reynaud has said: *"France can never die!"* This is only a sad phase in her glorious history ... an inglorious phase. Old Pétain has betrayed us, but we will find a way out.'

Julie burst into tears.

'Papa, I ought not to leave you. I cannot.'

'You must. No harm will come to me, an old man. But I shall be happy to know that you are safe in England, where there is still some sanity.'

'I promise you, Sir, that I will take every care of her,' put in Neil. 'She shall be taken straight to my aunt, Lady Hanley, who has a house in Devonshire. There, Julie will be safe. My aunt, I know, will take care of her.'

Old de Vallois sighed deeply.

'Julie's mother spent many summers of her childhood in Devon. I have heard so many stories of it. I feel my Julie will be at home there.'

Neil turned to the girl whose face was hidden in her hands. His heart ached for her. He knew that this sudden pain of parting with her father and her home ... all the divine tranquillity and sweetness of the life she had led in this Provençal village ... must be wellnigh unendurable to her. He loved her so much, and was so helpless to ease her pain. Awkwardly he said:

'Maurice will be in England, I *know*, to greet you, Julie. I feel in my bones that he is one of the many Frenchmen who escaped with the British Army from Dunkirk.'

Julie drew a long sigh and turned from him so that he should not see her wet, disfigured face.

'I will go into the house and get ready,' she said in a muffled voice.

'Only a suitcase,' he called after her. 'We must take only one each, as we may not otherwise get through. Pack no more than you will need.'

Gaston de Vallois nodded at Neil.

'And you, my boy, come with me and we will find you some clothes and make you look like a refugee rather than an Englishman in the Royal Air Force, *hein?*'

The two men walked across the sun-dappled lawn, following Julie's desolate little figure into the house.

The next hour seemed to Julie like a

fantastic dream. A horrible dream which had but one bright spot in it … the presence and companionship of her adored Neil. She found herself at length driving with him into the station at Aix, casting a last anguished look at her island. Beloved island! It stood there so alluringly in the summer haze; rising out of a sea that was like azure silk. She saw the dim shape of the crucifix, and sent a desperate prayer to the sculptured Christ before whom she had so often knelt:

'Let me come back, dear Christ, let me come back again and with *him!*' was her wild, innermost cry.

Then the island faded from sight. The little village of La Marita with its cobbled streets, its chestnut trees, the silver green of olives on the mountain slopes, was left behind her. Sadly she told herself that she would not see the grapefruit ripen this year, nor the gardeners carry great armfuls of spiced carnations to the market-square in Aix. Perhaps never again indeed would she see this beloved home of hers, nor walk down to the harbour to talk to old Taupin, nor laugh with Madame in the *auberge* where Neil had spent so much of his holiday. She had had no time to say goodbye to any of her friends.

Hortense, weeping and bewailing her departure, had helped her pack a few necessary clothes. She had put on the neat black suit and frilled white blouse which she used to wear to Mass on Sundays; an unaccustomed black straw hat on her silvery hair; unaccustomed gloves on her sun-browned hands, and a bag which contained a roll of notes which poor papa had pressed upon her at parting.

She looked strange to Neil ... a strange Julie ... but a very lovely and pathetic one. Poor little refugee! She was in his care and he was ready to give his life for her safety and happiness. He, too, looked strange in one of Papa Gaston's suits which was too big in parts, too short in others, and at first it made him so ridiculous that Julie had laughed through her tears. A silk muffler round his neck, a very French check cap on his head, sun-glasses, and a water-proof coat. He might be a Frenchman ... he might be anybody ... but certainly he was no longer Flight-Lieutenant Richardson. And he had been careful to pack no uniform in his case, in case it was searched.

He had worked out a plan. They would go to Marseilles. From Marseilles they would find a boat of some kind which would get them to England, perhaps via Gibraltar, and once there Neil could communicate with the R.A.F. in England.

Once having reached Aix, Neil met and talked to a retired English General and his wife who had lately settled in Provence, and had received private warning from a friend in the Consulate at Marseilles that it was imperative that he and his wife should get back to England at once.

General Benson was one of the old 'Diehards', and even now, although he respected the advice because of the source whence it came, refused to believe that France was really caving in.

'The South must surely be safe,' he kept saying, shaking his head. 'The Italians will never get through the Alpine defences.'

But he was forced to alter his mind as, in company with Neil and Julie, they made the journey to Marseilles.

The train was unbearably hot and packed with men, women, and children of every nationality. Czechs, Polish, French, and English, they were staggered by the surrender of Pétain, refusing themselves to give one inch to the Germans, pouring out of the country towards England. England, which promised them the liberty which Pétain's government was trampling underfoot.

In the carriage with Julie, Neil, and the old Bensons were another English couple who had lived for years in Provence and were having to leave all that they had saved behind them. The woman had a baby in her arms and it cried ceaselessly. The mother was tired and nervous, and Julie took the baby from her so that the unfortunate woman could snatch a few moments' sleep.

Neil, to whom the old general talked incessantly, cast an eye now and again at Julie and thought he had never seen anything lovelier than the sight of her with that baby in her arms. She looked at it, rocked it with a tenderness which might have been depicted on the face of a young Madonna. It gave him a deep pang. Julie, the clinging child with so much passion and fire in her, so much lovely laughter and gaiety, had also the makings of a mother ... a true woman indeed. He would have liked so much to have seen her with a child of *his* in her arms.

The train stopped at every station and packed more and more refugees on board. Julie made no complaint but sat quietly trying to soothe the baby whilst the mother collapsed into the arms of her rather helpless-looking husband.

They reached Marseilles when it was growing dark. Normally it would have been a very short trip, but as they were all to find out, nothing was normal in France now.

Marseilles was seething with refugees from all parts of France. Streets, hotels, open-air cafés were crowded.

General and Mrs Benson suggested that Neil and the French girl, whom they took for granted was his fiancée, should stay with them. Somehow or other they managed to find a taxi and Julie bribed the driver with a roll of notes to take them down to the docks.

The docks were already seething with a motley mass of humanity. Julie, clinging on to Neil with one hand and holding her suitcase with the other, stared about her, bewildered. So many times in her young life she had seen this harbour ... in peaceful days when she and papa had met relatives or friends coming by boat from Egypt or England. It was the same Marseilles, yet not the same. The harbour seemed sinister, shadowed by the catastrophe that had befallen France. Everybody seemed bewildered. Many were penniless and wondering what to do, where to go. Aeroplanes flew overhead, droning monotonously, and the eyes that looked upwards were all apprehensive. Already Marseilles had been bombed, and the Germans might take it into their heads to repeat the performance even though an armistice had been signed.

The little foursome who had joined together at Aix eventually found themselves in a struggling queue waiting to get on to an outward-bound ship. Julie was dazed and Neil worried. As the General had remarked, there were thousands of people and only two little coaling ships of four thousand tons to take them off.

It seemed that they stood for hours on that quay waiting their turn. Julie was dropping with weariness but she smiled and assured Neil that she was all right whenever he questioned her. None of them had had anything to eat since midday. There was no question of finding food now. The main thing was to get away from the shores of France, and as quickly as possible. They were now in a crowd of people who were mainly Britons. Everyone spoke to everybody else, exchanging fantastic stories. Many admitted that, when they had left their homes in the South of France, they had also left all that they possessed in the world. Some had parted with their Rolls-Royce cars and Packards, leaving them as tips to the porters who helped them with their luggage. The old and inform were being supported by the younger ones. Exhausted parents took turns in holding their fretful babies. Small children clung to their mothers' skirts crying for food and drinks which they did not get, and pitifully repeating that eternal word 'Why? Why?' To which there was no answer except *'Because the Nazis are here.'*

Julie could hardly stand, so tired was she, by the time they got on to one of those small coaling ships. Neil put an arm around her as they moved at last with the crowd, on board.

'Well, thank God, we're on,' he said grimly, 'even if it looks like being an uncomfortable trip. Thank God it's a warm night, too, as we shall be sleeping out.'

Mrs Benson was a delicate old lady. The General was forced to take her below.

'Below' meant no cabin, but a sack in one of the holds, which were deep in coal dust. There, the General's wife lay in company with the wives of millionaires, women with their jewel-cases clasped in one hand and something ridiculous, like a pot of *pâte de foie gras*, in the other; and Jewish families who had recently been hiding in Paris, and were now forced to flee in terror to London. They were a strange collection of people. All with a certain gay courage, an endurance which, in the face of their circumstances, was quite remarkable. For most of them had been spoiled and pampered, had never known hardship until now.

It was so utterly different from the tranquil and happy existence which Julie had so far led, that she knew she would have found it hard to bear but for Neil. With him she could suffer anything. He kept constant guard over her. When he found her a quiet corner on deck, he laid down his coat for her and rolled up a jacket and placed it under her head.

'Lie there, darling, and rest,' he said, I must just forage around and see if I can find anything for you to eat.'

She hated to see him go. She was terrified he might never find her again, but he had marked the place where he had left her, he told her with a smile, and the boat was small. Too small for his secret liking. There was life-boat accommodation for only fifty people and not a life-belt on board. He hated to think what might happen if they met with any armed resistance at sea.

Julie lay like one stunned, looking up at the stars ... those same stars which had shone so brightly over her island and her home. The little coaling ship was putting out from harbour now. Underneath her she could feel the shuddering of the engines. This was farewell to France! Farewell to the life she had known and loved. And all around her were others, like herself, losing all that they cared for. But there were no tears. Everybody seemed determined to be cheerful. In one corner of the ship a group of English people were singing 'God Save the King' as the ship moved out.

Strangely stirred, Julie sang with them the words of the British National Anthem. As the strains died away she said to herself:

'God Save the King – *Neel's King!* And perhaps now I can count him as mine...'

She was never more glad than when she saw Neil's tall figure making his way through the crowd back to her. She laughed up at him. He looked so comic in Papa Gaston's old striped suit and that collar which was much too big for him. He was very cheerful, and carried to her a tin and two biscuits.

'Our rations,' he said gaily. 'All that they can spare tonight.'

He threw himself down beside her and raising themselves on their elbows they ate the gingerbread biscuits and drank, in turn, the water. It was warm and unattractive. Everything was warm, and Neil's face and hands were black. You had only to walk through the ship and you were black with coal dust, he told her.

He had found out they were being followed by the little sister ship, and that their first stop would be at Oran. There they might be allowed on shore to get some provisions, because the ship was so short of them.

'I have brought you to strange things,' murmured Neil, looking down at Julie's face. A grimy little face ... nobody could be clean on this ship ... but in the starlight, still the loveliest face in the world to him.

She whispered back:

'With you I am happy, and I shall never be afraid.'

'Anything may happen to us, darling,' he said. 'But I know you will always be brave, I couldn't leave you in France, Julie, I *couldn't*. Once the Germans get control there, anything might have happened to you, and we still hope to find Maurice on the other side.'

She nodded.

The thought of Maurice kept her from saying all the things she would like to have said to him. They lay quietly there in this strange intimacy ... yet so far apart ... the shadow of Maurice like a drawn sword between them ... between their bodies if not their minds.

Those next few days would live for ever in both their memories ... days of danger, thrill, excitement, acute physical discomfort shared by them all ... hundreds of men and women who refused to whine, and who shared with one another the few ounces of bully beef and the gingerbread allotted to them.

The next day dawned clear and calm, a matchless sky, sea like blue glass. The terrific heat made their discomfort more acute, and no water was allowed for washing. Julie looked in despair at her dirty hands, and with the aid of some witch-hazel and some cotton-wool tried to cleanse her face. An English girl sitting near her was doing the same. They laughed together at what they called their 'facial treatments'.

One of England's most gifted novelists, who was on board, kept his own little coterie amused with his witty quips and jests. A famous Indian prince found an empty condensed milk tin and carried some water in it proudly to an ex-Queen, who was permitted to bathe her hands ... envied by all.

During that day of heat and slow progress, Neil and Julie stayed close together, trying to recapture some of the gay companionship which they had shared in Provence.

'Let's pretend that this is Jean Taupin's

boat and that we are making now for our island,' Julie said.

Neil, smoking the last of the few cigarettes in his case, fell in with her suggestion. But when he thought of Julie lying on the warm sweet sand, laughing up at him whilst he pressed the ripe cherries between her lips, he could no longer laugh or pretend. The future was too grim, for it was a future in which Julie could not be included. He had always to bring himself back to the thought of Maurice.

On the second day, the little sister ship fell out with engine trouble. Immediately an Italian submarine surfaced so near the ship on which Julie and Neil were aboard, that they could hear the voices of the crew. At midnight three torpedoes were fired. And then Julie knew the meaning of a moment's real fear. It was a dark night, and she sat huddled on the deck, her hand fast clasped in Neil's, her ears straining for the slightest sound. Neil put an arm around her. He could feel the short hard beats of her heart, shaking her slim young body.

'Courage, darling,' he whispered. 'I won't leave you.'

'They may get us, Neel.'

'We'll go together.'

She shut her eyes against his sleeve and threw a deep breath.

'I love you,' she said, desperate to tell him

the truth, in the face of possible death.

'I love you, too...' he said. 'It will always be the same.'

Their lips met and clung in a kiss of strange ecstasy. In this hour they belonged utterly to each other ... there was no Maurice ... only themselves ... and if death came they would face it together and unafraid.

Some of the old women and children had been put in the lifeboats. There was no confusion or terror on board. A complete absence of panic. Just a sinister silence ... all of them waiting for the explosion which might, or might not come.

Then the gunner on the little boat gave the Italian submarine a couple of rounds from his gun. The Italian submarine turned and fled. Everybody rose and cheered and Julie found herself weeping and laughing, together, in Neil's arms.

So passed another night. They slept side by side massed with the other men and women on that coal-blackened deck, under the cold ironic stars. Another dawn when Julie wakened to feel Neil's breath gently fanning her cheeks ... lay and watched him sleeping quietly, looking like a young boy with his roughened hair, his brown, sooty face. And she felt that her heart would break with love for him.

So they reached Oran and there made ready to go on shore, hoping that they would be allowed to buy food and perhaps spend a night in comfort. They were joined again by the old Bensons who had been having a rough time of it below.

But the British Vice-Consul from Corsica flew over with the information that the Colonies were capitulating and that the French authorities would lock up any English who attempted to land at Oran.

Neil imparted this news to Julie.

'That's that, my dear,' he said. 'So fade our hopes of a nice juicy *tournedo* and some fresh fruit and hot coffee.'

Julie sighed.

'I wouldn't mind some of my fish suppers at La Marita.'

Neil grinned.

'And I wouldn't mind some tobacco for my pipe, but don't let's talk of it, it'll be bully beef again for dinner.'

Old General Benson, refusing to be done out of the supper for which he had hoped, attracted the attention of some fishermen in a boat, threw them down a roll of francs and asked that they should bring back ham and bread and fruit which they would hoist up on deck with a rope and bucket.

The fishermen were friendly, and all the more so when Julie leaned over and smiled, and spoke to them in her native tongue. But the English party never saw the fishermen or their thousand francs again. The captain of the coaling ship had decided to go full steam ahead.

That night, Julie began to feel that aeons and aeons had passed since she had driven away from La Marita with Neil ... that thousands of miles of sea had been put between her father, her old home, and herself. She felt utterly lost, no longer the old Julie de Vallois. Her one dread now was separation from Neil. It did not seem possible to her that she could part from him again after this ... these incredible days and nights which they had shared.

Until she died, she knew that she would remember and treasure the thrill of her first glimpse of Gibraltar and the British flag.

Everybody on board crowded to the rails and waved wildly as the little coaling ship moved bravely through the blue waters towards the Rock.

'The Rock!' said Neil, and his hand went up in swift salute to his flag and his country. Then he smiled and pressed Julie's hand. 'Cheer up, darling. You'll soon be on English soil.'

In a small tremulous voice, she said:

'You won't let them take me from you, will you, Neel?'

'Of course not,' he said tenderly. 'You're right in my care until I get you safely to Aunt Alice's house.'

It was one of those exquisite mornings in

Gibraltar when the mighty outline of the Rock seemed to be etched in fine black lines against a deep blue sky. The Gibraltarians greeted the refugees from the little ship with unlimited generosity. The moment they arrived at the Customs there were large boxes of cigarettes from which they could help themselves. Then everybody was taken to the Colonial hospital, given beds in the cool white wards, a lunch that seemed to Julie and Neil the finest they had ever tasted … and (more appreciated than anything) … hot baths.

And now it was a question of waiting for a ship to take them back to England.

During those five days in Gibraltar, Neil, Julie, and the old Bensons were given billets in an empty flat in Irish Town. There Julie did the cooking, looked after the General's wife, and was, as Neil told her, an invaluable help.

Every morning, like a true Frenchwoman, she took her basket and walked down the main street to find cheap good vegetables, and good fresh fish and meat for their meals. She was an excellent little cook and the meals she served were a delight to them all after the privations on board the ship which had brought them from Marseilles.

She was bright and gay with a little apron over her dress, performing all the domestic duties in the flat because Mrs Benson was too old and infirm to be of any help. Neil and the General spent a great deal of their time with the officers of the various regiments now stationed on the Rock, and were shown the wonderful defences which had been put up on this side of Spain.

There were hundreds of refugees like themselves, waiting to hear of ships to take them to England. Neil chafed impatiently at the delay. Not only was it difficult to live this life in close association with Julie, yet having to check the ardour of his love for her, but he longed to get back to his job.

The arm stubbornly refused to heal. He attended the English Military Hospital daily, hoping that, under the attention of a British doctor, the wound would soon close up.

He and Julie made continual inquiries about Maurice, always hoping that they might find him amongst the crowds who had landed here from France, but so far they had not come across the young French airman, nor had anybody seen or heard of him.

Julie lived her life during those five days in a kind of daze, alternating between bouts of acute homesickness, wishing that she had not left her father and Villa Vertige, and the joy which she always knew in Neil's presence.

The old Bensons always retired early to bed, and almost every night Julie and Neil entertained English troops, shared with them their meals and drinks. Gibraltar was gay and optimistic. Alcohol and cigarettes were cheap. But most of the women had been evacuated to Casablanca. So Julie, young and lovely, found herself the centre of an admiring crowd wherever she went. It was five days of real happiness for her ... of almost hysterical gaiety which she and Neil enjoyed with the soldiers, sailors, and marines.

Neil sent a long letter to his aunt in Devonshire, telling her that he would soon be with her, and explaining about his precious 'refugee'. At the same time he wrote to headquarters informing them of his escape from France and asking for news of Maurice.

It was on the fifth day that a troopship put in to Gibraltar and took off the English who had recently landed there. That ship had the last of the B.E.F. on board. Men who had worked their way down from the north of France to Marseilles. One of the officers told Neil they had still had most of their guns and equipment when they reached Marseilles, but the moment they had begun to load it on the troopship, the French authorities had turned off the electric power so that the cranes would not work.

'Dirty dogs,' he cried. 'We had to blow up our guns and destroy our equipment.'

Neil refrained from telling Julie that story. He knew how it would upset her. She was so utterly loyal to her mother's country. She could not bear this betrayal by the French.

As they steamed out from Gibraltar, Neil and Julie leaned over the rails to take their last glimpse of the Rock.

'I was happy there,' Julie whispered. 'It was fun ... cooking meals for you ... going everywhere with you.'

'Cheer up, darling,' he said, although his heart was heavy within him. 'One day perhaps we will be happy like that again.' But he wondered how – or when – or where!

Food was scarce on the ship, but it was comparative luxury after the other voyage. There were unforgettable sights on the way. Broken wrecks of great ships, the relics of magnetic mines. And gradually they left the blue waters and the brilliant sunshine behind them. It grew cooler, greyer. And then one morning Julie found herself in Liverpool.

Big-eyed, thrilled, she took her first glimpse of a great English port. Neil laughed when she expressed her amazement at the intricacies of the tremendous docks ... the vast network of railway lines ... the rather dark, closely crowded streets and tall grim stone houses.

'This isn't all that we can show you,' he said. 'Wait until you see Devonshire, my dear. And I promise you that sometimes the sun does shine with us ... even if it isn't quite the same as La Marita!'

When they were in the train to take them

to London, Julie spoke of Maurice.

'In London they may know about Maurice, may they not?'

'It is possible,' said Neil. 'I shall go straight to headquarters and see what I can find out.'

She nodded and sat very quiet. Looking out at the suburb of Liverpool through which they were passing ... at all the sights that were so new and strange to her, her heart was sinking. She thought:

'Very soon I shall be with his aunt and he will leave me. I must try not to mind too much and not to be a coward when the parting comes. After all, I've known all the way along that it *would* come. I must try to be thankful for this great adventure that we have had together ... he and I.'

Neil, smoking a pipe and enjoying the luxury of his favourite tobacco, looked up from an English paper which he had been reading with interest.

'You have heard, I expect, of General de Gaulle?' he asked her.

'Yes, of course. He is a great man ... a great patriot.'

'He is here in London,' said Neil, 'asking all Frenchmen to rally under him. Maurice, if he is alive, will be amongst them. I know that. And somehow I feel in my bones that we shall find him here.'

'I hope so,' she said in a low voice.

Then their eyes met and a little tremor

shook them both. His hand found hers and pressed it hard. They were silent for a long, long time.

11

It is a long way from the village of La Marita in Provence to the quiet village of Mulverton in North Devon, which was the home of Neil's aunt, Lady Hanley. The home to which Neil took his precious refugee.

Neil knew very well that he could expect a warm welcome and every sympathy from Aunt Alice. She had always been the favourite of his few relations. His mother's youngest sister, Alice was still in her early forties, and one of those beings upon whom the gods seemed to have smiled from her birth. For she had everything. Looks, charm, intelligence, a husband and children whom she worshipped, and one of the most beautiful and picturesque homes in North Devon.

Mulverton was six miles from the nearest station. Lady Hanley herself drove to meet her nephew and the French girl about whom she already knew much. She had received Neil's long letter from Gibraltar, written while they were waiting there for the boat which finally brought them home.

136

So Julie reached the end of the long, unforgettable journey which had been a tremendous experience. She felt at the close of it all that she was no longer a young, uninitiated girl who had seen nothing of life. She was a woman now who had been through adventures which might have shaken the courage of many stronger and more worldly-wise than herself. At the same time it was an experience she would not have missed, because it had been shared with Neil. He had never left her. She had loved him before they left France, but now he was to her as a god whom she worshipped. He had been so exquisitely kind and understanding. He had shown her such utter tenderness at a time when passion would have been out of place. He had remained loyal to Maurice, and the first thing he had done on reaching England was to get in touch with headquarters and send out an SOS for Lieutenant Dupont, a request that any information concerning the young French aviator should be sent at once to his fiancée in Devonshire.

Julie hardly knew whether to be glad or sorry when at length she found herself driving through the wooded countryside of Devon, with Neil and his aunt. It had been wonderful sharing so much with him. Now it must all end. The moment Neil's arm was healed, he would return to his unit. Indeed, long before that she was sure he would go away and do what he could for his country.

The badly dressed shabby stranger who had travelled with her from Marseilles was once more a smart young officer in his Air Force blue. But she had loved that shabby stranger who had been so close to her through that great adventure. Yes, she was almost sorry that it all had ended.

She liked Neil's aunt at sight. Alice Hanley was tall and slim, with close-cut dark hair showing silver threads, beautiful hazel eyes, and a warm brown skin. She looked a typical English woman, in her well-cut linen tweed suit and sensible shoes. There were a couple of spaniels in the back of the small car, barking furiously at first, and then wanting to make friends. Parcels which Julie was given to hold. A jar of cream, a basket of strawberries, some letters and newspapers which, Lady Hanley explained, she had picked up in Mulverton while she was waiting for the train.

She welcomed Julie with a kiss and a smile which did much to ease the homesickness which the girl had been feeling since she left France.

'You poor child!' she had said. 'What you must have been through. Those vile Germans! Never mind, we'll soon get some colour into that little face of yours after we've had you for a few weeks at Mulverton

Court, won't we, Neil?'

Neil had laughed and said:

'Knowing you, Aunt Alice dear, I'm sure she will soon have a high colour. I remember how I used to put on weight and get disgustingly fat whenever I stayed with you, in my youth.'

Now the phantasmagoria of the past fortnight passed and reality claimed Julie as she sat, with a spaniel on either side of her, taking in the vista of the countryside. Her first real glimpse of the England which her mother had loved. And although deep in her heart she hungered wildly for Provence, Devon smiled upon her with a tranquil benison which laid a healing spell upon her. Julie had never cared for the town, but this was exquisite country indeed ... the best that England had to offer with its rich red soil, its cool green valleys, and the river Exe flowing like a silver ribbon under little stone bridges ... a river, Neil told her, filled with speckled trout which he used to fish for as a boy.

This was the England for which millions of men were fighting, Julie thought to herself with awe, as her large eyes photographed every detail which she passed. She was enchanted by the tumble-down white cottages, half-hidden by honeysuckle and roses, the flower-starred hedges, the little gardens, the luxuriant trees. Six miles of pure beauty as they climbed from the valley up a hill, up, up until they were hundreds of feet above the road on which they had originally travelled. Here was Mulverton Court. And when Julie first stood on the terrace, looking down at the valley and at the river which was now like a distant streak of silver, she caught her breath and said delightedly:

'*Ah! C'est merveilleux!*'

And then she turned from the lively Exe valley and saw for the first time in her life what 'one of the stately homes of England' could be like. Utterly different from Villa Vertige, which had its own peculiar charm, Mulverton Court was much bigger, more magnificent, with its perfectly kept lawns, its dark yew hedges, and wonderful trees. The rose garden at once made her feel at home, because it reminded her of the roses at La Marita.

The house itself was of the Queen Anne period; mellow pale rose bricks, charming porticos, and the loveliest of windows with circular fanlights ands square panes.

Lady Hanley took Julia's arm and drew her indoors.

'You'll be wanting to change and rest,' she said.

Julie gave a fleeting look at Neil. He looked back at her and for a moment love sprang naked and unashamed into that gaze which they were both holding. Alice Hanley intercepted it and her brows lifted.

'H'm,' she thought. 'So that's how the land lies. My poor old Neil and the little French girl! And what of the French fiancé? This looks bad to me!'

Julie was taken to her room … one of the many lovely guest rooms at Mulverton Court. As she walked through the house she had a glimpse of gracious, walnut furniture, of green and rose real English chintzes, soft brocades, delicate watercolours against white-panelled walls, many books, and flowers … flowers everywhere. Alice Hanley was an artist at arranging them, although, as she was quick to tell Julie, she hadn't much time now, what with knitting parties, canteens in Tiverton, and a dozen and one duties which the war imposed upon her. Indeed, half of Mulverton Court was filled with evacuees.

'Noisy little children,' Lady Hanley laughed when she told Julie about them. 'All from the danger zones, poor lambs. But I'm pleased to have them. All my own children have gone and my husband, too.'

Julie heard that she had three children. Two boys, one of whom was a medical student up in Edinburgh, one in the Army, and a girl in the Women's Auxiliary Air Force, and her husband, Commander Sir Percy Hanley, was at sea. All away, her dear ones, serving their country; Julie thought it was wonderful, just as she thought that

Neil's aunt, and her fine fighting spirit, were wonderful. Julie had always loved the thought of the British Isles because of her mother. But now she was going to love them for themselves; to understand why men were willing to die before they surrendered their country to Nazi Germany as poor France had surrendered.

Lady Hanley suggested that Julie should change into a thin black frock ... the only one she had brought with her.

'You will feel fresher, and then we'll have drinks on the terrace before our evening meal. I haven't asked anybody in to meet you tonight as I thought you would like to get used to your surroundings first of all.'

Julie smiled at her, her underlip quivering a little. Alice Hanley saw that quiver and her heart went out to Julie. No wonder Neil had fallen for Julie de Vallois, she thought. She was an enchanting child. Alice had never seen anything so attractive as those large dark eyes with that cloud of silvery hair.

She tried to cheer Julie up.

'Tomorrow I hope my young niece, Pat Wallis, will come over and meet you. Or I'll take you to see her. She is a V.A.D. in a Red Cross Hospital between here and Tiverton.'

'That will be lovely,' said Julie.

Lady Hanley left her. For a moment Julie stood looking round the charming room. The creamy shiny chintz with its pattern of rosebuds was perfect with the dark oak furniture and the rose-coloured carpet. Two tall windows looked across the garden down the green valley to the river. The sky reminded her a little of the skies at La Marita, flushed with the glow of sunset. It was all very beautiful and seemed far from war ... from the awful horrors of bombing, torpedoing, the nightmare through which she had recently passed. Then she thought of her father, alone in his deserted village, her pigeons, Co-co and Ton-ton, who would be missing her, although Hortense had promised faithfully to be feeding them ... and her island which seemed thousands and thousands of miles away. Her heart sunk. What did the future hold? How little she knew! She must just remain here, an exile, embarking upon a hopeless search for Maurice whom she might never find, but to whom she must remain loyal till she knew of his death.

Through the open window she caught the sound of a man's laugh. Neil's rare boyish laugh which she adored to hear. Her whole being flooded with love for him, with a yearning which must not be satisfied.

She started to unpack, her eyes blind with burning tears.

12

In a Red Cross officers' hospital near Mulverton, a young English V.A.D. was taking the last luncheon tray to one of her patients, before going off duty.

Pat Wallis was tired. She had been tired for weeks. She had almost forgotten how it was to feel anything else. Since the evacuation from Dunkirk, and with fresh convoys of wounded coming down to Devonshire daily, she had been putting in a hard day along with the other nurses and sisters.

But nobody in the ward who saw Nurse Wallis carrying that tray to the end bed near the windows, which looked out on to a very pleasant garden, would have known that she was so exhausted. Only someone who took a close look and saw the blue shadows under her eyes and the slightly pinched look about her nostrils might notice it. But the man in this room saw only a trim figure in the neat-fitting uniform, spotless veil, apron with a little red cross, and that wide, cheerful grin, which was one of Pat's chief charms. For the rest, she was not exactly pretty, but she had a pair of blue, curly-lashed eyes which could be called truly beautiful, and a turned-up nose which seemed in harmony with her broad sense of humour. She was a great favourite in the hospital. And if she was the sort to tear a hole in her apron, or break a cup easily, or get a smudge on that *retroussé* nose just before Matron's inspection, well – that was Pat and all part of her make-up.

Pat had been out here for the last three months. She had left a comfortable home in Cheshire, two younger sisters, a horse, and a couple of cairn-terriers, all of which she adored. At twenty-one she was determined to 'do her bit', like her only brother, Francis, a Gunner who had last been heard of at St Valery – and not since.

These were bitter, anxious days and Pat was fretting badly about Francis, whom she adored, about some of the other boy friends from home. Besides, nobody was safe these days. Even here, in England, one was liable to be bombed. But Pat's panacea for her worries was work … hard work … more work.

She set the tray on the enamel table beside the narrow white bed on which a young officer was lying, his head covered by a white capeline bandage (Pat had put on that capeline and was proud of it).

'Now, *Jeudi*,' she said cheerfully, 'here's a nice piece of fish. Take a look at it and see if you're hungry.'

The officer, so addressed, raised himself

on one elbow and grinned back at the V.A.D. His eyes were as blue as hers, and his face as white as though all the blood had been drained from it. There were scars all over that face ... superficial ones, rapidly healing ... both his hands were burned and in bandages.

When he spoke it was with a decided accent.

'Feesh! Ah, *poisson, c'est bon!*'

'*Poisson* is the word,' said Pat.

'I will eat it only if you will sit beside me,' he said.

Pat blinked her curly lashes.

'You must be insane. As if I have time to sit beside anyone.'

'But *me!* You can do it for *me*,' he said in a beguiling voce.

'Indeed I can't,' she retorted, but the look she threw him was very tender. The young V.A.D. had a decidedly soft spot in her heart for this patient. '*Jeudi*' he was known to all. A nickname that Pat had given him. With his uniform charred, there had been nothing left by which to identify him at the casualty clearing station. Even his identity disc was missing. It was said that he must have dragged himself from his aeroplane, which had been burnt out, and that it was a miracle he had survived. They knew only one thing about him ... that he was French ... beyond that he was a mystery. His head

146

had been wounded and he suffered from concussion. The past was a blank to him, and so far nobody had claimed him. But he had been brought here into Pat's ward on a Thursday, so *'Jeudi'* she had christened him.

The other nurses ragged Pat about *Jeudi*. He was Pat's 'foundling'. She had special care of him. For the last fortnight he had been very ill, but now he was much better, and during this last day or two he had become sufficiently normal to show Pat that he was more than ordinarily grateful for her ministrations. He had a sense of humour to match her own. In fact, he flirted with her outrageously, and as only a Frenchman can. And whilst Pat roared with laughter at his flattering words and persuasive ways, she experienced a very decided thrill whenever she came near *Jeudi*.

She wondered who he was and whence he came; what his home had been like, and whether he was married or single. In his bewilderment, he had discussed matters fully with Pat, and could come to no conclusion except that he was sure that he was not a married man.

'I don't know why,' he had said the other day, 'but I'm just sure.'

Then Pat had said:

'Well, I bet you have a girl friend.'

To which he had replied glibly:

'Ma chérie, I am French, I am sure I must

have many. But now – only one. My leetle English nurse.'

A satisfactory enough reply for Pat.

One of his injured hands had healed sufficiently for him to hold a fork. With this fork he managed to eat his fish. Then as Pat showed signs of leaving him, he dropped the fork with a clatter.

'*Mon Dieu.*'

She turned back.

'Now what is it?'

'My fingers hurt. I must be fed. I cannot hold the fork.'

She came back at once and sat beside him.

Lifting some fish and a piece of potato on to the fork, she put it near his lips. Instead of taking it, he bent his head and dropped a kiss on her hand. She turned fiery red and pursed her lips.

'Well, I don't know how to say "you're the limit" in French, but that's what you are, *Jeudi. Just the limit!* You are perfectly capable of holding that fork. You just want to play the idiot.'

'*Chérie,*' he whispered, 'you have the bluest eyes I have ever seen.'

'Listen,' said Pat, 'you're here to get well and not to pay compliments to the nurses.'

'I don't pay them to the nurses ... only to one.'

She tried not to smile. Under that starched white apron and gown her heart was beating quite fast, and Pat's heart had never beaten fast for any man before. She felt quite alarmed about it.

'You just carry on with your *feesh*,' she said.

'Ah! Now you mock my English,' he said reproachfully.

'I've got to have my own lunch and then go off duty,' she announced.

'What are you going to do?'

'Take a walk round the town and do some shopping, I expect.'

'The doctor said I can get up next week, then you'll take a walk with me. Yes?'

'Certainly not. Nurses aren't allowed to go out with their patients.'

'Then one of us must leave the hospital in order that we may see each other off duty.'

'You hurry up and get well,' she said severely for the second time, and tried not to look pleased.

A sister came walking down the ward, which was a pleasant sunlit room. There were only six officers in here. A mass of lovely flowers stood on the centre table with a gramophone and some books.

Pat saw Sister and made a rather feeble display of straightening *Jeudi*'s bedclothes, then turned to go. Sister, however, stopped her.

'You have a visitor, Nurse Wallis, a young officer. I have told him to wait in the nurses' sitting-room. Nobody seems to be there at the moment.'

Pat gasped.

'Oh! It *isn't* my brother, Francis, is it, Sister – or someone with news of him?'

'I'm afraid not. He says he is your cousin. I think Flight-Lieutenant Richardson was the name.'

The eager light sped from Pat's eyes. She had so hoped that it might be darling Francis who had turned up at last. So it was cousin Neil. A very nice cousin, and one of whom she was fond, although he was older than she by some years and she had never seen much of the Richardson side of the family. They were Mummy's relations. The last time she had seen Neil was at Christmas, when they had all met at Davos, skiing. Heavens! What a lot of water had rolled under the bridge since then!

She knew that Neil was flying and had recently been out in France. She presumed that their aunt, Lady Hanley, had told him where she was nursing. This hospital was only five miles from Lady Hanley's home. Well, it would be nice to have a word with Neil. Perhaps he would be able to go out with her, this being her half-day, she thought, hopefully.

Full of pleasant anticipation, she hurried into the nurses' sitting-room where Neil Richardson awaited her.

She found him with one arm in a sling, looking much the same as she remembered him. A trifle more mature, perhaps, and really, she told herself, he *is* a good-looker!

After they had exchanged greetings, Neil told Pat his news. How he had been wounded in May and that for some reason or other the wound refused to heal and kept breaking down. How he had convalesced in Provence and learned whilst there of Pétain's capitulation. He then mentioned Julie, casually.

'She and her father were very good to me in Provence and I brought her over to safety. She's engaged to a French airman and he is missing. We thought we might find him here.'

'I see,' said Pat, 'and you're staying with Aunt Alice at the moment?'

'Yes, and I'm livid about my arm,' said Neil gloomily, 'and in a day or two I shall go up to town and see if I can't get some work with the Squadron.'

'Well, how about taking me out as it's my half-day?' Pat grinned at him.

'That's what I've come to do. Aunt Alice wants me to take you back to Mulverton Court for tea.'

Pat cheered up visibly.

'That sounds grand. I'll ask Matron.'

Neil looked out of the window at the green lawn, which was dotted with figures. Some in wheel-chairs or chaises-longue, some walking on crutches, others sitting under the trees.

'This looks a pretty decent hospital,' he said. 'I wonder if you've got any chaps here that I know.'

'We've several R.A.F. boys.' Pat reeled off a list of names, and Neil broke in:

'Wait! Bracken! Is that Wing-Commander Kenneth Bracken? If so, I know him well.'

'Yes, he is a Wing-Commander, and I think his initials are K.B.'

Neil was delighted. He asked if he might go along to the ward and see his old friend, so Pat took him there.

Neil walked into the sunlit room, wherein there were six wounded men. He immediately recognised his friend, Ken Bracken. He had one leg in a splint, but otherwise looked hale and hearty. Bracken greeted Neil with enthusiasm.

'By God, it's good to see you, Richardson. How goes it?'

Neil sat down by his bed and the two men lit cigarettes and talked. They had not served in France together, but had been together on several occasions at home. They discussed the war, and the conditions under which they had both received their wounds. And then Neil found time to look round the ward.

His casual gaze lit on the man in the bed

opposite Bracken's. But it ceased immediately to be casual, and his expression changed to one of amazement and incredulity.

'Good God!' he exclaimed, jumping to his feet.

The Wing-Commander looked up at him.

'What's up?'

Neil's gaze was riveted on the young officer opposite. A man with bandaged head and scarred face. Those very blue eyes ... that wide mouth and cleft chin ... good God, unmistakable!...

'Who is it in that bed opposite you?' Neil asked Bracken hoarsely.

'Oh, he's a French fellow. We don't know his name. He's an airman, brought in in a bit of a mess and with nothing to identify him. For a moment he's our mystery man, affectionately named *Jeudi* by one of our V.A.D.s.'

Then Neil, with his heart pounding, said:

'I know him, Ken. I know who he is. His name is Maurice Dupont. He was with our Squadron as liaison officer, and has been missing for some little while. I must speak to him at once. Possibly, seeing me, he'll remember...'

13

Bracken looked interested. He addressed a big red-faced Major in the bed beside him.

'I say, Major, do you hear that? Richardson thinks he knows who our Frenchman is.'

The one eye which the Major had left to him gleamed appreciatively.

'Good show!'

Neil stood beside Maurice Dupont's bed. His pulses were hammering and there was a dry feeling in his throat. It was with mixed feelings that he looked down at the young airman who had been his brother officer, his friend, and was Julie's affianced lover. Feelings tinged with guilt, dismay, pleasure, so many conflicting emotions. But the main one was pleasure at having found Maurice alive.

'Maurice,' he said excitedly, 'Maurice, old chap, don't you know me? It's Neil. Neil Richardson.'

The young Frenchman lay still, his bloodless face unsmiling, his round blue eyes staring up into the Englishman's face without recognition. But there was considerable bewilderment written in those eyes. He said slowly:

'*Pardon,* but I'm afraid I don't remember anything or anybody.'

'But you *must* remember me. We were together... Look here... Château de la Marche ... La Chaume ... the place where our reconnaissance unit was stationed. You *must* remember ... just behind the Maginot Line ... try and think, Maurice, old boy.'

Dupont, who had heard himself addressed by no other name save *"Jeudi"* since his arrival at this hospital, continued to stare bewilderedly at Neil. A slight flush stained his cheek-bones. He struggled with his mind ... that mind which had been so shadowy, so muddled, since his escape from death. But the past remained a blank to him.

There were almost tears in his eyes as he answered.

'No, I don't remember, but tell me more. You say you know me. Who, then, am I?'

'Maurice Dupont. *Dupont.* Try to remember...'

'Dupont,' repeated the young Frenchman and passed a hand across his wrinkled forehead. *'Mon Dieu!* It strikes some kind of chord and yet ... yet I don't remember.'

'You come from Provence. You parents live in Aix.'

'Yes, yes. Tell me more.'

'You have been missing for some time. Your parents have been gravely concerned and your fiancée...' the words stuck in

Neil's throat '…has been worried to death.'

Maurice stared at the Englishman with painful intensity, and now his face was a dull scarlet.

'My fiancée!' he repeated the words in a whisper. 'Am I then engaged?'

'You are,' said Neil grimly, 'and she is here within five miles of you. I brought her back with me. Her father asked me to take care of her and save her from France just after Pétain surrendered.'

Maurice went on staring at Neil, his blue eyes completely blank. Neil added:

'For God's sake, man, you must remember *Julie*. Villa Vertige, her home. Don't you remember all the stories about her wonderful island? Her pet pigeons, Co-co and Ton-ton…'

He broke off, swallowing hard. He watched the colour fade from Maurice's face, leaving it dead white again save for the red scars. He met blank bewilderment in those blue eyes and he realised that Maurice was listening to him without recognition, without even a glimmer of understanding. It struck him then with a feeling of dismay how completely Maurice had lost his memory. If he could not even remember *Julie* … that was the ultimate test. What normal man on earth could forget that *she* belonged to him?

Neil sat down on the chair by Maurice's bed and tugged at his collar, feeling hot and harassed. He found a packet of cigarettes in his pocket and offered one to Maurice. As Maurice bent forward to take a light from the match which the other man struck, he said:

'*C'est terrible!* Every word you say to me is Greek ... a girl from Provence called Julie? It means nothing! Nothing at all.'

Neil pulled a handkerchief from his pocket and wiped his forehead.

'You have had severe concussion, you know. That's the trouble. Perhaps you'd better stop taxing your brain just now, old boy. Give it a rest. It'll all come back in time, I'm certain. You shall see Julie at once. When you see her, I'm sure you'll remember everything.'

He said those words not without a bitter pang. It wasn't easy to have the task of reintroducing Maurice Dupont to Julie de Vallois ... to be the one who must endeavour to bring them together again. It seemed like another ironic jest on the part of fate to have brought him here to this hospital .... right into this ward for the purpose of seeing Ken Bracken ... then throw him straight across Maurice's path. Had he never come here, never seen Maurice, what might have happened? Maybe Maurice would have remained a 'mystery man' for months. Neil had heard tales of the last war ... of men who had lost their memories and not returned to their families for years.

Loving Julie so completely and utterly, Neil would not have been human had he not preferred that Julie and Maurice should remain apart. On the other hand, it would have been inhuman to do less than he was doing now in order to reunite them.

He focused his attention upon Maurice again.

'Look here, old boy, I must see the M.O. and tell him that I have identified the old body' … he tried to laugh … 'and then you can be given your rightful name and be damned to *"Jeudi"*.'

Maurice, who had been lying still in brooding silence, brows knit, clenched one hand.

'It was Nurse Wallis who gave me that name,' he said almost suddenly.

'Pat Wallis is my cousin. I came here to see her. Think of the luck of it. If I hadn't come, I wouldn't have found you, my old friend.'

Maurice did not reply. He was not altogether sure that he was pleased he had been 'identified'. Of course, it was good to know who he was, and to hear about his parents, and to realise that he would eventually be reunited with them. But this 'fiancée' business did not please him so much. The Englishman said that Julie de Vallois was lovely and attractive but Maurice could not remember her attractions. She meant nothing to him. It was Pat Wallis who

158

meant Woman with a capital 'W' to Maurice. And, of course, if he already had an affianced wife, he would have to conquer the affection which had been rising within him for the young English nurse.

He had a cheerful spirit, however, and he made a noble effort to be cheerful with Neil.

'I am enchanted, *mon ami,* that you should have come and christened me and I thank you. You must at once give me my parents' address so that I can write to them. No doubt some word can be got to unoccupied France though Geneva.'

'And you must see Julie.' Neil forced.

'Well, look here,' said Maurice frowning. 'It's all rather difficult for me. I don't remember a thing about Mademoiselle de Vallois. To me she is a total stranger. Break the news to her that my memory has gone and that it will take me a little while to get used to the fact that I am engaged to her.'

Neil felt almost shocked by those words. It seemed incredible that such a position should have arisen.

'Look here, Maurice,' he said. 'I know you'll remember everything when you see Julie again. Shall I bring her to you now? I can drive back to my aunt's house at once.'

'Of course,' said Maurice dutifully, but he thought of Pat Wallis.

Neil smoked in silence, his mind turning in circles. God, it was asking a lot of a chap, he thought, when he had to force another fellow into the arms of the woman he loved.

Neil could not at this moment begin to speculate on the possibilities of this injury which had made a blank of Maurice Dupont's mind. But it was fairly obvious that it might make all the difference to him, Neil, and to Julie. The marriage which had been arranged *might now never take place*. For a moment, however, he felt it to be his bounden duty to stand by Maurice, and to make his own feelings towards Julie of secondary importance.

Then Pat came into the ward wearing her blue uniform and cap. She advanced down the ward, beaming. Upon reaching the French airman's bed, she smiled at Neil and said:

'Hello, Neil, have you made friends with our *Jeudi?*'

Then Maurice spoke in a high, strained voice, looking straight at her.

'Miracles never cease, *ma petite*. Believe it or not, your cousin turns out to be an old friend of mine and I am no longer the hospital mystery. I know who I am.'

Pat's face flooded with colour.

'Oh, Neil, do you *really* know *Jeudi?*'

'Yes,' Neil nodded. 'He and I were together in La Chaume. He was a liaison officer attached to my unit. His name is Maurice Dupont.'

160

'Maurice – Dupont…' Pat repeated the name slowly. 'But how *marvellous, Jeudi,* aren't you thrilled?'

'Of course,' Maurice said, and then turned his face from her.

Her professional eye caught the signs of rising fever. That was a hectic flush on his cheek-bones and his eyes looked bright and heavy. She advanced to the bed and lifted one of his wrists.

'Now, now,' she said. 'This has been too much excitement. Your temperature's up. I must tell Sister.'

Neil rose.

'If you'll excuse me I'll just nip along and have a word with the M.O. and tell him what I know.'

Pat looked down at Maurice after Neil had gone.

'Well!' she said with a smile and a laugh. 'So you're not *"Jeudi"* any more. You're a *lieutenant d'avion* of the name of Maurice Dupont. Would you believe it?'

'*Voila!*' he said grimly. 'And would you believe that I am engaged to be married? You were right, *chérie*. I have a fiancée waiting for me in the house of your aunt, Lady Hanley. *Mais c'est formidable!*'

Pat let go of the thin hot wrist. The smile faded from her face. She felt a queer sinking in her heart. The sort of feeling that had never attacked her before in her young life.

So *Jeudi*, her darling *Jeudi*, was engaged to be married. That wasn't so good!

She did not betray her feelings. She smiled again.

'But how splendid!' she said brightly. 'You're hearing all the good things at once. Didn't I tell you there was sure to be a girl friend?'

'*Chérie*,' he whispered and turned to her with a look which went straight through her heart. An unmistakable look of longing. She turned from it at once.

'I must go. Sister will give you something to take down that fever.'

Pat walked down the ward a little blindly and quite unlike herself. And the young Frenchman lay quiet and struggled with the mists in his mind, with the thought of all the things which the English airman had revealed to him. *Provence*. An island with a crucifix. A girl named Julie. It meant everything and nothing. He could think of nothing, really, except the little English nurse who had just walked out of the ward looking as though she had received a blow. And the blow was just as much his.

He repeated to himself the words which he had just said to her:

Mais c'est formidable!...'

14

Four people stood in the drive of Mulverton Court beside Lady Hanley's little car. Four people with serious faces discussing a serious problem.

'I think,' said Alice Hanley, 'that much the best thing – since the M.O. agrees – is for Julie to talk quietly to the poor boy and see if she can't gradually reawaken his memory. Andrews can drive you. He has plenty of time on his hands these days.'

'That's it,' said Neil with an expressionless face. 'What do you say, Pat? You've nursed Dupont for some time. You must know him quite well. Will it be all right for Julie to see him?'

The young V.A.D., concealing a very sore and disappointed young heart, smiled and nodded.

'Much the best thing. You take Mademoiselle de Vallois over to the hospital now and I'll stay here with Aunt Alice.'

'Yes, I must go to poor Maurice at once,' said Julie.

Alice Hanley looked at the three young people a trifle uneasily. There was tension in the air and she could feel it. Of course she knew, without doubt, that Julie was not in the least in love with her Frenchman. When Neil had come back with the startling news that he had discovered Maurice … that by the strangest of coincidences, the fiancé for whom Julie was seeking lay in the Red Cross hospital in this very district … Lady Hanley had observed Julie closely. She had seen the girl's big eyes grow even bigger, and her face dead white. She had looked stunned rather than ecstatically glad, although she had hastily proclaimed her pleasure and relief at the discovery.

After Neil and Julie had driven away, Lady Hanley walked with her niece into the house, feeling worried about things. But she did not express that worry to Pat. She was a reserved woman and the soul of discretion. Cheerfully she said:

'This seems to be one of the miracles. How marvellous the little French girl finding her fiancé here.'

'Absolutely wonderful,' said Pat, without giving any indication that her little world was being shattered around her. She could only think of Maurice Dupont as *Jeudi*, her protégé, her darling patient … the first man in the world to thrill her practical young heart.

Generously she added:

'Mademoiselle de Vallois is the most beautiful little thing I've ever seen. No wonder old Neil took her under his wing and rescued her.'

'Yes, she is sweet,' said Lady Hanley. 'When she arrived yesterday she looked like a scared lost little kitten. She makes one want to cherish her. But our Neil mustn't do too much cherishing' ... she laughed lightly... 'Julie is engaged to his friend.'

'Yes,' said Pat slowly, and began to realise why people said of love that it rarely comes without suffering. She was suffering now, untold pangs of jealousy at the thought of Julie sitting beside Maurice's bed. For, of course, Maurice would soon recover his lost memory and, if he didn't, he would very quickly fall in love with Julie all over again.

In the car which Andrews, Lady Hanley's old chauffeur, was driving down the steep hill on to the main Tiverton Road, Julie sat very still beside Neil, clasping her bag in two small hands which were inclined to tremble with sheer nerves. Neil was obviously concealing what he felt by being over-enthusiastic about the matter.

'What could be better than this?' he said. 'To have found Maurice so quickly and within a few miles of my aunt's home! It's amazing. I was staggered when I saw Maurice opposite old Bracken's bed. You can imagine how I felt.'

Julie stared blindly at the Devon landscape. 'Yes. I can understand.'

'They call him *Jeudi* because he came into hospital on a Thursday,' said Neil with a slight laugh. 'Poor old Maurice! He looks just the same as ever, in spite of his wounds.'

Julie said in an expressionless voice:

'It's so awful that we can't get in touch with his people to relieve their anxiety, or even tell my father. *Awful* being so completely cut off from France.'

He stole a look at her and saw the cherry-red lips quivering. Although he had meant to be very platonic and practical, his hand went out involuntarily and covered hers.

'Poor little darling! It's all so damned tough for you. I wish to God I could help.'

Every nerve in her responded wildly to the caress, but she tried not to betray her feelings. She said:

'You've done everything for me. Brought me to this beautiful peaceful English home where your aunt is so sweet and kind to me, and now you have found Maurice...' her voice broke a little '...what more can you do?'

He drew his hand away. The thought of Maurice was very prevalent in his mind and a steel barrier between them. He had an almost irresistible desire to put an arm about Julie and draw her closely to his side. It seemed long, much too long, since he had touched that sweet red mouth with his. He was sick with longing for her, and now he was taking her back to Maurice. He ought to be glad, *glad* that he had found the poor chap.

'God, it's the very devil,' he said to himself.

And Julie thought:

'I must do my best to help Maurice and be kind to him. He is wounded and his memory has gone ... it is up to me to be doubly loyal and to carry out all the vows I once made to him. But oh, Neel, Neel, how unbearable it is to love you so desperately!'

It was not a happy drive. Spasmodically these two spoke of Maurice and his chances of a speedy return to health. Dutifully Neil pointed out to his 'passenger' the special beauty spots in the drive through the valley and then they reached the gates of the hospital grounds ... one of the big ancestral homes of Devon which had been turned into an auxiliary Red Cross hospital. Just before they entered the building together, Julie's courage failed her a little. She gave Neil an appealing look.

'*Mon Dieu!* It's going to be very difficult...'

For a fleeting second he pressed her hand.

'Be brave, Julie darling. Try to forget everything else but Maurice. I'll help you all I can...'

Blindly she followed his tall figure through the spacious hall into the big sunny ward in which Maurice was lying.

Neil Richardson forced himself to go

through the necessary ritual of making the introductions. Sister had, with discretion, put screens round the Frenchman's bed so that the reunion with his fiancée should not be too public. Between the screens, Neil grinned cheerfully at his friend.

'I've brought Julie to you, old boy. I know you'll remember her soon. I'll talk to Bracken and then Julie can come back with me to Mulverton. The M.O. doesn't think she should stay too long. You don't want to get too worked up.'

A rather hollow laugh … and then Neil vanished.

Julie stood looking down at the young man who had been her childhood's friend and to whom she was betrothed. With a fast-beating heart, she scrutinised the familiar face with the round bright blue eyes. The fair hair was hidden under white bandages. The cheeks were scarred. The amusing underlip which jutted out a little was just the same (she used to call it his 'Maurice Chevalier' lip). But there was none of the old Maurice in his expression. It was as though a stranger lay there staring up at her. A very polite stranger who said in stilted English:

'It was good of you to come, Mademoiselle. Won't you sit down?'

It seemed fantastic that Maurice should look at her, speak to her like this. She broke into rapid French.

'Maurice, my dear, my *dear,* surely you remember Julie? I can't believe that you don't know me. Look at me closely. *Think.*'

His brows contracted and his face flushed. For a moment he struggled with himself, then broke into a smile which she found pathetic. He answered her in his own language.

'My dear Julie. If you are indeed my fiancée I am deeply grateful to you for coming to see me, and I know I should be profoundly thankful to have discovered my identity at last. But it is all a mystery to me. I can remember nothing. *Rien de tout.*'

Julie drew off her gloves and her little hat and laid them in her lap. She shook back her cloud of silvery hair. It was a characteristic gesture and the man lying in the bed knew that he had seen someone do that before. Somewhere in the dim recess of past time he had been on intimate terms with a girl who had that cloud of beautiful fair hair.

She said, still speaking in French:

'Try to remember Aix-en-Provence ... our poor country, Maurice. Your parents ... your house in Rue Helios. My home at La Marita. Villa Vertige; poor Papa. Old Hortense, who always made such good coffee for you. Madame Huillard down at the *auberge.* Jean Taupin, our fisherman, who used to take us in his boat to the island where we bathed. Oh, Maurice!...'

169

She broke off. She was genuinely eager to reawaken his memory. To help him. Yet even while she described the old places, the old life, she felt lost and afraid. And it seemed not as though she had broken faith with him, *but with Neil,* to whom she had given her uttermost love on that island. She felt that she had no right to connect it with memories of Maurice. It was theirs, *theirs.* Maurice seemed to play no part in it.

She talked on … mentioning a dozen little names and incidents which might strike a chord in his brain. And he listened, harassed and depressed because, although sometimes the things that this girl said to him evoked a glimmer somewhere … it was a glimmer that soon faded out.

'I can remember nothing,' he kept repeating despondently.

She drew breath, leaned forward and took one of his hands.

'Never mind, *mon pauvre,* don't try to think any more. It will only distress you. It will all come back in time. The doctor told Neel so.'

He pressed her hand in sympathy. His eyes were soft as they regarded her. She was very lovely and kind, and he told himself that he should feel a most fortunate man to have such an exquisite creature acknowledging him as her future husband. Apparently they had been engaged for some months, and had been about to be married this autumn. How exciting it all must have been, he thought, but for the little English nurse to whom he had given his heart since his arrival in England.

Maurice Dupont told himself that on no account must he betray his feelings to Julie. She was in love with him. He presumed that she must be, as they were engaged. However, it was no hardship to raise her small hand to his lips and kiss it in his facile French fashion.

Then he gave her one of the old humorous smiles which she remembered, and murmured:

'I've come through hell and discovered an angel. I am the most fortunate of men.'

Her old affection for him was there, even though her love had never been really his. With eyes full of tears, she bent and touched his forehead with her lips.

'Poor Maurice! Thank God we have found you and I can look after you now.'

'Let us talk English,' he said abruptly. 'It is curious, but since I have been here I have felt more English than French. I am ashamed of my country, Julie. I do not acknowledge the Government at Vichy. I fight now for England. I have offered my services to General de Gaulle, and the moment I am well, I trust I shall be able to fly with the Royal Air Force.'

Julie nodded.

'I understand how you feel. But those who govern France today do not voice the true feelings of the people. One day those monstrous Nazis will be beaten back and we shall regain our country. I shall always love Provence ... my dear Provence...'

Her voice broke and she put a hand under her eyes.

The young Frenchman's heart beat in sympathy. He lifted her left hand and kissed it again, then said:

'Tell me more about yourself, Julie. Does it distress you very deeply because I do not know you? Forgive me if it does. You are charming and I assure you always of my love and fidelity...'

She sat still. The tears dried on her long lashes. Her heart felt frozen as she remembered Neil, who was on the other side of the screen talking to his friend, Wing-Commander Bracken.

15

Perhaps it was merciful for Julie that the Sister on duty in the ward took her away from Maurice. The interview had sent Maurice's temperature up. He was feverish and complaining of violent pains in the head which warned the Sister that the charming French girl who was his fiancée was not doing him much good at the moment.

'It is the excitement,' she explained to Julie, 'Doctor said that, in his condition, his emotions should not be taxed too highly for a day or two. Come again tomorrow, my dear, and no doubt he will be a little stronger.'

Never had Julie been more glad to get away from anybody, fond though she was of Maurice and compassionate because of his condition. When Neil led her out of the hospital, he saw that she was, herself, in a state of high nervous tension. She looked on the verge of a breakdown and his whole heart went out to her. Poor tragic little Julie! He could fully understand what this must mean to her; what his own state of mind would be under similar conditions.

Her large dark eyes mutely beseeched him, and it was an appeal which he could not resist. He knew that she was soundlessly asking him not to take her straight back to Mulverton Court, where she would have to face Aunt Alice, Pat, and perhaps some strangers. Aunt Alice invariably had a crowd up there for tea. He knew that Julie would be expected to appear in the guise of an immensely elated young woman who had just discovered her missing lover. It would be too much for her. Neil quietly took matters into his own hands. There were limits to everybody's endurance, he thought, and perhaps Julie had reached hers.

When he had put her into the car, he told the old chauffeur to drive to the 'Red Lion', which was half a mile from Mulverton Court; a charming old inn mainly used by fishermen who came down here in the season after salmon and trout.

'We'll give the family a miss and have a quiet cup of tea together,' he told Julie, as he took his place beside her.

She could not even answer him, but sat with her face buried in her hands, struggling for a composure which seemed far from her. That interview with Maurice had shaken her to the foundations. Not only had it brought home fully the realisation that she no longer loved him even as she had loved him in the old days ... that she had never loved him in the complete and passionate way in which she loved Neil ... but it had brought back the most painful memories of the life she had left behind her. Everything seemed to her to have gone. Her country, her home. Her peace and happiness. She faced nothing but exile and the loyalty which she owed to Maurice ... and the farewell to her heart's love. A farewell which was drawing nearer every hour ... every day!

Neil did not talk to her. With unseeing gaze, he surveyed the fair green valley and the silver water of the bubbling river beside which they were driving. He knew exactly what was in her mind, and his own heart was sore within him. He could comfort neither her nor himself. He only knew that he must be alone with her for a little while. They had both done their best for Maurice. If they snatched an hour now... 'One moment from annihilation's waste' ... surely poor Maurice would not begrudge it, even were he to know.

At the 'Red Lion' Neil put out a hand and took Julie's small cold fingers.

'Pull yourself together, darling, we'll have some tea here and face it out,' he said.

She raised her head and in answer to the pressure of his hand stepped out of the car. He was shocked by the dead whiteness of that small face, the pinched nostrils, and the despair written in her eyes. She had not looked like that all through their adventuresome trip from Marseilles. She had borne the discomforts without complaint and smiled through every setback. Even on that night when the Italian submarine had fired at their ship, she had been brave and gay. But now she looked almost beaten, and that was a look he could not bear. Julie must not feel beaten. She had too much courage. Did he not know it? Had he not had every proof of it in Provence? She must not be reduced like this to a crushing sense of loss and sorrow.

He had adored her in Provence for that sweet gaiety, that infectious laughter, that glorious vitality and enthusiasm which had emanated from her like a glowing light. The Julie he had known at La Marita had seemed to dance through life and all his memories of her were exquisitely joyous. A Julie laughing at him, lying back in the sun-warmed grass on her island. Julie, singing her Provençal songs; sharing a picnic with him, swimming in the translucent water; raising a brown face wet with salt water, her body warm and beautiful and vigorous beside him on the sands. That was the Julie whom he had grown to love with all the power of his body and soul. It was intolerable that circumstances should be as they were, trying to blot out all her loveliness and laughter.

He himself was deeply depressed and tired of the struggle now that Maurice had been found, and the end, so far as Julie and himself was concerned, was in sight.

He told Andrews to take the car back to the Court.

'Tell her ladyship that Mlle de Vallois and I are walking back, and not to wait tea.'

What Lady Hanley would think he did not know, and for the moment did not care. It was unbearable that life must be led to please everybody else in the world except themselves. If snatching this hour with Julie was an egotistical act, then it must be so.

Their mutual need of it was all-consuming.

How glad Julie was to be alone with him for a few moments, she could not express to him except by the deep grateful look in her eyes when at length they were seated together in a little room at the back of the Red Lion Hotel, making only a poor attempt to eat the big Devonshire tea which had been placed before them.

Neil made a valiant attempt to appear cheerful, or, at least, ordinary.

'I don't suppose you have ever been in a room like this before, eh?' he smiled at her.

She answered the smile wanly as she looked around.

Certainly it was all strange and new to her. This typical English 'parlour' leading out of the bar. The black shiny horsehair sofa and chairs, the whitewashed walls hung with old-fashioned advertisements, a big case over the mantelpiece containing a stuffed trout – tables spread with little blue and white check cloths. On each, a Toby jug filled with a variety of simple garden flowers. Casement windows overlooking the tangled cottage garden.

It was cool and dark and secluded in here after the brilliance of the summer's day outside, and fortunately they had the parlour to themselves. Six o'clock was the busy hour at the 'Red Lion', when fishermen gathered at the bar to relate their stories of the day's catch.

'Try and eat some tea, Julie darling,' said Neil gently.

Obediently she stirred her cup, took a sip, then began to spread a scone with some butter and jam. He watched her with a sense of hopeless love and longing. What a pathetic child Julie looked! He could never, somehow, regard her as a woman. Although she had been all woman in those blinding moments when he had held her in his arms – this afternoon she was just a tragic child in her blue and white cotton frock, and the sandals which he remembered her wearing in La Marita. (When she had taken them off there, he had been amused by the white ribbons on her brown feet; those marks under the straps which the sun could not reach.) She had tied her fair cloud of hair back with a ribbon and, bending thus over her tea, struggling to eat and not to weep, she might have been a home-sick schoolgirl knowing that at any moment she will be banished from home and sent back to the long dreary term.

At last he could bear it no more. His own tea had been sadly neglected. He kept think-ing of all that Julie must face with Maurice, and now and again he had half regretted bringing her to England; wondered whether it would not have been better to leave her in the home where she had been born and brought up. Although, he asked himself, what would her fate have been in a France overrun by Germany and governed by traitors? He would have had to leave her there alone with her father. He, himself, would not have been able to keep in touch with them.

He got up, and walked to the back of her chair, put his arms about her neck. Stooping, he laid his cheek against her hair. Immediately Julie dropped her knife, seized the two brown hands, pressed them against her breast and covered them with desperate kisses.

That simple action of hers was more poignant than any words, any voluble protests of love could have been. The young airman standing behind her, feeling the impassioned touch of those soft red lips, shut his eyes and wondered how in God's name he was to fight this thing. A man has more battles than one to fight in this world, he thought grimly; wars for his country, wars within himself, and it was with him now as it had been in France ... he could more easily have faced physical dangers than resist the temptation of this girl whom he loved.

He began to wonder whether the loyalty they were both trying to show Maurice was a mistake; whether he should not take her away quickly ... marry her ... leave Maurice to work out his own salvation. Maurice did not even remember her. Why the hell should she remain blindly faithful to her promises to him? Why shouldn't they do as they had once planned, and tell him the truth?

The repeated caresses from Julie drove Neil crazy. Suddenly he pulled her out of her chair up into his arms and set his lips to her mouth in a kiss that drove all thoughts from her mind, save love for him. The colour surged back into her white cheeks, the blood seemed to flow once more in burning torrents through her, reviving her, bringing her back to the deep consciousness that she had been born for this man and this one alone.

Pliant, yielding, in that close embrace, she lay against him, two small hands locked about his neck. In between the kisses, they murmured to each other wildly and disjointedly.

'*Je t'adore!*' she kept saying frantically, and he answered her in that language which he had loved to speak with her in Provence.

'*Je t'aime,*' he said... '*Tout, tout pour toi,* Julie, my darling ... my heart's love!'

How long they stood there, exchanging those wild kisses, those wild words of love and desire, neither of them knew, neither of them cared. Then somebody knocked on the door and they drew apart, Neil to search blindly in his pockets for his pipe, Julie to powder her flushed face and rearrange her hair. A young maid cleared away the tea. When they were alone again Neil took

Julie's hand and raised it to his lips.

'We haven't done this for a very long time, Julie,' he said. 'We were very good at the Villa Vertige, after my operation. We were good on the ship and in Gib., but my God, darling, sometimes it's more than flesh and blood can stand, and I'm damned if I know what to do with you or myself. I don't like the word "defeat", but I'm very near it.'

She looked at him with eyes which were shining. No longer the pale, dejected schoolgirl, trying pathetically to eat her tea, but the lovely radiant Julie of La Marita days whom he loved to see. That was what added to his heartbreak; to know that he had the power to transform her into this joyous woman. Yet by doing what convention would call 'the right thing', he must reduce her to that other unhappy child.

'Mon très cher,' she whispered, 'dearest, dearest Neel ... it is frightening – this power of my love for you.'

'And mine for you, Julie. That's why the whole thing is so difficult, that's why it's been so difficult right from the beginning. We just didn't take what you might call a fancy to each other. We fell completely, damnably in love. And there is Maurice. There has always been Maurice and, as far as I can see, there always will be Maurice.'

She spread out her hands with a foreign little gesture.

'I don't love him, Neel. I am very fond of him and glad that he is alive, and that we have found him and can look after him, but I *don't* want to be his wife.'

Neil Richardson pressed a thumb down on the tobacco in his pipe, then lit it, puffing the blue smoke into the air thoughtfully. He said:

'I know all that. And as far as I can see, poor old Maurice neither recognises you nor cares much whether he marries you or not.'

'That's how I feel about it, and yet if I were to tell him now that I want to break my engagement and marry you, it would seem so ... so mean and cowardly in the face of his illness... It would be easy if he were a strong man and in his right mind, but he is a sick man and has lost his memory – after coming through that terrible evacuation from France. To let him down now would seem an abominable thing to do.'

Neil closed his eyes tightly, and then opened them again and looked at her.

'That's how I also feel when I think about it, darling, so we are in a cleft stick.'

She cupped her burning cheeks with her two hands.

'It's so unbearable,' she moaned. 'Supposing he gets back his memory ... supposing he falls in love with me all over again and becomes as he used to be ... wanting to make love to me ... *wanting* to marry me...

I don't know how I would stand it.'

'The whole thing's torture,' muttered Neil, 'but I'm damned if I see any solution. We both of us agree that we can't take advantage of his present situation and quit on him now. So for the moment we'll have to put up with it, and the sooner I leave Mulverton Court the better.'

The colour ebbed from her face, and back came the old tearing pain in her heart. A little shudder passed through her. She looked away from Neil's brown handsome face, through the open casements, at some blue delphinium spikes in the flower border. In a small voice from which all joyousness had fled, she said:

'Yes. I suppose you're right. And I must try not to be a coward. I felt I couldn't bear any more when we left the hospital just now, but I've *got* to bear it. I must try to look upon it as my "war" job. Yes, that's what I'll do...' She pressed her hands together and spoke earnestly: 'I'll do my best for Maurice and try to forget myself ... even though I can never forget my love for you.'

'I knew you were brave,' said Neil quietly, 'you have more courage than I, but it's the right way of looking at things, darling Julie. Let us both do what we can for Maurice as part of our war work.'

They moved towards each other again, and for a moment his arms went around her, holding her tightly.

'Neel,' she whispered, 'when will you go away?'

'Will it make it easier if I go immediately?'

'In a way, yes. In a way no, I would be so lost without you. It gives me strength to look at you and hear you speak. And when you do go, it will be for a long, long time. I know it. So don't leave me alone just yet, darleeng – not until you have to.'

'It's weak of me,' he said, with a smile. He smoothed the golden tendrils of hair back from her forehead. 'Somehow I think it would be less of a strain if I left. But next week I have this medical board in Tiverton and perhaps they'll pass me fit for service again. Things will be decided for us.'

She shut her eyes.

'Till then I like you to be with me.'

'All right, darling, til then I'll stay.'

He glanced at his wrist-watch and sighed.

'Ought we to go back?' she asked wistfully.

'We ought to, yes.'

'I've been so happy here in this little room ... I shall always like it, your quaint fisherman's inn,' she said, looking around her.

'Darling child,' he said, then gathered her closer and the world with all its sorrows and difficulties was blotted out for Julie again as she surrendered to his long kiss.

16

It was about a fortnight later, on one of those perfect afternoons in July when the gardens of Mulverton Court baked in the hot sunlight, that Julie lay on the grass at Maurice's feet, reading to him.

During the last week, every afternoon after lunch, she came out here under the huge cedar to read to Maurice. There was nothing he liked better, he said, than to listen to her sweet musical voice. It soothed him, and he saw to it that she read always from the English classics, prose or poetry. The more Maurice read of the war news, the more pro-British he became. He refused to speak French, beyond a stray word of endearment, even with Julie.

For over a week now he had been Lady Hanley's guest, convalescent in this beautiful peaceful home of hers which offered everything that could help to heal a wounded soldier's body and mind.

So far, Maurice Dupont's bodily wounds had healed extremely well. The bandages were off his head, and the thick fair hair was once more visible. The scars on his face and hands were fading from angry red to a pallor that would soon make them scarcely visible. But the mind of Maurice Dupont remained a blank so far as the past was concerned. He could remember nothing that had happened before his crash.

He had seen Julie every day for a fortnight now. She was his devoted companion, his 'little nurse' since he had left the hospital.

No one, except Neil Richardson himself, could have guessed the agonies of doubt and misery which beset Julie all this time; the difficulties within herself which she faced whenever she was with Maurice. But she was doing what she called her 'war job' and doing it well. She believed it to be her duty. Maurice believed that it was because she loved him. And although his mind wandered continually to the blue-eyed, cheerful Pat, whom he saw now only on the occasions when she visited her aunt, he did not let Julie know it. He was to her as he believed he ought to be ... a future husband. Always charming, gallant, gay. Very much the old Maurice who had been her companion in Provence.

Julie today was reading a lovely poem by Elaine Emans. A note of sadness thrilled through her voice. Maurice sat back in his deck-chair, eyes shut, harbouring his own sadness of thought.

'Be never chary in remembering
All that to you was lovely, were it a thing

Joyous or sad; wild iris you have come
Upon beside a stream, the golden hum
Of bees in clover, hours taut with magic
Of young love, music, and the gently tragic
Farewell to certain places; hilltop wind,
And silver lit with candles, sunlight thinned
Perceptibly in April woods; and grief
Incomparably brave, and calm belief
That life has purpose. Be not cautious lest
You keep too much of what is loveliest.'

When she had finished, Julie shut her own eyes, trying not to let the tears force themselves between her lids. Maurice looked down at her. She wore blue linen slacks and a thin silk shirt. Her brown arms and throat were bare. Her hair seemed more bleached than ever after a spell of the Devon sunshine. She was very lovely, he thought. An enchanting companion, and he wished that he loved her. He wished that he could remember the days when he must have loved her very madly and wanted her for his wife.

'"Incomparably brave",' he repeated some of the words she had just read to him, '"And calm belief that life has purpose." Yes, that must be so, Julie. Life must have purpose, else it would be so futile ... all the suffering ... the sacrifices ... what the English call "setbacks".'

Julie nodded.

'This verse tells us to be generous with our

memories,' she said in a low voice, 'and I agree. We should never forget the loveliest things that have happened in our lives ... even though they hurt.'

He bent and ruffled her hair with his scarred hand.

'You are too young and too beautiful to harbour memories that hurt. You must be happy,' he said gently.

She could not answer for an instant. She was thinking of those lovely memories of Provence and her island. *'Farewell to certain places'* the poem had said. What a tragic farewell it had been to her beloved island! ... to all that had meant Neil and the tempest of love which had shaken them – flung them so crazily into each other's arms.

Then she flung off her sorrowful mood, and when she raised her face to Maurice, she was smiling. She shut the book of poems and said:

'There's too much trouble in the world. Don't let us brood over it. Let us think of the things that can make us laugh. That day, for instance, when you were standing on the quay down in La Marita, making an oration to me; telling me that you were the best fisherman in Provence ... and then, with your hand on your heart, you took a step backwards and fell straight into the water and Jean Taupin and I had to drag you out. How we laughed... Oh, Maurice! It was funny!'

Maurice shrugged his shoulders.

'Did I ever fish in La Marita? Did I ever fall into the water and make you laugh? I cannot remember.'

She sighed and stood up, putting her hands in her pockets; slender and straight as a boy. She looked sadly at the figure of the young man in the deck-chair. He was the same Maurice of Provençal days and yet so different. She had always seen him either in his uniform or those very French suits which he used to wear in mufti ... big stripes ... bright ties and socks. This was a very English Maurice in a grey flannel suit which Lady Hanley had given him ... one of the many left behind by her son Peter, who was now in the Army. He and Maurice were of similar build, so Lady Hanley had been able to deck the French aviator out with all that he wanted in the way of clothes. And soon he was hoping to be well enough to get back into uniform and fly again.

'Never mind, Maurice,' said Julie. 'One day it will all come back. You may even remember the moment when you dined with me at the Vendôme in Aix and put this on my finger...' She pointed to the diamond ring which she was wearing, and added: 'You bought it in Paris and were so pleased because it fitted, and afterwards we went into the Casino and you played *chemin de fer* and ran a bank and made 30,000 francs. It was the sensation of the *salon* and you gave champagne to everyone. You were so excited and pleased because we had become engaged...'

She broke off. Turned away from Maurice's gaze and stared blindly through the sunshine at the house. Neil was in there somewhere. Neil who she adored. It seemed so utterly wrong and fantastic that she should be out here endeavouring to revive another man's memory of an engagement from which her whole soul shrank.

In a queer voice, Maurice said:

'It worries me to hear you tell me these things, Julie. I have a dim bewildering vision of that night in Aix ... of running that bank, and making that money. But a vision so dim that it is as though it happened in another life. Your words recall it but it does not become real. Nothing seems real. Ah! It is terrible for you. For you more than for me. I must seem so distant, so ungrateful for all that you have given me ... darleeng...' He caught at her hand and used the English word of endearment as he pulled her closer to him.

She set her teeth, put an arm about his shoulder, and patted it. She said:

'Maurice, dear Maurice, don't upset yourself. Do not even try to think, if it worries you. And *don't* apologise to me. I am quite content...'

'You mean that?' he asked. 'You are really

content, Julie, and do not look upon me as a wooden log, uninspired, boring for you?'

She shook her head, deliberately shutting out the thought of Neil.

'It's time you took some exercise,' she said. 'Come! We will walk down to the swimming pool.'

Maurice fell in with her mood, stood up, took the stick with which he was learning to walk again, and moved slowly beside her over the velvety lawn on to the gravel path. Here one of the two old gardeners who had been left to work at the Court was shearing the borders, making the knife-edge which was Alice Hanley's pride and joy. To the left, the gardens sloped down to another level on which, some years ago, Sir Percy had built a fine modern swimming pool for his family. Some of Lady Hanley's evacuees were splashing in it, and their laughing voices rang through the summer air. Julie thought:

'It must be a thousand years ago since I laughed like that ... since I was a child without a care in the world!'

Suddenly she saw a figure in Red Cross uniform coming out of the house toward them. She paused and said:

'Here is the little English V.A.D. whom you like so much, Maurice.'

Maurice Dupont's heart gave a quick throb. He woke up suddenly to the full joy of being alive on this summer's day and waved to Pat Wallis, who waved back. Rather guiltily he wondered what his young fiancée would have said had she known just how much he 'liked' the V.A.D. who had been so good to him.

Pat reached them and the two girls exchanged greetings. Pat explained that this was her half-day and that she had promised her aunt to spend it here. This evening they were all supposed to be going to the cinema in Tiverton.

Julie, glad of the excuse to get away from Maurice, murmured that she had some sewing to do ... she was making herself a dress ... and walked up to the house, leaving Maurice and Pat together. It never entered her head that they were unduly attracted by one another – she just knew that they were good friends and would enjoy a talk.

Pat looked thoughtfully after the slender figure in the blue slacks. She said:

'How lovely Mlle de Vallois is! *Aren't* you a lucky boy, *Jeudi?*'

His face flushed.

'*Mon Dieu!*' he said. 'It's good to hear that old name again.'

Pat laughed with some embarrassment. She was distinctly embarrassed at finding herself alone with the young Frenchman. She had not really bargained for a *tête-à-tête* with him, but Julie had slipped away so quickly. Pat had not the slightest intention, either, of letting

Maurice know just how much she missed him; how foolishly she resented the new case in her ward who had been put into Maurice's bed; how badly her sleep had been disturbed lately by thoughts of *him*. She had *'got it'* badly, and it didn't seem much use telling herself over and over again that it was all no good, and that she had no right to be in love with another girl's future husband.

'Weren't you just going for a walk?' she asked Maurice.

'We were, yes.'

'Come on, then,' said Pat. 'We'll take it. It will be good for you.'

She took off her coat and cap, and threw them on the grass. Maurice walked beside the small, plump figure and thought how deeply fond he was of this girl. Bless her, he thought, with that turned-up little nose, her sweet blue eyes. Her presence animated him and they were soon laughing and joking together as they used to do in the ward. They left the rose garden and the swimming pool behind them, and found a quiet seat in the woods adjoining the grounds of Mulverton Court. Once there alone with Pat, Maurice forgot Julie altogether. He took both Pat's work-roughened hands in his and raised them to his lips. *'Chérie,'* he said, huskily, 'I do not think that this can continue. I have got to tell you what is in my mind.'

Pat's brave young heart thrilled to the look

in his eyes, to the note in his voice, but she tried to draw away her hands.

'Don't *Jeudi*,' she said. 'You mustn't, you know.'

'But I think that I love you very much, Pat,' he said.

She swallowed hard.

'You mustn't say that. There is Julie.'

'I know that there is Julie. But she is like a shadow-love from a past that I cannot remember. I remember only *you* … *you* from the moment I woke up in that hospital. And I have been wondering lately if it would not be right for me to tell Julie the truth.'

For an instant Pat struggled with herself. She knew herself to be deeply in love with this man, but she came of solid English stock … of a family in which honour and integrity were put before anything else … in which nobody ever poached on another's preserves. She knew perfectly well that if that beloved young brother of hers who was missing could be beside her here now, he would say to her: *'Cut and run, Pat, old girl … do the difficult thing and the right thing. You'd never be happy if you snatched this fellow from the other girl…'* Yes, that was what Francis would say, and she wanted to keep faith with him. He would hate to come back and find his sister had 'done the dirty' on anyone. And because she believed that Julie de Vallois loved Maurice, Pat fought back all her innermost longings to surrender to the embrace which she knew was waiting for her.

She sprang to her feet shaking her head violently.

'I won't listen to you, *Jeudi*, *I won't*.'

He stood up and caught at her arm.

'But you love me,' he persisted. 'You do. You must say it, Pat. Say it – just once to me!'

She put her face in her hands and did not answer him.

17

Maurice drew Pat's fingers away from her face. He was much moved to see that usually happy cheerful young face distorted with pain. The blue eyes beseeched him.

'Don't, *Jeudi!* You mustn't. It isn't fair on me – or Julie, or yourself.'

For an instant he struggled with himself and then let his arms fall to his sides. For an instant he stood there before her in dejected silence, and she, too, endured that same struggle. She was so stoutly convinced that it was her duty to stand aside because of the little French girl to whom Maurice was engaged. But at the moment it seemed to her incredible – incredibly sweet – that

Maurice should prefer her, freckle-faced, snub-nosed, to that lovely little thing!

She turned from the sight of Maurice's downcast face to the woods around her. In the green gloom here it was cool and fragrant as only an English wood can be. Here and there through the emerald lace of the leaves, a shaft of sunlight made a rich pool of golden-red amongst the scattered leaves of last year's falling. High in the branches there was bird song from a dozen feathered throats. Out of the thicket darted a rabbit, peeped at Pat with startled eyes and twitching ears, and disappeared again with a leap and a bound.

An English wood on a summer's afternoon. It had its own peculiar beauty, and a spell which Pat could feel despite her misery. It was so far removed from the horrors of war. The horrors which she could not get away from within those white hospital walls where she worked. And there was a deep pain in her heart because this young Frenchman had already come through the shadow of death and might return to danger. And she would have liked to have sent him with her love, and the knowledge that there was a binding link between them. Instead, she knew that she should say goodbye to him today and never see him again. And yet that would be difficult without betraying what she felt to her aunt, to her cousin Neil, to Julie.

She made a valiant effort to regain the old friendly ground with Maurice.

'Oh, for lord's sake!' she broke out with a twisted smile, 'don't let's make idiots of ourselves, *Jeudi*. Don't let's spoil everything like this. We can't … we mustn't! I refuse to burst into tears and make a scene and dash back to the hospital. I came out to have a good half-day and go to the pictures, and I'm jolly well going!'

Maurice raised his head and looked at her with some amazement. This was truly English … the kind of attitude that his French soul could not altogether understand. He was all ready for a 'scene'. He was bewildered to see the little nurse grinning at him and talking about going to the pictures. Slightly baffled, he shrugged his shoulders and turned from her.

'Oh, well, if that's how you feel…'

She took his arm and gave it a little shake, her lower lip was quivering. She knew that she was hurting Maurice, but she was mistress of herself once again. She wasn't going to let Francis down … no, not if she never saw him again, the poor sweet. And she wasn't going to let Maurice know that she yearned to throw herself on his breast and kiss that attractive 'Chevalier' mouth of his.

'Oh, buck up, *Jeudi*,' she said, 'let's walk back to the house and eat a huge tea. *Venez, mon brave!* There! That's my best French.'

He moved slowly with her down the woodland path, out into the brilliant sunshine again and through the grounds. He still could not understand Pat. He felt thwarted and still inclined to sulk a little.

'The sooner I get well and return to my Squadron, the better,' he said.

Pat swallowed hard.

'We'll have you leading the French Air Force under General de Gaulle yet, old thing. You know, I'm quite excited about seeing you in uniform.'

'I don't think *you* get excited about anything,' said Maurice stiffly.

She gave a little laugh which had a miserable note to it, and shook his arm again.

'You are a baby, *Jeudi*. You know perfectly well how I feel really.'

His eyes softened and he took her hand and pressed it until she winced.

'And you are an angel ... so wonderful...' he said huskily.

That made her feel a great deal better. The vivid flower-beds of Mulverton Court became suddenly a kaleidoscope of colour as her eyes swam with tears.

They found tea being served on the stone-paved terrace with its wonderful view of the Exe valley. Lady Hanley was already sitting by the tea-table under a big striped umbrella, pouring out for the family. Julie sat beside her, a quiet, cool little figure in a grey linen dress which had a cherry-coloured belt. There was a cherry-coloured ribbon tying up her fair hair. Pat looked at her without any animosity, indeed with the frank admiration that she always felt for the French girl, whom she considered so beautiful, which fact in her eyes made Maurice's preference for her, Pat, all the more remarkable.

Julie greeted them with a smile.

'You had a good walk?'

'Grand,' said Pat.

'Excellent,' said Maurice, laying aside his stick and seating himself in one of the basket chairs.

Lady Hanley, big silver teapot suspended in her hand, looked around her.

'Has anybody seen our Neil?'

'He's gone into Tiverton to a medical board,' said Julie in an expressionless voice.

'But was he expecting to go today?' said Lady Hanley with some surprise.

'No,' said Julie. 'He had some message from the hospital after lunch apparently. And just after Pat came, he drove off with Andrews.'

'Well, well,' said Lady Hanley. 'I wonder what they'll say about him now. Personally I think that shoulder of his is healed at last.'

'He'll be lucky if he can get back to the air,' said Maurice gloomily.

Lady Hanley gave him her bright friendly smile.

'Don't be in too much of a hurry, my dear boy, your turn will come.'

Julie busied herself handing around sandwiches and the Devonshire 'splits' which Cook knew how to make so well. But her thoughts were not here at the tea-table, with any of these people. They were with Neil … speeding with him in that car which was leading him to the local hospital. She had seen him just for a moment before he left, and he had told her that he thought it more than possible that this time he would be passed fit for service again. She knew that he wanted to get back to his Squadron; that his was a nature which chafed against inaction in times like these. So many times he had expressed his dislike of hanging about his aunt's lovely peaceful home while his brother officers were risking their lives daily in these aerial attacks which took place frequently over the Channel. He wanted to get back to the old hazardous existence. She knew well that he had not earned the name 'Devil Richardson' for nothing. He had always been the most intrepid of flying men. But the mere thought of him going back to it all filled her with dismay. Her feelings were so hopelessly mixed. She was patriotic … she was anxious that the man she loved should do his job, and yet to say goodbye to him in such circumstances as the present ones, would, she knew, be nothing less than agony. For although she loved him with her whole soul, in the eyes of the world she must make that goodbye a casual one and pretend that the only thing that mattered to her was the presence of Maurice, her fiancé.

Alice Hanley became conscious of a slight atmosphere of constraint during the tea-party. Maurice was not as gay and amusing as usual. He seemed depressed. Pat looked white and tired, and Julie seemed to be in a state of nerves. What was the matter with all these young people, Alice wondered. Of course, she knew perfectly well that Julie was not in love with Maurice and that it was Neil for whom she cared. Well, the sooner Neil left Mulverton the better. It was all very distressing. She tried to cheer them up.

'Aren't you children going to the pictures and then coming back for a late supper?'

None of them had a ready answer.

Maurice mumbled something about having a headache. Pat said she was ready for anything. Julie murmured that a cinema had certainly been suggested this morning.

Lady Hanley gave it up, and after tea left them to themselves. She had plenty to do. Sir John Quinley, who was commanding the Home Guard of the district, was coming up in a moment to see her. She had promised him a pair of guns which Peter had left behind. And there was some trouble with the mother of one of her small evacuees which had to be attended to. Alice sighed to herself as she left the three young things at the tea-table. How glad she was that she had no love troubles to add to the troubles of the war, she told herself wryly. She was too old for that, and her heart was firmly with the husband who was somewhere at sea in his ship. If she could get him safely back and carry on with the delightful existence which they had led when he first retired from the Navy, and get her boys back too, it was all that she asked of God.

An uncomfortable silence prevailed after Lady Hanley's departure. Maurice, Julie and Pat were not a happy trio. Finally, Maurice decided that his headache was getting worse and retired to his room. Pat, having no desire for a *tête-à-tête* with Julie, took herself off with a pair of shears to cut some flowers for the hospital. Julie sat alone on the sunlit terrace, watching the shadows lengthen, feeling more homesick than usual for Provence, wanting passionately to see poor Papa again, picturing vividly this hour at Villa Vertige.

She sat there dreaming sorrowfully, until she heard the sound of a car coming up the steep hill, and then she sprang to her feet and, with both hands pressed to her breast, watched for the car which she knew was bringing Neil home. Home with his all-important news.

18

Julie stood taught, listening, as Andrews drove the little car into the courtyard, and into the garage just behind the house. The next moment she heard firm familiar footsteps and she saw Neil coming round the corner of the house. Neil in uniform and with his arm no longer in a sling. That was the first thing which struck her and made her heart miss a beat. His arm was no longer in a sling. Of course, that must mean that it was now all right.

She was trembling when he reached her. He saluted her gravely, then took off the forage cap which sat at an angle on his smooth brown head, and laid it on the table beside her. Grave and unsmiling, he looked at her. Then he answered the unspoken question in those large brown eyes.

'I'm passed fit for service, Julie. I go back to my Squadron tomorrow.'

She gave a little cry that was soundless, both clasped hands against her lips. The gesture, which was one of fear and pain, smote him to the heart. He hated Julie to suffer. And, most of all, he hated to be the one to cause that suffering. Yet he could not avoid it. How sweet she looked in that grey dress. He did not remember having seen her in it before. And the cherry-coloured ribbon, forming a snood for her silver-fair hair, was entrancing. He said:

'You mustn't mind, Julie. I'm glad I'm going. In a way it will put an end to the strain.'

Her hands fell away from he lips. With her large burning eyes she looked up at him.

'If it's better for you, I'll try to be glad, too,' she whispered.

'It's always better for a man to have work,' he said, almost roughly. 'No fellow in this war likes mooching around doing nothing. I want to be with the others.'

She said nothing for a moment. In her heart she was crying out:

'Yes, it's always easier for a man. He can lose himself in his work. In the thrill of the battle. I can understand that. I wish to God, I, myself, could go and fight … but to be left behind to deal with Maurice … to be a *woman*… Oh, God, that isn't so easy!'

Neil spoke again.

'It's a damned good thing that arm of mine is right at last. It's taken long enough.'

She thought of the time when he had come to her at Villa Vertige for his convalescence. Of the breakdown in his room … of the days when she had nursed him … of all the wild happiness they had shared. She said:

'You want to go. I know that. So I will try to be glad.'

He took refuge in his pipe, lit it and then sought for words to comfort her.

To make love to her would be easy. The easiest thing in the world, since with his whole being he wanted to draw that small piteous figure into his arms. But he must not. He must set his face to sterner things. Tomorrow he would be back with his friends, ready to fly again. He must leave Julie as a thousand other men had to leave the women they loved, and that was all there was to it. But he knew what she was thinking and feeling, and he wished to God that he could leave her knowing that she belonged to him rather than to Maurice Dupont. That would have taken much of the acid out of the wound in both their souls.

'Where are all the others?' he asked abruptly.

She told him, trying to smile, trying to get clear of the awful feeling of misery and depression which choked her like a thick fog. She said:

'I don't think Maurice is very well, he has gone up to his room.' Then she added: 'What time do you leave tomorrow?'

'The early morning train.'

'Do you know where you'll be stationed?'

'I have a pretty shrewd idea.'

She caught her breath.

'You will … go into action?'

He gave her his swift, sweet smile.

'I hope so, Julie. So far as I know I'll be where they're having a bit of a party these days. You know, my dear, I'm longing to crack at those Heinkels and Messerschmitts and the rest of 'em.'

She nodded grimly.

'That I understand. I wish to God I could go with you.'

He smiled again.

'What a darling little pilot you'd be. What would you do with those golden curls … tuck them all in a helmet?… Bless you…'

'Oh, Neel,' she said, 'it'll be a long time before I see you again.'

'The hell of a time, darling' … the word slipped out … he found it hard to remember that he must not call her that. Yet he felt always that she was so much more his than Maurice Dupont's. They had been through so much together … so much, from the moment of their first mad embrace on the island at La Marita, till their arrival in England.

Suddenly he said:

'Do you know that I haven't heard you sing since we left Provence? I was thinking about it last night. How lovely they were, your songs, and how I loved listening to them.'

The blood burned in her cheeks and she gave him a swift warm look through her lashes.

'I loved singing to you, Neel,' she whispered.

'Do you remember *"Parlez-moi d'amour"?*'

'Yes – you whistled it to me before I ever sang it to you. You knew it was my song. It was one of the first links between us.'

'It'll always be dear to me,' he said in a low voice, 'and I'd like to hear it again before I go. Come and sing to me, Julie. Come into the drawing-room. Nobody ever uses it. But the piano is there. Aunt Alice's Bluthner. Uncle Percy is a bit of a musician. He's the only one in the family who plays. Come along!'

She hung back. 'It will disturb Maurice.'

'Nonsense. He'll hardly hear. He's on the other side of the house.'

She smiled at him.

'Do you really wish to hear me sing again?'

He nodded.

'And supposing I make *you* sing? Don't forget I know you have a voice. On the island you sang to me.' She began to hum: *'Vostre cros car e gen…'*

The sound of the old Provençal poem disturbed him vastly. It brought back such rich and poignant memories of their early love. He took her arm and walked with her into the cool of the house, into the long L-shaped drawing-room which was full of Alice Hanley's treasures. Here green blinds kept out the hot sun. The curtains were soft green brocade matching the deep sofa and chairs. The whole room seemed full of the greenish light which was strangely soothing. In one corner stood the ebony grand piano, and on it a tall vase of roses, and a silver framed photograph of Sir Percy Hanley in full dress uniform.

With an arm through Julie's, Neil walked to the piano and looked at the photograph. The figure in naval uniform was a fine one and the face that of an idealist, with serious eyes and delicately chiselled lips.

'He's a good fellow,' said Neil.

'He always looks to me the highest type of English gentleman,' said Julie softly, 'and your aunt loves him very dearly, doesn't she?'

'Yes, theirs was a boy and girl affair, and they are in love to this day, despite their grown-up family. It would be the end of all things for Aunt Alice if anything happened to *him*.'

Julie shivered and clung to Neil's arm a little.

'Isn't that how any woman would feel about the man she loves ... it would be the end of all things if he were taken from her.'

He pressed her arm to his side.

'We mustn't think that way. Men and women have to face these things in wars, my dearest. Come along, sit down and play to me and I shall be for a moment transported from this room back to the little *salon* at Villa Vertige, where you so often played for me. Now, you see how sentimental I can be!'

Julie's large eyes were brilliant with unshed tears as she looked up at him.

'I adore you for it,' she said, and took her place at the piano, and opened the keyboard.

Neil sat down in one of the arm-chairs from which he could see her. Yes, this big lovely room, full of soft green gloom and the scent of dying roses, was peculiarly soothing even though it was tinged with sadness. This time tomorrow he would be back at his job … in a Mess … perhaps in an aeroplane … a Spitfire or a Hurricane, somewhere … anywhere. But today he was alone with Julie, and she was singing to him again and he remembered … remembered…

It was as though his aunt's drawing-room dissolved into a mist. He sat in Gaston de Vallois' ornate little *salon,* with its striped taffeta curtains looped back from the windows looking upon the formal garden, and through the two tall cypress trees to the sea. He could see the snow-leopard rug by the fireplace, hear the sweet high chime of the ormolu clock, smell that faint odour of sandalwood and old silk and polish which he always associated with Villa Vertige.

Julie's low sweet voice was singing the old familiar song:

'Parlez-moi d'amour...'

Tightly he shut his eyes. The pipe in his hand remained suspended. His body seemed alive with memories. La Marita. Further back than that ... the château at La Chaume. Maurice, sitting on the edge of a bed, grinning at him, whistling the same tune. *Julie's tune.* And yet again the same haunting refrain without the accompaniment of a piano... On the hot grass under the umbrella pine ... there she had sung for him, and then burst into tears, and he had lain close to her, comforting her as best he could, knowing that their love was without hope.

Suddenly he opened his eyes and said harshly:

'Don't go on! Stop it, Julie, stop it, I say. I can't stand it!'

Her hands fell away from the keyboard. Neil had sprung to his feet, his whole body shaking, his face contorted. There were no more visions of the past. Only stark reality. Here in Lady Hanley's beautiful drawing-room, where the shadows were deepening, he was forced to realise that it was the last hour he might ever have alone with Julie, and that tomorrow he would be leaving her forever.

She sat rigid on the piano-stool, looking at him with her great dark eyes. And suddenly, as though impelled by something too potent to resist, she got up and moved towards him.

When she was close to him she tilted back her head and shut her eyes, her arms suspended at her sides. She looked as though she was making a gesture of supreme surrender. He caught and held her wordlessly, his lips against her offered mouth. It was an embrace as mad, as violent, as annihilating as that which had taken place between them on the island, that unforgotten day. Reckless of anybody coming in and finding them, they clung and kissed. And when at length Neil Richardson released the small yielding figure, his face was white as death. He looked … he felt … like a man who has run a race and lost it.

He said:

'Before God I love you, Julie. I love you and I can't go on. I can't go away tomorrow and leave you like this. I shall have to tell Maurice.'

She gave a gasping sigh. A great light radiated her face. In a kind of ecstasy she looked up at him.

'Yes, tell Maurice,' she said breathlessly. 'It's too much for both of us. Let us end it all, my Neel. Let us end it, *darleeng*. We have tried to fight, but it is no good.'

He nodded, his face grim and set.

'We'll go to him now. We'll tell him at once. The sooner the better. It's more than flesh and blood can stand. He has got to know how we feel. It's the only honest thing

211

to do to him as well as ourselves.'

Julie as on the point of replying, but the words died on her lips, for suddenly the drawing-room door burst open. Maurice Dupont came in. He staggered rather than walked. He looked changed, strange, like a man who had received a violent shock. His fair hair was dishevelled and his eyes bloodshot. He came stumbling towards them, panting. Julie and Neil stared at him dumbfounded. Then looking at Julie, Maurice spoke in rapid French:

'That song... *"Parlez-moi d'amour"* ... I remember. I remember everything. Julie, my little one, light of my soul! I remember...' He sobbed the words hysterically... 'La Marita and you ... Papa Gaston, my dear parents in Aix ... the day that I fell into the water and we laughed... Oh, God, I remember *all, all!* Julie, something in my head has given way. It is as though a torrent has been released. I remember you again and how much I love you. Oh, my love ... my love!'

He fell at her feet and buried his face against her knees, sobbing and shaking. Julie stood rigid, looking down at him in horror. Then without speaking, she raised her eyes and stared at Neil, who returned that look aghast, unable to break the frightful silence.

19

It was Neil who spoke first.

He had all an Englishman's horror of an emotional scene, but he felt a queer compassion for this young aviator who was his brother officer ... who had worked with him in France ... who was instrumental in bringing him into contact with Julie. He bent down and touched Maurice on the shoulder.

'Why, it's wonderful to think you've recovered your memory, old boy,' he said, hot and embarrassed. 'Pull yourself together ... you'll be all right now. Don't give way, man, buck up for God's sake!'

Maurice made no answer, but a shudder went through his whole body and he continued to cling desperately to Julie's knees. She, on her part, was in a state of mental turmoil from which she could not extricate herself easily. Everything seemed to be spinning around her. A few moments ago she had been locked in Neil's arms and they had reached the momentous decision to tell Maurice the truth. She had meant to break with him and give herself into Neil's keeping.

Now this thunderbolt had fallen at her very

feet. It had its ironic side. The very song which she had sung to Neil, a prelude to their vital discovery that they could not live without each other, had penetrated the fog in Maurice's brain. She remembered that it was what the Medical Officer at the hospital had told her might happen ... suddenly, something ... something either big or trifling ... would bring back the past to Maurice. He had heard her singing that song which had once been his favourite, which he used to whistle so often while he was away from her, and it had done the trick.

She was glad that Maurice had bridged that darkness and silence in his mind and that he was himself again. But, unfortunately, the return of memory had re-awakened his old feelings for herself. This was not the calm, rather stilted young man who had listened to her reading poetry to him this afternoon. Not the Maurice who had been affectionate and friendly, playing his part as her fiancé. This was the old Maurice, madly in love, pouring out his heart to her in his own language, as she had so often heard him do in the past.

She realised that she was in a hideous dilemma. How could she be brutal enough to break with Maurice now. He was thanking God for her, here at her knees, recalling a dozen incidents in their past life ... sobbing words of passionate pleasure because he remembered everything. She realised that he was still a sick man who must be taken care of and humoured, otherwise that over-excited brain might snap altogether. The more she thought about it, the colder she grew, and the more obvious it became that this was the end between Neil and herself.

She bent over Maurice and mechanically stroked the fair hair which was beginning to grow thickly again, covering the scars.

She, too, spoke in French.

'My poor Maurice ... hush! Don't upset yourself. There is no need. Yes, yes, it is a marvel that my song has restored your memory. We will have so much to talk about. But now you must go and lie down. Yes, I'll come with you, but you must not excite yourself like this, my dear.'

Maurice staggered on to his feet, pulled a handkerchief from his pocket and blew his nose violently. His face was scarlet, wet with tears, pathetic. He gave them both a woebegone smile which had something in it which, in its very essence of childish simplicity, drove hatred and jealousy from Neil Richardson's heart. For he knew what Julie was thinking, and he, too, was well aware that this unexpected turn of events had put the final barrier between them. He wanted to hate Maurice and could not. He could only stand there feeling, as Julie did, that he had been hurled suddenly from ecstatic heights into an abyss of despair. He did not have it in him to open his lips and tell this emotional, exiled Frenchman that he, Neil, meant to take Julie away from him. He stood still and grim, and watched Julie with an arm about Maurice's waist, and his around her shoulders, move slowly through the drawing-room towards the door.

Once at the door, Julie turned to Neil. She said:

'I wonder if you would find Pat and tell her what has happened? She is a nurse. Perhaps she can help Maurice.'

Neil nodded, but did not speak. The door shut behind the tragic pair, but Maurice's voice could still be heard, babbling in his own language, pouring out a torrent of words ... excited recollections of his native land, his family, all that had been a blank to him since his crash and evacuation from Dunkirk.

Neil Richardson felt that he was beyond moving, even beyond lighting the inevitable pipe which was his usual refuge in times of stress. With an expression of utter hope-lessness he looked around the room in which the greenish light was fading as the sun sank behind the trees. The scent of dying roses became overpowering and sickened him. He felt that this was a room of death ... the death of all his hopes concerning Julie. Suddenly he turned and almost ran out of the room, out on to the terrace into the glory of the sunset. He began to call for his cousin.

'Pat! Pat! Are you there?'

The young V.A.D. appeared round the corner of the house carrying a basket of flowers, and gave him her usual friendly grin.

'What's up, Neil? Your voice is enough to wake the dead, old thing.'

Neil gave an unnatural laugh and now found his pipe and stuck it in the corner of his mouth.

'That just about describes it, my dear Pat. The dead *has* been awakened.'

She came up to him, set the basket on the table and drew the back of her hand across a moist young forehead. It had been warm work cutting those flowers.

'Idiot, what do you mean?'

'Maurice Dupont has recovered his memory.'

The grin faded from Pat Wallis's face; she dropped the shears with a clatter on to the table.

'Good heavens! Since when? How?'

'Julie was singing. A song which she often used to sing to him, and somehow or other it struck a chord. That's all.'

'Good heavens!' repeated Pat, and her blue eyes looked blank for a moment.

Neil said:

'You'd better go up to his room. Julie

wants you. I think he's in a bit of a state.'

Pat's hand flew to her throat.

'Oh, it hasn't hurt him, has it?'

'I don't suppose so, but he's pretty shaken. Not quite got control of himself. Julie thought you might help.'

The nurse in Pat asserted itself although the woman in her was sorely troubled. She went quickly into the house and up to Maurice Dupont's room, wondering how this return of memory would affect him. In the hospital ... and since, he had been just *Jeudi*, her protégé and – so nearly – her lover. But now that he remembered the past, *Jeudi* might well disappear into the background for ever, and Maurice Dupont might become what he had been before, *Julie's* lover ... in every sense of the word.

On the landing she met Julie, who looked, thought Pat, absolutely ill, with her pale cheeks and enormous, shadowed eyes.

Julie stared back at Pat, then made a gesture in the direction of Maurice's door.

'He's asleep,' she whispered, 'fast asleep. *Mais c'est extraordinaire*,' she lapsed into the French she had just been speaking to her fiancé, then corrected herself and went on in English: 'It is extraordinary. For about ten minutes he spoke without ceasing. He was in a terrible state ... then when he lay down on the bed, holding my hand, he shut his eyes and went suddenly to sleep.'

'Perhaps that's the best thing,' Pat whispered back. 'Do you think he's all right, or do you want me to have a look at him?'

'Please,' said Julie, 'you have nursed him, you understand these things. Look at him and tell me if you think he is all right, or if we should send for the doctor.'

With a heart that knocked despite all her efforts to be calm, Pat tiptoed into Maurice's room. She saw him lying there on the bed with a chintz-spread across his legs. His fair head was sunk deep in the big linen pillow. Julie had drawn the blinds. The room was dim, but Maurice's face was clear enough to Pat, a face that had become dear and familiar all the weeks he had lain in hospital. She went close and bent down. He seemed to be sleeping tranquilly, like a child. She put her fingers on his pulse and then he stirred. The pulse was a little fast but nothing to worry about. He caught her fingers, pressed them, and murmured:

'Julie!'

Pat turned and walked out of the room. She felt broken-hearted. Somehow she resented with all her soul hearing that name on his lips, knowing that it was Julie who was uppermost in his mind. She knew that it was perverse of her. This afternoon in the woods she had had her chance with Maurice and had turned him down. She had tried to keep faith with herself and with all that her much-loved brother had taught her of loyalty and honour. She had sent Maurice back to Julie. Yet now when he was so *completely* hers, she found it hard to endure.

Once outside the bedroom, she pulled herself up sharply.

'Pat, my girl, you're "yaller", that's what you are! Get a grip of yourself, for lord's sake!'

She managed to smile at Julie, who was waiting anxiously in the corridor.

'I don't think you need worry,' she said. 'His pulse is O.K., and I think that sleep is just due to exhaustion. It must have been a terrific reaction for him remembering everything in a moment like that. When he wakes up, I'm sure he'll be quite normal again.'

Julie nodded. Pat glanced at her curiously. It struck her again that the French girl looked terribly ill. Did she love Maurice as much as *that?* Well, it was her prerogative, and if she was going to make Maurice happy, then she, Pat, had no right to be miserable.

Down in the hall, Lady Hanley waylaid them.

'I've just heard the news from Neil. It's wonderful! Julie, you must be delighted, my child.'

'Of course,' said Julie. 'It is indeed marvellous!'

Then she felt as though she could not say

another word either to Lady Hanley or Pat. If she had to act a part one moment longer she would break down and scream. She ran past them out into the garden. Alice Hanley looked after her and sighed. Her secret conviction that Julie was not in the least in love with her fiancé increased. She began to talk to Pat about the young Frenchman's condition.

Out in the garden Julie walked quickly, aimlessly, away from the house. She was near to breaking point. She had had a few difficult moments with Maurice up in his bedroom. He had seemed frenziedly glad to have recovered his memories of the past, and in an equal frenzy he had pulled her into his arms and covered her face with kisses.

'Ma petite gazelle!' he had called her, half-laughing, half-weeping.

And that old pet name had struck chill in her very soul. 'Petite gazelle!' Yes, that was what Maurice had christened her because she used to run so fleetly up the mountain-side ... over her island ... along the seashore, at La Marita. She had once boasted that he could never catch her.

It was awful to have Maurice in this state. Awful to be held and kissed by him so shortly after that embrace which she had exchanged with Neil.

She walked on and on until she came to the gate which led into the woodland. That same pathway which Maurice and Pat had taken earlier in the afternoon. And there, sitting on that same solitary wooden seat, she found Neil, smoking his pipe. Neil, who had fled from the house like herself, wanting to be alone.

He heard her light footsteps on the rustling leaves and turned his head in her direction. Then without speaking he held out a hand and pulled her down beside him. Putting away his pipe, he wrapped his arms around the small figure which trembled so violently and held her in silence for a long time, stroking her cheeks, her fair shining hair, her quivering shoulders.

At last she made a little sound … almost a moan … with her face pressed against his shoulder.

'*Mon Dieu! Mon Dieu!* What can we do?'

He knew great heaviness of heart as he answered, but with no hesitation. He could see clearly enough what they must do.

'It's all over, Julie. You must see that for yourself, my poor sweet. In the face of Maurice recovering his memory and his old feeling for you, we can't possibly do as we had decided and tell him about us. Can you imagine the effect it would have upon him when he is so full of love and joy about you? It might be very serious … might send the poor fellow crazy. Don't you agree?'

She nodded. No words came. He felt her

small hands tighten about his neck. He felt a desperate resentment against fate for doing this thing to her and to him. There was nothing he wanted more now than to get back to his Squadron and kill as many Germans as he could. Yes, he had a violent desire to *kill*. A primitive desire, because this woman, this child, Julie, who trembled against his heart and was, he knew, broken by her love, had been taken from him. He said:

'You do see, don't you, darling, that it would be monstrous of us to ask Maurice to break your engagement now?'

Then she spoke.

'Yes, I see it. I saw it when he came into the drawing-room and fell at my feet. It's the most terrible thing that has ever happened.'

He did not smile at her exaggeration. It was no exaggeration as far as Julie was concerned, nor, indeed, for him. For what worse thing could happen to them than to have to say goodbye? They had been anticipating it for weeks, months, yet somehow both of them had always had *hope,* and that hope had materialised into a very real thing this afternoon. For a few supreme moments they had both believed that it would be right to tell Maurice what they felt, and to ask him for Julie's release.

Neil put a hand under Julie's chin and

raised her face to his. He looked with utmost love and pity down into those velvet brown eyes which were swimming with tears.

'We have faced this before, my sweet. We must face it again. Do you remember how you once decided that Maurice should be your war-work? That is how you must regard it, darling. He fought for France … as our ally … he is going to fight again for us over here. And he needs you. As long as he needs you, you can never desert him.'

She gave a long sigh and nodded.

'Yes, everything you say is right.'

'You know I don't want to say it. You know I would give everything in the world this minute, to be able to take you into the house and tell everybody that we are leaving Devonshire together.'

'Yes,' she repeated.

'You know, too, when I told you in the drawing-room an hour ago that I love you, that it's true?'

'Yes.'

'And that I'll always love you,' he went on, 'and that whatever I do in the future will be for you. Whether I fly, walk, eat, sleep, whatever it is … it'll be for *you. Tout pour toi –* that will be my motto, always, Julie darling.'

'Oh, darling,' she said, and although she made no sound, the big tears rolled tragically down her cheeks.

He pulled out a handkerchief and wiped

the tears away. Deep in his heart he asked himself why Julie must be the one to suffer. Even if he, Neil, chose to endure leaving her, why must she, poor little darling, be condemned to so much misery? Why must Maurice Dupont, alone, be considered? But he did not ask himself those questions long, because he knew the answers. He had had no right from the very start to take Julie's love from Maurice, and he had no right to take it now. For a few moments this afternoon he had believed that it would be the honest thing to tell Maurice the truth. That would still apply in his mind, were Maurice a normal healthy fellow who could 'take' a reverse. After all, a good many men had to accept the fact that their fiancées had changed their minds. But, unfortunately, Maurice was neither fit nor normal, and even if he had been well, the very fact that he was an exile and had nobody in this country, except Julie, to care for him, made it impossible for that engagement to be broken. It would be like hitting a man when he was down.

'Listen, darling,' he spoke to Julie again, still holding her gently against him, 'I don't want to seem to you that I'm pushing you into this marriage with Maurice. God forbid! I shudder at the thought of it, but I just consider it my personal duty to clear out and leave the field free for him. If you can't go through with the marriage then that's up to you. But I've got to be counted out of it, darling, I've *got to be* if I want to keep my self-respect.'

She drew away from him and sat for a moment in silence with her face in her hands. Then she raised her head and said:

'I understand. I shall never let you lose your self-respect. I realise everything is finished. Perhaps it is as well for all of us that you go tomorrow. All I can say is that I'll do my best for Maurice. But I shall love you till I die.'

Intensely moved, he took both her small hands and kissed them repeatedly.

'Oh, my darling,' he said. 'My little darling!'

She wanted those kisses and yet could hardly bear them. She tore her hands away and stood up.

'I must go back. We will be missed and it will seem so strange that we should come out here together like this.'

He sighed and gained his own feet.

'All right. You go in. I'll stay here and smoke a bit longer.'

For an instant she stood looking up at him, her fair lovely head thrown backwards in unconscious supplication, but when he made a gesture as though to take her in his arms, she drew back.

'No, don't, don't. I think it would *kill* me!

And I could never say goodbye. I'm not going to say goodbye now. I shall just say "God be with you", my darling beloved Neel. I shall pray for you every day of my life.'

With that, she turned and ran down the woodland path and out of sight.

He sat down on the bench again and stared blankly through the trees where the shadows were ever darkening.

Overhead, three Spitfires, flying in formation, made a steady droning noise very familiar to him. He could not see the 'planes but he looked up through the trees, his eyes grim, his lips set, and spoke aloud.

'*Salut!*' he said. 'Happy landings, my friends, and thanks be to God, I'll be back with you tomorrow!'

20

It was the last day of July. A day of wind and cloud and intermittent sunshine, a little cooler than it had been, although the Devon countryside was still luxuriant and fair at the height of this, one of the fairest summers England had ever known.

Lady Hanley drove her car into Tiverton to collect Julie, who was attending First Aid and Home Nursing lectures at the Red

Cross Depot. As she waited for the girl to appear, the two spaniels in their customary place behind her, their paws on the back of her seat, their eyes ever asking for 'a walk', Alice Hanley smoked a cigarette and did a bit of thinking. So busy was she these days that she rarely had time for quiet reflections, but the French girl who had sought the protection of her home had occupied a good many of those thoughts lately.

In fact, Julie and her Maurice were altogether a problem to Alice just at the moment.

Since Neil's departure from Mulverton, Julie had been like a dead thing. She showed no particular emotions. No hysteria or open grief. She just seemed without life, and looked ill, with a hopeless expression in those large lovely eyes which went straight to Alice Hanley's heart. The sort of look that she had seen once in the eyes of a pet dog after it had been kicked by a boy in the village.

Julie had, of course, been mentally kicked. First by the wrench from her father and her home, and, secondly, by the parting from Neil. She had never discussed it with Alice, but Alice knew perfectly well that Julie was frantically in love with her handsome nephew, and that the girl had no business to be engaged to Maurice at all. At the same time, it was a problem to which Alice saw no solution. The young Frenchman seemed heart and soul devoted to Julie. Since the recovery of his memory he had expressed a strong desire to hasten on their wedding. At the end of this week he was due for a medical board and might be passed fit for active service again. Last night he had said in front of Alice and Julie that he wished to be married before he rejoined the Air Force.

How Julie was going to stand up to this wedding Alice Hanley was not sure, and that was what worried her. Julie suffered but was unquestionably brave. She never spoke of Neil. When Alice gave her news that Neil was stationed somewhere on the East coast and was taking part in these almost daily aerial battles which the Germans had lately been launching against Great Britain, the girl listened in silence and gave no sign that the news affected her one way or another. But Alice knew exactly what that information meant to Julie.

Alice was surprised that Maurice was so blind to Julie's condition. He was just a little wooden-headed, and like most men unobservant and, thought Alice Hanley, conceited. Maurice took it for granted that Julie was in love with him.

Julie seemed to care for nothing at the moment except her Red Cross work. She was passionately eager to pass her examinations and become a V.A.D. like Pat. Pat was another worry to Lady Hanley. What had happened to that child lately, she did not know, but she seemed to be avoiding Mulverton Court. Made an excuse not to come every time her aunt asked her.

Alice, smoking her cigarette in the car, turned her anxious reflections to her own family. She had enough to worry about there, but something to look forward to. Her beloved Percy was, as far as she knew, somewhere in the West Indies and she might not see him for some time. But Peter, her son, was due home on leave next week, providing there was no invasion to cancel the arrangement. It would be nice, thought Lady Hanley, to have a thoroughly selfish week engrossed in her son. She would shed all these nieces and nephews, protégés and evacuees. She had had enough of them lately.

She had a very real welcome in her eyes, however, for Julie when she emerged from the depot. Julie in a new, very English grey suit, a grey felt hat on her fair head. She looked business-like and determined, carrying a little dispatch case which held her books and papers.

Lady Hanley started up the car and turned in the direction of the Mulverton road.

'Well, dear, how did you get on?'

'Very well,' said Julie proudly; 'you see I took my examinations in France, so it is easy for me. I shall soon be able to call myself a nurse.'

'And what about that spine?'

'Oh, it is nothing, it was well years ago, only Papa was afraid for me. But nothing shall stop me now from working.'

Alice Hanley glanced at the lovely young face which, despite its summer tan, was drawn and thin.

'Well, don't you go at it too hard, young woman, or you'll have Maurice on your heels. By the way, while we're on the subject of Maurice, you know, don't you, Julie, that he wishes to fix an early date for your marriage.'

A moment's silence. Julie's large dark eyes stared ahead of her, then she said in a flat voice:

'I will do as he wishes.'

'My dear,' said the older woman gently, 'it must also be as *you* wish. You're not marrying because you've *got* to, are you?'

Julie gave a little shiver. Her thoughts turned as they turned a hundred times a day to Neil. Never, never would she forget that he had told her that she must look upon Maurice as her war-work. Never would she forget that he loved her but had gone away because he *must*. She was going to marry Maurice. She had quite made up her mind to that, but there were moments when she wondered how she could face it when it came to the actual day. She said:

'If Maurice asks me, I will arrange the day.'

That calm detached reply left Alice Hanley no less worried than she had been before about this child. But it was always her method not to interfere unless she was asked for her advice. So she changed the conversation and discussed the news which she had seen on the Tiverton posters.

'We're bringing down those Nazis like ninepins,' she said cheerfully. 'I think Mr Hitler's bitten off more than he can chew.'

'*Sales Boches,*' was Julie's muttered reply, and then, of course, she began to think of Neil again. What agony it was always to think of him, never to hear from him; always to wonder if he was all right, knowing that that he faced incredible dangers and took incredible risks every day of his life.

Night after night, Julie knelt before the little crucifix which she had brought from La Marita and hung in her bedroom at Mulverton Court. Knelt there till her back ached and her knees hurt, praying desperately for Neil and for the courage to live her own personal life as he wished her to live it. But sometimes she felt that one day nerve and sinew, flesh and blood, would give way … that the spirit he had instilled into her would be defeated and that she would break. Break for love of him, and be no longer able to live.

Yet the Julie who had tea with Lady Hanley and Maurice and some friends, smiled and talked and helped Lady Hanley pour out tea and hand round cakes. And those not knowing might have thought she was happy and contented and very lucky living here in this lovely place with her fiancé at her side.

The fiancé, himself, looked upon Julie with mixed feelings. Since that sudden unnerving return of memory, he had, in a way, been like the old Maurice, yet not the same. Hysterical appreciation and excitement at his recovery had died down and given place to a more thoughtful and cautious state of mind.

His passion for Julie was still alight. There was nothing he wanted more than to marry her now and settle down. And he had plenty to do, struggling to recover his health so that he could fly again, and carrying on a huge correspondence. He was in touch with Geneva and with the American Red Cross, doing his utmost to get messages through to his parents and to Julie's father in unoccupied France. Hoping to receive news, in return, of them. At the same time he was rather a troubled man whenever he considered Pat Wallis. He had undergone a queer reaction ... swerving from the love that had grown in his heart for her ... back to the old strong attachment to Julie. But as the days went by he thought quite a lot about Pat. Thought of her with no little embarrassment, and with regret. He missed her. Was sorry that she no longer came to Mulverton Court. Sometimes he wondered if he had ever answered to that old nickname of *'Jeudi,'* or ever longed for the moments when the blue-eyed cheerful little nurse brought trays and hot-water bottles to his bedside.

He felt that it was his duty now to put that part of his life behind him and to marry his fiancée without delay.

That same night after Lady Hanley had retired, he stayed a few moments in the lounge alone with Julie and brought up the subject of their wedding.

'It's almost certain, *ma chérie,*' he said, 'that next week I shall be passed fit and have to leave Mulverton. Do you not think then that it would be a good thing if, instead of wasting the days, I get a special licence and we are married – say at the beginning of next week?'

Julie did not answer for a moment. It struck Maurice as he looked at her that she had grown much older and was much changed from the Julie of La Marita days. She looked tall and very slender in her black dinner dress. She wore on her breast the little jewelled cross which was very familiar to him. Lately she had been pinning her long fair hair high on her head and that took away a great deal of the youthful appearance which used to charm him. This was a changed, grave-eyed Julie but infinitely desirable, and he took it for granted that the alteration in her was due to all the sorrow and hardship she had experienced after she had left home.

When she spoke her voice was very quiet.

'If you think it would be right for us to marry next week, then let us do so, Maurice.'

He came up to her, passed his arms about her waist, and rubbed his lips gently against her neck.

'*Ma petite gazelle,*' he whispered, 'you must not be so sorrowful. *La tristesse* is not for you. You were made for laughter. Maybe when we are married, you will forget all your past troubles and laugh again. Yes?'

She nodded dumbly.

'And what has happened to your old perfume, *Baiser?* It was most alluring. Can you get no more?'

'It comes from Paris. Maybe it can still be bought in London.'

'You shall have a big bottle for your wedding, and a fur coat. Yes, I shall buy you a fur coat for the winter to keep my *petite gazelle* from the English fog and cold.'

She did not reply. She did not tell him that she preferred not to have that old perfume any more. *Baiser* … to kiss… Neil had loved it. She never wished to use it again. As for the fur coat, she would like to go out into fog and cold without furs, without clothing

… to be chilled … *to die* … be buried so that she could no longer suffer like this. She wondered if, indeed, one could die of love, or heartbreak.

'Kiss me, my Julie,' whispered Maurice.

She closed her eyes and her whole body stiffened, yet it was with a gesture of surrender that she put her slender young arms about Maurice's neck and obediently lifted her lips for his kiss. And if her whole soul recoiled from that kiss she did not let Maurice know it. She said, at length:

'I'm just a little tired. Shall we say good night?'

He gave one of his happy laughs and playfully pulled one of her long fair curls from its confining pin.

'Eh bien, darling, but what date shall we say for the wedding?'

She swallowed hard, groped blindly in her mind for an answer, then said:

'Next week? August 4th?'

His expression changed.

'Dieu! What a date. The anniversary of the last war in which my father fought and my two uncles died and most of the friends of my father. No, not such a sinister date as that, *chérie.* Let us say August 5th.'

'August 5th,' she repeated, like a machine.

'Bien! And I shall wire to our dear friend Richardson *le Diable,* and ask him to be best man. It is essential that he gets leave and

comes to our wedding.'

Then, suddenly, Julie de Vallois came to life. She was shocked by that suggestion – so natural on Maurice's part – resentment, indignation, almost terror combined to draw a protesting cry from her.

'No! No! *No!* Please don't do that.'

Maurice stared. Julie's young face, which had been so pale, so calm, had flushed to bright scarlet, and her big eyes were burning, stricken. In complete bewilderment he continued to stare at her, then said slowly:

'But, my *dearest* Julie, why not? He is the best friend of us both. Surely he is the one and only man to stand beside me during our marriage?'

21

Julie did not answer. She had relapsed into a stricken silence, terrified that she had given herself away in an unguarded moment.

Maurice's round blue eyes blinked at her comically.

'*Nom de Dieu!* What on earth has come over you, Julie?' he asked in French.

Then she answered swiftly in the same language.

'Nothing. I just thought it would be

wrong, very wrong, to bring Neil all the way down here to be your best man when he has only just gone back to his Squadron. I felt it would be selfish.'

Maurice breathed again. The slight stupidity of the kind-hearted, gay young Frenchman ... the lack of a real understanding which Lady Hanley had seen in him ... was Julie's saving grace tonight. He said:

'Nonsense, *chérie,* it will not be at all selfish, and Neil will want to come.'

Julie bit her lip on a laugh. Although inwardly she could have wept.

'You think so?'

'Of a certainty,' was Maurice's jovial response. 'I shall wire him tomorrow. Do you know, for a moment I feared that perhaps you did not like him any more. That would have been a grief to me as he is my great friend.'

Julie turned away and looked blindly at a vase of exquisite yellow roses which had opened into big dewy blooms in the warmth of the room. She did not see the roses. She only saw Neil's face ... that thin brown face contorted with pain when he had told her that he could not let Maurice down. Poor simple-hearted Maurice! More than ever tonight she saw how right Neil was. To tell him the truth would be like hitting an affectionate Newfoundland dog that sat wagging its tail asking for favours, trusting in the hand that patted its head. She felt sick with her misery, but there was a great deal of sincerity in her voice when she said:

'You are right there, Maurice. He is your *great* friend.'

And after that they said no more but parted amicably enough, and as Maurice went off to his bedroom and she to hers, she heard him whistling a favourite song of his:

'Plaisir d'amour...'

She went into her bedroom, switched on the lamp beside her bed, and stood for a moment looking around her, looking like one lost, lonely and afraid.

This room where she could always have solitude, where she could be herself and need not put on an act for the world, had grown dear to her. Tonight it was as usual charming with the single lamplight shedding a soft lustre on the creamy glazed chintzes with their deep frills, the glossy oak, the rosy carpet. Her bed was turned down and her nightgown and wrapper spread there waiting for her. She had her own bathroom adjoining; all the luxuries which were available at Mulverton Court. Dear Lady Hanley treated her as though she were her own daughter ... did everything to make her feel at home. She had even found a water-colour which she had had stored away, of a lake in Connemara, the country of Julie's own mother, framed it and put it up over Julie's fireplace. There were books, both French and English, by her bedside. There were flowers on her dressing-table.

But, with wild unhappiness, Julie surveyed the lovely room and then turned to the crucifix which she had hung on the wall by the side of her bed. Maurice's whistling echoed in her ears. *'Plaisir d'amour.'* God, she thought, was there any pleasure in such love as this which racked her from head to foot unceasingly? She had tried to blot it out and failed. She had done her utmost to forget Neil, and remembered him every hour of the day and half the night.

She thought of the rest of that song which Maurice whistled, and suddenly spoke the words aloud through clenched teeth.

'Chagrin d'amour.'

That was more like it. The sorrows, the disappointments, the heartaches of love.

Then she gave a little moan and flung herself on her knees before the crucifix. With her rosary between her fingers, clenching and unclenching convulsively, she cried like one from whom all courage has fled. Cried terribly, but without sound, fearing to let anyone else in the house hear. With passion and grief she prayed, wild hopeless prayers.

'Jesu! Maria! ... Mother of God, intercede for me, help me! Bring him back to me ... bring him back again because I can't bear it!'

In agonised intercession she knelt there, the fair curls falling from their pins, tumbling about her neck, her face contorted and wet with her wild tears. And then she passed from this storm of passion into a hopeless silence, face hidden in her hands, mind and soul almost numb with grief.

Surely it was a sin, she thought, to pray for the return of a forbidden love. Neil would not wish her to pray in such fashion. He had told her to be brave and to try to settle down and marry Maurice. She felt weak and cowardly and remorseful when she brought herself to thoughts of the young Frenchman who believed in her. She knew that somehow or other she must go through with their marriage next week' that somehow or other she must cease to torment herself with memories of Neil's embraces ... of all that he meant and all that he might have been. Frenziedly she tried to remind herself that there had been a time when she had been fond enough of Maurice to accept his proposal. (Ah! Then she had been so very young and inexperienced, and there had never been any other man in her life except Maurice!)

Why had life done this thing to her? Why had Neil Richardson been thrown across her path just to teach her the ultimate meaning of love, to show her a happiness that was beyond description ... only to leave her again?

She could find no answer to such questions, but at length she raised her swollen eyes to the Figure on the crucifix. She tried to remember what she had been taught in her upbringing as a good Catholic. She had been told that one suffered in this world in order to gain glory in the next. She gave a forlorn little laugh at this thought, wiped her face with a chiffon handkerchief which was already a soaked and crumpled ball, and looked ruefully at her rosary. She was afraid that she was not feeling a very good Catholic tonight, she did not want glory in the next world, she wanted happiness in this one. In other words, she just wanted Neil.

Then she composed herself sufficiently to say her nightly prayers. To pray for *his* safety. Her vivid imagination followed him this very night in a bomber flying over Germany. He would be piloting it across the country which he knew well, seeking military objectives. And in the silence and darkness he might suddenly meet with brilliant flashes of fire from German anti-aircraft guns ... perhaps with German fighters sent up to intercept his death-dealing 'plane. And Neil himself ... Devil Richardson ... might meet a stray bullet and then would come the end, a dreadful hurtling through space, and down, down to a darkness and silence from which there was no returning.

That picture made her forget herself and

her own personal griefs. With passionate fervour she prayed for Neil's safety.

'Dear Mother of God, watch over him... Angels guard him, let him be safe, for nothing else matters!' she cried with burning faith.

It was late when Julie rose from her knees, ruefully rubbing them, and prepared for bed. When she had switched off her light she was calm again and filled with a renewed determination to be brave and never to let Maurice suffer as *she* was suffering. It was such a pity, she thought, that he loved her. How easy everything would have been had there been somebody else in Maurice's life.

She pulled back the curtains and stood a moment looking out at the night. A summer's night of moonlight which made the yew hedge and the cedar tree in the garden below look black as ink. The faint perfume of night-scented stocks and of jasmine filled her room. There was a white mist curling in the deep valley below, so she could not see the river. But from the far-off woods there came the plaintive hoot of owls. She did not like that sound. It was eerie and depressing. It made her shiver and draw her wrapper close about her. Then she heard the owls no longer. For there came the steady droning of 'planes. Looking upwards she could see three dark shapes, cutting across the luminous summer sky. Were they English?

Were they German? She could not tell. But her heart beat in her throat at the sight. It might even be *him* flying across England *en route* for enemy territory.

There were no more tears in her eyes. She had none left. She was exhausted and almost stupefied as she crept into bed and closed her eyes, thankful that at least in sleep there would be some respite from the long agony of her love.

22

The next morning after breakfast Julie and Maurice went together to Lady Hanley to announce the fact that they had fixed the date of their wedding for Monday, August 5th. Maurice was going to apply for a Special Licence, and make arrangements to be married in the lovely little Saxon church in Mulverton village. After this, he said, they would go to London together. Maurice expected to be passed fit for service and he would take his wife wherever he might be stationed.

Lady Hanley accepted this news with many an anxious glance at the young couple. Maurice seemed gay enough, but Julie, as Alice had noticed yesterday, looked tired, the poor child; as though she was going into a decline, thought Alice. She managed to get hold of Julie alone for a few moments and questioned her.

'Are you quite happy about this date, dear?'

'Oh, quite,' said Julie, with a smile that Alice could see held little happiness. Sitting at her writing bureau, Alice looked at the pile of correspondences before her and sighed. She heard Julie add:

'Of course, I am desolated that I must marry without the good wishes of my darling papa, but, thank God, we are sure that we will win this terrible war, and then Maurice can take me back to Provence.'

Lady Hanley removed the tortoise-shell glasses which she wore for writing and reading, and held out a hand to the girl.

'Poor sweet! It *is* rotten for you, but I'll do my best to act the heavy mother. You must give me the pleasure of helping you to get a little trousseau together and we'll try to make it as lovely a wedding as possible. My son, Peter, will be home and we will ask everybody to come and drink what remains in the Hanley cellar, and we'll all make pigs of ourselves – eh?'

Julie smiled her little wintry smile again, but her eyes were soft with gratitude as she pressed Lady Hanley's fingers. She had grown deeply fond of this gracious and kindly aunt of Neil's who had been such a fairy godmother to her since her exile in this country.

'Don't worry about the trousseau,' she said. 'You have done too much for me already.'

'Nonsense. We'll take a trip into Exeter and see what we can find in the way of pretty-pretties for the bride. You'll want to be married in a going-away dress, eh? No time for satins, veils, and orange blossoms.'

Julie shuddered at the thought. *That* sort of bride could only have been with *him*. Then she said:

'Just an ordinary dress, yes, please.'

'I shall miss you when you leave Mulverton Court.'

'I shall miss you, dear Lady Hanley.'

'Oh, well,' said Alice cheerfully, 'perhaps Maurice will be sent to a place where you can't join him, then you shall come back to me. I want you always to think of this home as yours.'

Julie's eyes filled with tears.

'You are so very good,' she whispered, then added: 'But I hope to pass my V.A.D. exams this week. Whatever Maurice does I should still like to help in a hospital. I could not bear to do nothing.'

The conversation between them ended in an agreement that they would go to Exeter tomorrow morning to buy one or two things for 'the bride'.

That night there came a trunk call from

Ipswich for Maurice Dupont.

They were at dinner. Maurice left the table and answered the telephone in the library. He came back a moment or two later, his jovial face downcast.

'Is it not a shame! It is our good friend Richardson. He has had my wire, but does not think it will be possible for him to get leave for the wedding. He says he will do his utmost but cannot promise.'

'We must hope for the best,' said Alice Hanley, and stole a glance at Julie. The girl's face looked bloodless in the soft light of the candelabra on the long table. Yet there was distinct relief in her eyes, and Alice guessed what was passing through her mind. Obviously the poor child did not want Neil to be at her wedding.

Maurice was saying:

'Neil is hanging on to speak to you, Julie. Hurry, *ma chérie,* he is not allowed many minutes more. I told him that he must say a few words to my bride.'

Julie stood up. Her face looked even whiter. Her eyes were enormous. She half hesitated. With all her soul she wanted to speak to Neil and yet did not want to. What was there to say?

'Hurry!' repeated Maurice, smiling.

Then Julie walked quickly out of the room into the library and shut the door behind her. Every nerve in her body quivered. Her hands shook as she lifted the telephone to her ear. She said:

'Hello.'

Neil's voice answered her ... that deep charming voice which seemed to have the power to stir her to the heights or hurl her into the depths.

'Hello, Julie, my dear' ... he sounded a little awkward... 'Maurice said I must speak to you ... you understand?'

'Yes,' she said breathlessly. 'Oh, Neel, my dear, *dear* Neel, how are you?'

'I'm very fit, my dear, doing a hell of a lot of work. Just happened to have this evening off.'

'You're taking care of yourself?'

He laughed.

'Up to a point.'

'But you must, you must.'

'How are *you?* That's much more import-ant.'

Her small hand clenched against that young heart which beat so rapidly and which seemed to shake her thin body.

'Well. Quite well.'

'I've thought a lot about you.'

'Oh, have you, *have you?*'

'Of course.'

'I've thought about you, too,' she said with an ache in her throat.

'And you're going to be married next Monday?'

'Yes...' she admitted it almost in terror.

'I don't want to be best man. You understand? I couldn't be. I hate to hurt Maurice, but he'll understand if I say I can't get leave.'

'I don't want you to be here.'

'I knew you'd understand. Julie, you will be happy, won't you?'

She answered him, thankful that he could not see her face.

'Yes.'

'I still love you, God help me,' he said. 'It's still *tout pour toi.*'

Somehow or other she kept an iron grip on herself though her whole body seemed to shiver with pain as she answered.

'And I love you. *Tout, tout pour toi!*'

Came a man's impersonal voice:

'Your time is up. I'm going to cut you off now.'

In an agony Julie cried down the telephone.

'Oh, Neel, *Neel.*'

'Goodbye, darling,' he said.

She said his name again frantically, as though trying to reach him across those hundreds of smiles which separated them.

'*Neel.*'

Silence answered her. She beat frantically on the telephone.

'Neel, Neel!'

Then came a girl's laconic voice, much nearer:

'Have you finished, Mulverton?'

Julie put down the receiver. Tears were pouring down her cheeks. She could not move, could not go back to that dining-room. She wanted with all her soul to bridge that distance between Neil and herself, to feel his arms around her just once again, to die if need be against his lips.

Then Alice Hanley came into the room. She took one look at Julie, then, nodding to herself, walked up to the girl, and laid her hand on her shoulder.

'Pull yourself together, darling; you've got to go back and eat your pudding and tell Maurice funny stories.'

Julie's wet eyes stared at her wildly.

'I can't, I can't!'

'Yes you can, and you're going to. Where's that Irish fighting blood of yours? Now, come along, here's my powder-puff, dry your eyes, do up your face, and *smile*. Maurice won't notice anything, he never does, bless the idiot! But if you've made up your mind to marry him you must go through with it. No more telephone conversations with my delightful nephew.'

The steady practical voice did much to restore Julie's shaken self-confidence. Obediently she wiped away her tears and dabbed her face with the powder-puff Alice Hanley gave her.

Then suddenly she whispered:

'What do you know? Have you guessed...?'

'Of course, my poor lamb. I'm not blind, deaf, and dumb like your duffer of a Maurice. It's just as well he *is* a duffer, and just as well that you should continue to imagine that I know nothing. We won't discuss it. Just put it all behind you, sweetie. Now not another word. Come! Into the front line with you, and no weakening of the defences.'

Like one in a trance, Julie allowed Neil's aunt to lead her from the library and back to the kindly dimness of the dining-room where Maurice, unperturbed, sat eating and enjoying a really good peach.

And after dinner, Alice Hanley took matters into her own hands quite firmly. She announced that Julie had been working much too hard, was looking dead beat, and was to go straight to bed. Maurice immediately seconded the suggestion and begged Julie not to overdo things.

'Now that Lady Hanley mentions it, I see that you are very fatigued, *ma petite*,' he said kindly, smiled at her in his ever-cheerful fashion, and kissed both her hands. 'Run up to bed this instant, is it not so?'

So Julie with a grateful glance at Lady Hanley escaped to her room and went straight to bed, conscious not so much tonight of mental ills as of a physical exhaustion which was threatening to beat her down. She had not even the strength to kneel down and pray tonight before her crucifix. After her bath she lay like one in a stupor hearing only Neil's voice bidding her that last 'goodbye'. She kept murmuring it: 'Goodbye, goodbye, my beloved Neel...' until Lady Hanley came, herself, bearing a glass of hot malted milk which she insisted upon Julie drinking.

'No nonsense, my child. You ate very little dinner, and you're as thin as a rake. No ... you've nothing to worry about, Maurice hasn't noticed anything, he's just grumbling because Neil can't get leave.'

Julie sat up in bed, her great desolate eyes staring at Alice while she sipped the hot milk, and Alice looked back at the small figure with the fair hair floating above the pinched young face, the hollows in her throat, the thin shoulder blades very apparent under the transparent lace of her nightgown, and she longed to do something to help this poor hurt young thing, but could not. She wondered what she would have done if this had been Catherine, her own daughter; how she would have handled the situation. But, somehow, she could not quite see Cathy, as she as called in the family, getting into such a fix. Cathy was such a normal, healthy, thoroughly English young woman of twenty with a passion for outdoor sports and a friendly cheerful regard for the male sex. Cathy had never yet had a serious love affair, so far as her mother knew, and she was at the moment just about to get a commission in the Women's Auxiliary Air Force. Proud as Punch of her uniform, braving risks near a big aerodrome on the East coast which often made her mother shudder. No, Cathy could never be in Julie's shoes. Julie was quite out of the ordinary with her extreme fragile beauty and that ardent nature of hers. She loved much too much, that was her trouble.

Alice's main anxiety of the moment was to keep Julie from breaking down in health. The child looked very near the end of her tether this evening. As for being 'the happy bride' next week ... why it was ludicrous!

Almost Alice persuaded herself to suggest that Julie should postpone this wedding, but in the morning the girl seemed to have recovered her nerve and courage, and even suggested herself going in to Exeter to do some shopping. So for the next few days Julie struggled to play her part. She started to buy the little trousseau which Lady Hanley insisted upon giving her. Maurice made arrangements with the Vicar of St Mary's at Mulverton. The special licence and the wedding-ring were bought. But Alice Hanley looked on, far from satisfied about the whole thing. She had never enjoyed preparations for a wedding less. Julie did not mention Neil's name, did not even flinch when Maurice occasionally mentioned it. But her large eyes were unnaturally bright, and it seemed to Alice that there was a flame inside that delicate body which was consuming her ... that she would not be able to stand up to it for much longer.

Maurice, in his excitable French fashion, felt his own emotions rushing up and down like mercury in a thermometer during those few days preceding his wedding. He had one disappointment to face. The Medical Board would not pass him fit for service and gave him another month's convalescence because of his wounds. That made him moody and restless. He was intensely anxious to fight for this country which had given him refuge. He was intensely bitter against the Men of Vichy who were ruining his country. One of his chief ambitions as to get to London and personally see General de Gaulle whom, he told Julie, he looked upon was the saviour of France.

But it was on August 3rd, two days before his wedding, that his spirits went down to their lowest ebb. The sudden reappearance of Pat Wallis at Mulverton Court was mainly responsible. Pat, having turned down so many of her Aunt Alice's invitations, had come to the conclusion that she could no longer keep away without rousing all kinds of suspicions as to the reasons for her absence. She was quite determined to tell Aunt Alice that work would prevent her from attending the wedding, but on the previous Saturday she accepted an invitation to tea.

She found herself in a queer tense atmosphere that she did not quite understand. The bride-to-be looked as though she were about to die, in Pat's opinion. She had never seen a girl so thin, so nervy, although Julie managed to laugh a great deal; and indulged in an almost hysterical gaiety. Lady Hanley looked worried, and young Peter Hanley, who had arrived home on leave, openly announced to his cousin Pat that he thought Mulverton Court had become a refuge for neurotics.

'What's the matter with everybody?' he asked. 'Mother's got "nerves". You look like a thunder-cloud, that French fellow's an odd chap, and Julie's as pretty as a picture but seems on the point of bursting into tears any moment, even when she smiles. What's the explanation?'

Pat remained silent. She had plenty of explanations to make about her own attitude. She was almost angry to discover how deeply she was affected by seeing Maurice again. But she could not account for Julie's attitude, nor for her Aunt Alice's attack of nerves. She just told Peter to put it all down to the war – which he did. He was so utterly thankful to get away from the camp where he had been working strenuously, to exchange uniform for some old clothes, and to lie in the sun in his old home, and feel thankful to be alive.

Maurice renewed his association with his former nurse, and felt the strangest reactions when he looked into those very blue eyes and heard her half-bantering voice murmur the old name:

'How are you, *Jeudi?*'

'*Jeudi.*' That woke memories. It disturbed him … much too much, considering that he was about to marry Julie. He laughed and flirted with Pat in his facile French fashion, but underneath it all he was troubled. He stole more than one covert and puzzled look at her. What was there about this girl that attracted him definitely? He had undergone many swift revulsions of feeling these last few weeks. Before he had remembered the past, he had wanted to hold this girl, Pat, in his arms … he had loved her. It was queer. Most unsettling. Yet, when he turned from Pat to Julie his love for Julie was still there. Miserably he asked himself if he was a man who could love two women at the same time … or was it some freakish trick that life was playing on him?

The whole party sat out on the terrace finishing tea when a long-distance call came through for Lady Hanley. She threw her son Peter an appealing glance.

'I'm too tired to answer it, darling. Be an angel and see who it is, and unless it's important, take a message. It's probably something to do with my plan for entertaining Polish officers. Lady Orkney is supposed to be helping me, and I think she's in London this week.'

Peter, dark-haired, hazel-eyed, good looking like his mother, sauntered into the house. He came back rather more quickly, his sun-burned young face grave.

'I say, Mother, bad news.'

Lady Hanley let the big silver teapot fall back on the tray with a slight clatter.

'Peter, it's not your Father...'

'No, no, darling. It's about poor old Neil.'

Poor old Neil. Those words were enough to send the blood rushing to Julie's cheeks. She had been about to give a piece of cake to one of the spaniels. With the cake still in her fingers she sat paralysed, staring at Peter Hanley. Maurice spoke next.

'Mon Dieu! What has happened to Neil?'

'It was his Squadron-Leader from Ipswich who phoned. He said that Neil had left word with him that if anything ever happened, he wanted you to know, Mother.'

Lady Hanley gained her feet.

'Oh, my heavens! Shall I go to the phone? Is he waiting?'

'No, Mother, he's gone. He just gave me the message for you.'

Lady Hanley looked from her son round the little circle at the tea-table. Finally her eyes came to rest on Julie and two emotions gripped her. One of immense pity for the girl who was to undergo the final ordeal ... the other of anxiety that Julie would this time be sure to give herself away.

She wished she could stop Peter from saying any more, that she could break the bad news more gently to the unhappy girl. But Peter, to whom Neil was only a cousin and whom he rarely met, went on with his announcement without softening the blow.

'Apparently he went out on a bombing flight last night over Germany. Two of the Squadron are missing and Neil is one.'

Maurice jumped to his feet.

'Missing!' he repeated. 'That's bad. They must have brought him down. He would take big risks if I know him, Richardson *le Diable*.'

Pat said:

'Oh, God! What rotten luck, poor old Neil,' and thought bitterly of her cherished brother Francis. He, too, was missing ... had been missing since St Valery.

'It's tough,' said young Peter Hanley. 'This fellow said that as Mother was Neil's next-of-kin she would, of course, be receiving official intimation, but that if he heard anything he would let her know personally. Neil seems to have been very popular. He said how damned sorry they all were in the Squadron.'

Everybody had said something. Everybody except Julie. She sat there with that morsel of cake crumbling between her fingers, her small face colourless, her body cold as ice.

Inwardly she was saying so much...

'So you are missing, my darling. You've gone. Gone where we cannot reach you. Gone beyond the stars, perhaps. Neel, *Neel*. You must have known it when we said goodbye. You must have known that you would never come back. You who are so strong, so brave, so full of life. You whom I adored, Neel, my *darling*...'

'Maurice!' said Lady Hanley sharply... 'Look after Julie...'

The young Frenchman turned round and muttered an exclamation. Julie had slid gently, silently, out of her chair on to the ground.

23

Maurice picked Julie up in his arms. She was so light, so fragile, that he could lift her easily. He picked her right up and carried her into the house and laid her on the sofa in the lounge.

'*Mon Dieu!*' he exclaimed. '*Ma pauvre petite* ... the news has been a shock to her.'

It did not enter his head even then that it was queer that the news should be quite such a shock to Julie as this, and Lady Hanley hastily prevented him from thinking any further. She sent Peter for brandy; Pat was already loosening Julie's clothes, making various suggestions. But Lady Hanley was determined to take things into her own hands and prevent Julie from betraying herself further.

'It is just the heat, overwork, and then on top of it, that news which has been a shock to all of us about Neil,' she said in a brisk voice. 'Now, off you go, Maurice. Leave her to me and don't worry. You're looking a bit white about the gills yourself. Pat, you look after *him*. Here comes Peter with the brandy... Peter, ring the bell ... you and one of the maids and I can easily carry Julie up to her room.'

Peter did exactly as his mother asked. Maurice, with an anxious look at his Julie's unconscious form and death-white face, walked back to the terrace and sat down rather heavily. Pat followed him, her brows knit, her freckled face puckered. She was a bit perturbed by this incident. For the first time it had flashed through her mind that Julie de Vallois was not in love with Maurice.

She was supposed to be marrying him the day after tomorrow, but she did not love him. It was Neil whom she loved. Poor cousin Neil! Aunt Alice could talk about heat and overwork, but a girl doesn't faint when she hears that a man has been reported 'missing' unless he means more than an ordinary friend. And, of course, now Pat came to think about it, Julie had been very queer and not at all well ever since her arrival in Devonshire. She had seen a lot of Neil in Provence. She had shared the adventures of the journey to England with him. The more Pat thought about it, the more firmly she became convinced that Julie was in love with Neil.

She did not voice that opinion aloud. Nothing would have induced her to. She looked gloomily at the young Frenchman who was staring across the sunlit garden, then said:

'Buck up, *Jeudi*. She'll be all right in a minute. It was just an attack of faintness. I don't think that she is very strong, is she?'

He turned puzzled eyes to her.

'No, I do not think she is.'

'Let's have a cigarette.'

He took out his case, gave her one and took out one for himself. Then he said:

'It is terrible news. I do not like to think of my friend Richardson *le Diable* as a dead man. I *cannot* think of it.'

'Oh, come!' said Pat. 'Don't be so pessimistic, *Jeudi*. He's probably a prisoner of war at this moment, cursing his luck but very much alive.'

Maurice muttered something in French about the Germans which Pat did not understand – which was as well. They sat together in silence for a while, smoking, until young Peter joined them; then all three of them indulged in speculation about Neil and his fate ... a discussion mainly between the two men while Pat smoked and listened. But she remained very anxious in her own mind as to the cause of Julie's sudden collapse.

Upstairs in her bedroom, Julie came back to life, but it seemed to her more like death. Alice Hanley sat beside her holding her hand. With a taste of brandy on her lips and a handkerchief wrung out in eau-de-Cologne across her forehead, her stricken eyes stared up at the older woman's compassionate face.

'*Neel*,' she whispered.

Alice Hanley had known that that was the first name Julie would utter. She was glad she was alone with the girl. She bent over her.

'Now listen, Julie, my dear, you're all right. You're quite all right and your secret is safe with me, but you must try and pull yourself together and not let Maurice guess.'

This request did not seem to penetrate Julie's intelligence. She sat bolt upright, the colour tearing across her cheeks, her heart thumping wildly.

'What has happened to Neel?'

'He's been reported missing, my dear. But that may not mean the worst. It may be that his machine was shot down over enemy territory and that he is now a prisoner of war. If so, it will be some time before we hear, but at least you will know that he is safe for the duration.'

Julie put both hands to her cheeks, her teeth clenched.

'He is dead. I know he is dead. *Oh, mon Dieu, mon Dieu!*'

Lady Hanley seated herself on the bed and put an arm around the small quivering figure.

How could she be cross with Julie for giving way like this? She knew the child's highly emotional temperament, all the misery that she had been repressing for weeks. Alice had seen this collapse coming and she was not surprised now that it had come. In silence she held Julie close while Julie rocked to and fro, face hidden in her hands, tears pouring down her cheeks. Then when the first passionate abandonment of fear and grief had passed, Alice said gently:

'Julie, I beg you not to distress yourself like this. There is nothing whatsoever to indicate yet that poor Neil is dead.'

Julie turned and buried her head against Lady Hanley's knee. In a hoarse choked voice, she said:

'Oh, help me, *help me*. I can't bear it.'

Alice continued to hold her, smoothing the tumbled fair hair back from the hot young forehead. Her own eyes were wet with tears. Oh, this love, she thought, this young, passionate, torrential love! How it must hurt! And how, indeed, would she be feeling at this moment if she had heard that her Percy was 'missing'? For all her years, her placid nature, her English stoicism, she would be suffering the same agonies of grief and anxiety that racked poor little Julie.

'My darling child,' she said, 'I would help you if I could, but what can I do?'

Julie raised a tormented face.

'I can't marry Maurice the day after to-morrow, I can't... *I can't....!*' she said in a gasping voice.

Alice Hanley sighed.

'I think that stands out a mile, my dear. It's been obvious to me for the last few days. No, you can't marry Maurice on Monday. Something will have to be done about it.'

Julie flung herself back on her pillow.

'I would if I could. Neel asked me to be brave and to be kind to Maurice. But I've come to the end of my strength. Please, dear Lady Hanley, don't think me too weak and cowardly. Somehow, while I knew that Neel was alive and well I could go through with it. Isn't that strange? But now that he has

264

been shot down ... perhaps a prisoner ... perhaps dead ... I couldn't go through marriage with Maurice not while I am so anxious, so dreadfully miserable.'

'Poor child! I think I understand. You're not a coward at all. You've been very brave.'

'I love him so much,' said Julie, pressing both hands against her eyes. 'Oh, Lady Hanley, I love him so much.'

Alice Hanley drew another sigh.

'Perhaps you'd better tell me all about it, perhaps it will do you good to get it off your mind, my lamb.'

So Julie told her. And Alice Hanley listened to the story of the meeting between her nephew and this girl, in that Provençal fishing village. So vividly did Julie tell the tale that Alice could almost see the beauty, the glamour of La Marita. She could see those two young things swept into each other's arms on that enchanted island; their fight for honour and loyalty. Poor little Julie! It was all too much for her as for Neil. Alice Hanley knew exactly what he must have suffered, too. It could not have been easy for him, and on the whole, she thought he had come through the ordeal with flying colours. His initial mistake was, of course, in having gone to La Marita for his con-valescence. Poor stupid Maurice was to blame for that, never dreaming that such a tremendous love might flame into existence between his fiancée and his friend.

'Well, well, *well!*' she said when Julie had finished. 'It *is* a tangle and no mistake.'

'But you see, don't you, that I can't let Maurice down... I can't tell him about Neel.'

Lady Hanley considered this for a moment before replying, then she said:

'I quite understand my nephew telling you that he couldn't be instrumental in your breaking with Maurice. But you have just told me that he also said that if you couldn't go through with the marriage, you were not to do so.'

Julie flung out both hands with a gesture of despair.

'But Maurice loves me, and if he loves me it would be so cruel to turn him down. I would feel I had done something terrible. All I ask for is time, a little more time to get over *this*.'

'Well, my dear, if you want that, I think I can fix it. I shall just tell Maurice that you are ill and that the wedding must be postponed. I have a friend in the local doctor. He's a dear old man. He brought my Catherine into the world when we first came to live here. I shall take him into my confidence, and he will, I know, help us. He will just tell Maurice that you are not fit to marry for a month or two. It would be no untruth, my poor little Julie, to say that your health has been undermined by all that you have lately been through. We might even bring in this old trouble with your spine. Maurice will understand that you aren't fit for the responsibilities of marriage just at the moment.'

Julie sat up and stared at Lady Hanley with her great tear-wet eyes. The look on the small face was almost painful to witness. She whispered:

'Oh, if you could arrange that, how wonderful it would be! Just to postpone the wedding for a month, that wouldn't hurt Maurice very much.'

Alice smiled at her.

'You're a kind little thing. Some girls can think only of their own hurt. I know a good few of these hard-headed modern young women who would have sent Maurice flying long ago and careered off with Neil. I rather admire you both, but I'm not sure you're not a pair of quixotic idiots. However, that's for you and Neil to decide, and if you have a month's respite it should give you enough time in which to make up your mind definitely whether you will marry Maurice or not.'

Julie gave a deep sigh.

'You talk of Neel and me as though he is still alive... You bracket us together. It sounds so wonderful when it can never be.'

'Forget the word "never",' counselled

Lady Hanley. 'It's always good to hope, my dear child. I don't say that poor Neil is alive, but I refuse to believe that he is dead until I have official confirmation of the fact.'

'Oh, I pray, I pray he is alive,' said Julie huskily; 'but in any case, in the end, I know I must marry Maurice.'

'Well, now, look here,' said Alice in her briskest voice, 'this is where you stop worrying and just let yourself relax completely for a few days. You are going to have a nice nervous breakdown ... which is precisely what I think you have had, my poor lamb. I am going to ring up for Doctor McKenzie and then we shall inform poor Maurice that the wedding arrangements have to be cancelled. There, now! Aren't I an intriguing, interfering woman?'

Julie caught the older woman's hand and kissed it.

'You're an angel,' she whispered.

Alice Hanley bent and kissed Julie's flushed cheek.

'Just you lie down and try to sleep and not worry about Neil too much, and I'll give Maurice all kinds of loving messages from you and keep him happy. You can rest in peace until you have made up that little mind of yours.'

After the door had shut behind Alice, Julie lay back on the pillow and shut her eyes. She felt as though they were burning. Head and heart were throbbing. Every nerve seemed to ache. She alternated between a feeling of wild relief that she need not marry Maurice on Monday, and her desperate anxiety for Neil. Again and again she pictured that flight to Germany last night. 'Devil Richardson' doing his bit for England. Swooping down on some military objective, meeting with the defeat which had so far evaded him. His 'plane, on fire, perhaps, whirling down to earth. That had been her nightmare for so long, and now it seemed to have happened. Somehow she could not share Lady Hanley's optimism; could not console herself with the belief that Neil was alive and a prisoner.

She murmured his name again and again. 'Neel, Neel, my darling.'

Downstairs, Alice Hanley carried out her plans. In her opinion it was the only thing to do to save Julie from further collapse. Certainly she had no intention of letting the girl go through that marriage ceremony on Monday.

When Maurice was told that Julie had had a breakdown which necessitated the postponement of his wedding, he was obviously disappointed, but he took it well. Lady Hanley spoke to him first, and later to Doctor McKenzie.

The old Scottish doctor, who had attended the Hanley family ever since they had come to Mulverton, had made a careful examination of Julie and had told Lady Hanley that she need have no conscience about what she was doing. The girl was, in truth, quite unfit to face a wedding for some weeks to come. He repeated this to Maurice.

'Julie de Vallois is suffering from overstrain, brought on, no doubt, by recent events of the war and so forth. Then she seems to have been sleeping badly and eating very little and working hard for an examination. I should say that she has never been robust and her constitution has just not stood up to things. The heart is organically sound but a little strained. Her blood pressure is all wrong and what she needs now is complete rest and freedom from worry of any kind.'

Maurice listened gravely to this medical opinion and then expressed his utmost desire that Julie should do exactly what the Doctor thought best for her.

'I would not dream of permitting this marriage while she is so delicate,' he said.

Doctor McKenzie patted the boy's shoulder.

'Not that I suggest that having you as a husband would be an added worry, my dear young man,' he said, 'but marriage for that young lady at the moment... No, I think it is out of the question.'

'Does she need a nurse?'

'No, Lady Hanley has very kindly offered to look after her. All she wants is extreme quiet, no visitors, plenty of bed and sunshine, and perhaps at the end of the month ... we can think again about a date for the wedding.'

Maurice was completely satisfied by this explanation of Julie's collapse. Indeed, after Doctor McKenzie had left, he went out into the garden to seek Pat Wallis and tell her the news, and was surprised to find how little he was affected by the postponement of his wedding. It came as no crushing blow. He was just immensely sorry that Julie was ill, and apologetic that he had not seen for himself that she was heading for a nervous breakdown.

He talked it over with Pat.

'I think I understand,' he said, 'poor *petite* Julie has been much changed since she left Provence. Parting from her father and her home almost broke her heart. Do you not think it is that, Pat?'

Pat did not answer for a moment. She still had her own opinions about Julie. Then she said:

'Poor little Julie! Somehow there is something very pathetic about her.'

Maurice shrugged his shoulders.

'*C'est la guerre*. In La Marita she was gay, she sang all day; she danced. She was the happiest of creatures.'

Pat was silent again. She thought she understood why Julie had changed.

Maurice added ruefully:

'It appears from Lady Hanley and the Doctor that I am not too good for the patient. No love-making, he said, no excitement. I am to be banished from the sick room. I was not even allowed to go up to see Julie just now.'

The rueful look in his eyes went suddenly to Pat's heart. Maurice was such a baby sometime. She felt so much older than he was, although she was much younger. She felt almost maternal about him at times. She found herself sliding an arm through his and laughing.

'Poor old *Jeudi!* I'll have to flirt with you and cheer you up.'

Very readily he pressed her arm against his side and stuck out that Maurice Chevalier lip which always made her heart slip a beat.

'So! You will flirt with me, will you? Well, that's nice and Julie will be glad that you will keep me from being broken-hearted. *Chère petite Pat!* You have always been so sweet and so kind to me.'

She walked with him through the gardens with a new feeling of pleasure, of close contact with him, a feeling that she had not had since he had recovered his memory. She no longer felt guilty about Julie. She knew about Julie and Neil, she told herself, and wondered if Maurice would ever have to know.

Meanwhile ... sufficient until the day! It was Pat's moment and she seized it. She flirted with him quite flagrantly until it was time for her to return to hospital. And by the time she had gone, Maurice had forgotten even to ask permission to go up-stairs and say good night to his future wife.

24

Two days later ... the day which should have marked Julie's wedding to Maurice Dupont ... Lady Hanley sat on the edge of the invalid's bed reading a letter which she had just received from Neil's Squadron-Leader.

Maurice had gone into Tiverton with young Peter. The house was quiet in the drowsy warmth of the August day. The only sounds that drifted up through Julie's open windows were the laughing voices of the evacuees down by the swimming pool.

Julie had recovered from that first wild passion of grief and despair which had seized her when the bad news about Neil had first come through. Since then she had been veritably in a state of extreme physical weak-ness. It was what Doctor McKenzie called 'a state of shock'. At night her temperature rose and they were forced to give her sedatives to make her sleep. During the day she lay nerveless, too exhausted even to read ... mercifully drowsy through the long hours, seeing nobody except Neil's aunt who, these days, had ceased to be 'Lady Hanley'. Julie had christened her *'Marraine'*, and it was a name that Alice appeared to like. She felt as though she had become a godmother to little Julie.

Twice a day Maurice was allowed to come into the room. He stayed a few moments, then went out again. He had been admirable in his behaviour so far as Julie was concerned. A tender word, a gentle kiss on the hand. Just the facile, surface lovemaking of the Frenchman at his best. No reproaches because of the postponement of the wedding, no probing into her feelings. He just hoped, he said, that she would soon be up and well – 'his *petite gazelle*' again.

Grateful for this respite, Julie lay supine here in a room filled daily by Lady Hanley with the loveliest of flowers and fruit that Mulverton Court could supply ... and she tried not to think or worry, as Doctor McKenzie had prescribed.

Today's letter which was now being read to her was the first news of Neil Richardson since the telephone message from Ipswich, and the official telegram from the War Office which Lady Hanley, as her nephew's next-of-kin, had received.

Julie lay quiet, hands clasped together, listening to Alice Hanley's gentle voice:

'It is with deep regret that I have to send you this unhappy news of Flight-Lieutenant Richardson, who was one of my finest pilots, and who had already distinguished himself in France.

'He was immensely popular with his brother officers and will be sorely missed. Not that we have any of us given up hope that he may have been picked up, whilst still alive, by the enemy or one of our own ships, in which case he will be eventually landed in England.

'Flight-Lieutenant McLellan, who was with him on the bombing raid, can supply only the following information:

'He and Richardson were on their way across the sea to launch a night attack on a target in Holland when they sighted a formation of eight aircraft ahead. Two of these they recognised as Messerschmitt 110 fighters and they dived to the attack.

'The last thing McLellan saw of Richardson was that he appeared to be having a dog-fight with one of the Messerschmitts and his rear gunner had opened fire, immediately after which one of Richardson's petrol tanks was set alight.

'After a minute or two of this four-to-one contest, our boys turned back towards the English coast and nothing more was seen of Richardson's 'plane. McLellan got back.

'There is every hope that Richardson, who is a superb pilot, may have landed his machine and got out of it in time, although at the moment none of our 'planes who are looking for him have sighted either him or the wreckage of his machine.

'I wish I could give you better news, but you will, I know, like to hear that Richardson will get his D.F.C., which he had already earned in France, and we are all proud of him.

'Yours sincerely

'_____.'

Julie listened to this in silence, then reached out her hand for the letter and read it herself. There were no tears in her large feverish eyes, only a look of intolerable pain. She handed the letter back to Lady Hanley and said:

'I knew this would happen. Somehow I have always known it. I only hope...' she bit hard on her lip ... 'that he did not suffer.'

'Come, Julie darling, I'm not going to let you imagine that our Neil is dead. As this letter says, there is every hope that he is still alive.'

Julie looked through the open window. Two tortoiseshell butterflies fluttered in, hovered a moment in the beam of sunlight dancing with the dust, then flew out again. She gave a deep sigh.

'I will try to hope.'

'I'm glad he's got the D.F.C.,' said Lady Hanley, blowing her nose rather violently.

'Is it,' said Julie, 'that he will receive the decoration ... even if he doesn't come back?'

'It will be sent to me ... and then ... you shall have it, my dear...'

Then Lady Hanley pulled herself up with quite a sense of shock. She found it difficult these days to remember that Julie was still officially engaged to that young man, Maurice Dupont. She bent down and kissed the girl.

'Courage, my child. And no tears after I've left you.'

Julie smiled up at her.

'Dear *Marraine*. I don't believe I have any more tears to shed.'

Lady Hanley went quickly out of the room. She was quite horrified to find that she had plenty, which gushed freely into her handkerchief now that she was out of Julie's room. She went along to the bathroom to wash her face. Really, she thought, she was getting far too sentimental about Julie and Neil. She had written to Percy about them last night. She had never come across such a case of 'real love', she had said to her husband. That child from Provence was practically dying of it. How dear prosaic unsentimental Cathy would laugh at such a thing! But Alice Hanley could not laugh, neither could she stop herself from hoping quite shamelessly that, if Neil got back, these two would come forward with the truth and get themselves married. It was ridiculous to carry on with their sacrifice when they felt like this. Of course, if poor old Neil had gone beyond the stars ... well, Julie maybe would be glad to have Maurice take care of her. If she was still alive to be taken care of! It always gave Lady Hanley a shock to see the transparency of the girl's face, the almost brittle thinness of her wrists and those ever-deepening hollows in the soft childish cheeks.

She went along to her bureau to attend to the day's correspondence. Later on, when Peter came back with the car, she had to go and do her four-hour shift at the canteen. But first she must write the daily letter to Percy. Every day she wrote to that beloved man who was 'somewhere at sea,' and twice a week to her children. To Cathy; to her youngest son, David, who was a medical student, at the moment spending his holiday improving his knowledge in the wards of a hospital near Bath.

Sometimes Alice grew weary. She was nearing fifty, and despite all her zeal, her courage, her love of work, and her unfailing devotion to her family, Alice Hanley had, lately, flagged a little. It was as though she was pulled up now and then by a touch from the hand of Time, warning her that she was not as young as she used to be, and that she must go a little slower. She rarely had a moment to herself and seldom found time to sit down and enjoy to the full this glorious Devon home of hers.

She was not going to give in, neither was she going to rest until the war ended and Percy was back. Sir Percy was eight years older than his wife. He had been retired from the navy soon after the last war. Alice knew that it had been hard for him to be dragged from his peaceful life down here, back to that most exigent of services – the Navy. But he had gone without a murmur and his letters seldom voiced a complaint. But occasionally he wrote in a way that told her how much he yearned to get back to Mulverton – and to her.

She hadn't seen him now for six months. He was due for some leave, but he might not get it if he was at the other side of the world – which he might well be. She often thought how marvellous their reunion would seem to them. They would have another honeymoon, old though they were compared to these children like Neil and Julie. Theirs was a love without such wild fervour, such reckless giving of mind and body. That belonged to youth alone – theirs was the deep steadfast devotion which had weathered the years of vicissitudes, the ups and downs, of a long married life.

At tea-time Peter came back alone with

the car and announced to his mother that he had left Maurice at the hospital. He wished to see his old friends, and he would be coming back on the bus.

Peter had his own ideas about Maurice's desire to stay in Tiverton. Ideas that he had been forming these last two days since his association with the Frenchman. Ideas connected with cousin Pat Wallis. It seemed to Peter that, for a man engaged to be married to Julie, Maurice was remarkably interested in Pat. But Peter, like his mother, was discreet and said nothing.

Maurice Dupont, meanwhile, entered the hospital where he had first met Pat Wallis and asked to see her. His feelings were very mixed.

Pat was on his mind again. Somehow or other, the postponement of his wedding with Julie had had a peculiar reaction upon him. It was as though a bubble of excitement and anticipation had burst and left behind a complete lack of emotionalism. He felt tender, affectionate, protective towards Julie. He would always love her, but whether he was still *in love* had become doubtful to him. Lately through that slight veil of denseness in Maurice, had crept the realisation that Julie was by no means a woman frantically in love. She had, indeed, become distant, almost a stranger to him. He felt that there was something so delicate, so ethereal about her now that she had ceased to be a girl to whom he could make frantic love. She was not warm flesh and blood; healthy, gay and responsive – like Pat.

He was rather ashamed of these feelings. Yet he argued with himself that he had fallen in love with Pat before his return to memory and that it was only natural that reactions like these should set in. To himself he confessed that he was in 'the devil of a mess' about both women, but the fact remained, shocking though it was, that he did not really grieve because he could not marry Julie today.

He called here at an hour when he knew the little V.A.D. would have a few hours off from duty. Pat came outside the hospital and he was moved to see how her face lit up at the sight of him. Julie's face didn't light up like that. He had begun to notice it, to resent it.

He saluted Pat and greeted her in his most charming manner.

'You promised to mend my broken heart,' he grinned at her, 'so how about a leetle walk with me, eh?'

Pat grinned back. She was all too delighted, but she asked dutifully after Julie. Julie, he assured her, was getting better, but did not seem inclined for any visitors – even himself.

'Today would have been my wedding day,'

he reminded Pat. 'What a lot you must do and say to console me.'

She eyed him quizzically.

'Sometimes I wonder, *Jeudi*, my boy, if you need all that consolation.'

His bright blue eyes beamed at her.

'The sun is shining and we are young, and it is good to be alive,' he said. 'Let us enjoy ourselves while we may.'

'Nice French philosophy,' she laughed.

But she went with him, and the two figures … the young man in the grey flannel suit and the girl in her uniform, walked through the beautiful gardens of the hospital laughing and teasing each other. Pat's loyal young heart was rocketing a little, and she knew that it was not much good fighting against this strong emotion that Maurice always roused in her. And whether she was right or wrong, she as glad, *glad* that Maurice had not married Julie this morning and that he didn't seem to mind.

Just before they were out of sight of the hospital, a white-veiled figure came flying across the lawn after them. A voice called:

'Nurse Wallis, Nurse Wallis.'

Pat and Maurice paused. The other nurse breathlessly reached them and held out a square white envelope to Pat.

'For you, Wallis. It's just come and is marked urgent, so I thought you'd better have it before you took your stroll.'

'Oh, thanks awfully, Watson.'

Nurse Watson cast an appreciative glance at the fair-haired young Frenchman, who smiled back at her, and then returned to the hospital, telling herself that Nurse Wallis had all the luck.

But Pat did not look at this moment like a girl who had any luck. She had read her letter and her face had changed. Under the tan she looked suddenly grey. Maurice saw this and his own expression altered.

'What is it, *chérie?* Not bad news, I hope?'

She did not speak, she could not, but her eyes were brilliant with tears and her lips quivering.

'Oh, Francis,' she said under her breath, 'Francis!'

Maurice knew then that this was something to do with her beloved brother. So often in the past Pat had talked of this elder brother for whom she appeared to have complete hero-worship, and who had been missing since the disaster at St Valery.

Dumbly she handed Maurice the letter; he took it, then putting an arm through hers, drew her further across the lawn and under the shade of a tree, where he stood with her, and read the letter.

It was from her mother ... Lady Hanley's sister. It told Pat plainly, tragically, the news which the family in Cheshire had just received. Second-Lieutenant Francis Wallis was no longer 'missing'. The War Office had stated that he must be presumed dead. There was no longer, therefore, hope of his return.

Maurice folded the letter and handed it back to her and shook his head gloomily.

'Poor boy! Just a kid, eh? And you loved him very much.'

Pat broke down completely.

'I adored him. We did everything together when we were children. And, somehow, I always felt he'd turn up again. Oh, *Jeudi,* what a cruel senseless war it is! My poor mother! It will break her heart as well as mine.'

Then suddenly Maurice's emotions ran high. He could not bear to see the brave little English girl reduced like this to bitter tears. And suddenly he took her in his arms and held her there, covering her wet face with kisses.

'You shall not break your heart, my darleeng. I love you. Yes, I've always loved you. And when Julie is better I'm going to tell her so.'

There came no protest from Pat this time. No hesitation. Nothing but a very human longing for comfort in her great loss. And suddenly she relaxed in Maurice's arms and raised her lips to receive the first kiss of passion he had ever given her.

25

All the pent-up emotion in Pat Wallis' heart, all her love for Maurice and her grief for her brother culminated in that kiss which she and Maurice exchanged. For a moment she stood acquiescent in his embrace. Gradually his warmth, his tenderness aroused the response in her for which he had been hoping. The colour stole back to her cheeks. The tears dried on her lashes. Her face looked unutterably beautiful to him in that moment of surrender which was as touching as it had been unexpected.

He who was so experienced in love, like all young Frenchmen of his age, was fully aware that this young English girl had never before known more than a light kiss or indulged in more than a passing flirtation. And because of that knowledge, all that was best in him arose to meet the occasion. He did not make burning love to her, which he longed to do. After that one fervent kiss he held her gently, smoothing the brown hair back from the young face which had been so distorted with grief. Gently he kissed the tip-tilted nose with its faint golden sprinkling of freckles, the curly lashes which had always fascinated him, the firm chin which had a cleft in it like his own. He said:

'Poor little darleeng! You are very sad for your brother. But I love you. I love you with all my heart and you must let me comfort you.'

Then Pat broke through the mists of enchantment and drew herself back to reality with a bump. Never before in her life had she known such a wild thrill of mental and physical rapture as she had felt when Maurice caressed her. She was deeply in love with him; always had been; but there was still Julie. Still the fact that Maurice was not free to make love to her.

Trembling a little she drew away from him.

'Please, *Jeudi*, let me keep my head. I admit it's swimming a bit at the moment.'

Then he laughed at her gaily and frankly.

'What a delicious person you are, my Pat! So very *practique*. And how could a head swim? That is one of your English idioms, eh?'

She managed to laugh too. That was the best of *Jeudi*. He generally managed to share a joke with her. She put up her hands and tried to tidy her hair, but her heart was racing madly. One glance at that attractive Maurice Chevalier lip of his and she knew that she wanted to fling herself straight back into his arms.

'I'm afraid I let myself go a bit,' she said in a low voice; 'you know I do care for you, *Jeudi,* more than I dare tell you, but ... well ... you also know what there is between us. I mustn't let the news of Francis get me down to such an extent that I forget Julie.'

Maurice took her firmly by the arm and began to walk with her to the farthest end of the grounds where, hidden by the trees, he knew they would be undisturbed. He sat down on the grass beneath one of these trees and drew her down beside him.

'Now listen, my darleeng. This is where we must talk. We have so much to say to each other. I know there is Julie, but I have come definitely to the conclusion that Julie does not love me any more. In fact, I wonder if she ever did.'

Pat's blue eyes flung him a puzzled look.

'What's made you think that?'

'Everything about her. I think I have grown so used to the idea that I was to marry Julie ... it was an arrangement from my boyhood ... that I have not worried about her attitude. But lately I have seen for myself that Julie is not in love with me.'

'I think I've always seen that too, *Jeudi,* but I haven't liked to say.'

'Ah! You have seen it too!'

'Yes,' Pat nodded. But she said nothing about Neil. If Maurice had not guessed about Julie and Neil, she was not going to enlighten him. That was not her business. But she had to confess to herself that she felt a distinct relief that Maurice was now alive to the fact that Julie did not love him. She said:

'And you're quite sure you are no longer in love with Julie?'

Maurice leaned back against the tree trunk and folded his arms:

'Yes, of that I am now sure. I have passed through a stage of great confusion. I have been tormented and troubled in my mind. When I first recovered my memory it seemed to bring back my old feeling for Julie. But that passed. Now, I am back where I was in this very hospital, weeks ago. It is *you* I love, *très cher,* it is you whom I will always love.'

Pat caught her breath. She hunched her knees and clasped her arms about them, looking up a moment at the blue sky which showed through the tracery of green leaves.

'Oh, *Jeudi,*' she cried, 'I don't know what to think. You know the last thing I'd ever do would be to grab another girl's fiancé, and yet … I don't feel a bit guilty about Julie, somehow. It would be so different if I thought she couldn't live without you.'

He gave a wry smile.

'I am inclined to think, *ma petite,* that it is that she cannot live *with* me. Somehow I have been convinced of it since the hour she postponed our wedding. Her health has been affected by this terrible war. My poor friend, Richardson *le Diable,* did wrong not to have left her in Provence with her father. She is, I think, dying of homesickness. And she doesn't find me the consolation.'

Pat remained silent. Dear old *Jeudi,* she thought, still so dense that he couldn't see daylight. Why did it not enter into his head that Julie had given her heart to poor cousin Neil who was, at this moment, possibly lying at the bottom of the sea with his wrecked bomber? Poor, poor old Neil! And thinking of Neil, Pat's reflections swung back to her lost brother. The tears sprang to her eyes. She covered her face with her hands.

'I can't think just now, *Jeudi.* I'm all to bits. I must ask Matron to give me some leave and let me go home. I'd like to be with my own people just now. I'm due for leave quite soon, so I don't feel too bad in asking for it.'

He put an arm about her and drew her to his side. Taking her right hand he put the palm against his lips.

It was a hard capable little hand. So completely the reverse of Julie's slender helpless fingers with their rosy tips. Yet somehow he loved Pat's hands which already had done so much for him. There was something about her British courage, her fine

289

sense of honour, her humour, which appealed to the very highest in him. And that is the woman whom a man should marry, he told himself; not necessarily the woman who violently excites his passion, but the one before whom he bows his head in homage.

'I adore you, Pat,' he said. 'You are to me as no other girl has been. It is you I must have for my wife. Whatever is your decision, I shall break my engagement to Julie the moment she is well enough to talk things over with me.'

All Pat's training, her self-discipline, melted away in the face of this speech. She was only human and she was in love for the first time in her young life. She had lost the brother whom she had worshipped, but she had gained a lover and she could not resist the desire to surrender again.

'You know I'm crazy about you, *Jeudi*,' she whispered, 'and because I know that Julie isn't going to mind, I won't stop you from breaking that engagement.'

Joy flamed through him.

'And you will marry me when I am free?'

She gave an excited little laugh.

'I'll take you home and see if you pass the family test.'

'*Mon Dieu!*' he exclaimed. 'Must you always tease me, even when I am making love to you?'

'I expect so,' she said.

But the look in those cornflower-blue eyes of hers told him all that he wanted to know, and the smell of her hair was like hay in the sunshine, he thought. She was sweet and fresh and adorable. And this time his kiss was much longer and his caresses more fervent. And it was a very shaken and rather dazed Pat who finally pleaded that she should be allowed to draw breath.

She sprang to her feet and brushed her uniform skirt and looked with dismay at her rumpled white blouse.

'Heavens! What have you done to me? The nursing staff will think I am just a bad lot and the Matron will probably ask me to take permanent leave if she sees me like this.'

Maurice stood up. He took a comb from his pocket and passed it through his thick fair hair.

'I, too, had better assume some of this English dignity. Have you left lipstick on my face? No, of course not, because you do not use it when you are in uniform. But that is distinctly refreshing.'

She shook her head at him.

'I wonder how many girl friends there have been before me, *Jeudi?* I wouldn't like to think.'

He put an arm through hers and started to walk with her through the avenue of trees back to the hospital gardens.

'You have no need to worry, *chérie.* I have

loved nobody but you. Even dear little Julie has been only a boyhood's infatuation.'

'And to think how you nearly married her!'

He blinked with a sense of shock, and said:

'Yes, *today!* I must have been crazy.'

'We all seem a bit crazy.'

'But you are going to be happy, now. And when I am free, you are going to become engaged to me. Is it not so?'

Pat bit her lip. Only for an instant she hesitated. She was quite sure of her love for Maurice. And yet, somehow, it seemed fantastic to look ahead and imagine herself as this young man's wife. To be Madame Dupont. *She,* Pat Wallis, the wife of a Frenchman! And at the end of this war when France had risen again, she would have to live in France. It would be goodbye to her British nationality. That seemed a little queer when she had always been such a thoroughly English person; so burningly patriotic.

Maurice seemed to read her thoughts. He pressed her hand in his and said:

'The thought of the future must not make you anxious, my dear little one. Julie will tell you I am really not a bad fellow when I am at home. And my parents are the most excellent creatures who will love and welcome you. And never shall I ask you to forsake this England for which I am not going to fight.'

Gratefully she returned the pressure of his fingers.

'You are a dear, *Jeudi*.'

'And what now?'

'Now,' she said, as they reached the hospital. 'I shall see Matron, and if I can get even forty-eight hours' compassionate leave, I'll take the first train to my home.'

'I will see you off,' he said. 'Where is your home?'

'In Cheshire ... a little village named Applethwaite. We have always lived there. We have rather a nice old Georgian house. My father is a retired Colonel of the Indian Army. My mother, as you know, is Aunt Alice's sister. I have two young sisters, Peggy and Phillipa, whom we call "Pip". She is only thirteen and a bundle of mischief – still at school.'

'I shall love all your family,' said Maurice gravely.

'I think they'll love you,' she said.

Then the corners of his mouth turned up.

'But, oh, you English! What names! Pat, Peggy, and Pip! Of a certainty you are an unromantic nation; and what devastation if you all have fiancés and they address their letters to Miss P Wallis. I shall be careful to put your name in full, *mon Dieu!*'

That made her smile. She realised, with deep gratitude towards him, that he had done much to ease the bitter sting of her brother's loss. For months now her family had expected to hear that Francis was dead, but it was bitter none the less. She hoped that it might even help the family, divert their attention a little, if she could go back and tell them about Maurice. Tell her mother that she had lost a son, but would shortly be gaining a son-in-law.

26

It was on Julie's first day up and out in the garden that Maurice broached to her the subject of their engagement and asked for his release.

That request came as such a surprise to Julie that her astonishment vied with the unutterable relief.

It was a fortnight since the calamitous news of Neil's loss on that bombing expedition. During those two weeks, Julie had lain more like one dead than alive, seeing little of anybody except Lady Hanley and the doctor.

Doctor McKenzie would have kept her in bed, but a new spirit had entered Julie and roused her to sudden action. After the first shock of Neil's death, after the first deluge of grief had swallowed her up, drowning her in its intensity, Julie had emerged with a strange new courage and with determination to face life. Instinctively she felt that to give way to grief would be against all Neil's philosophies of life. He would not want her to lie and weep for him. He might even despise her for weakness, for cowardice. He was himself a man of great courage, and he would never have allowed a great sorrow or loss to defeat him. He was dead, but Julie believed that his spirit lived on, undefeated. And because of that she, too, must not admit defeat.

As soon as she had gained a little physical strength she told Lady Hanley that she would get up, and go back to work again. Her one wish now was to prepare again for her Red Cross examination, but this Doctor McKenzie forbade. He put his foot down on it just as her father and his physician had done in Provence. She was *not* of the physique to stand hard nursing. A few weeks in a hospital and she would soon be back in her bed, he told her.

Julie protested, but Alice Hanley argued with her that if she wished to give her services to the country it would be foolish to attempt work beyond her strength and then become an invalid again. Far better to go carefully this summer, anyhow. There was still her wedding with Maurice in the offing and, until then, she had far better go down to the canteen and work, Lady Hanley said, just for a few hours each day. Then she could have plenty of rest in between times.

Finally, Julie agreed with this. She was now longing to be well enough to start work in the canteen. She could not bear to do nothing. She did not want too much leisure in which to think. Thinking brought too much heartache. Better be fully occupied, to be so tired that she must sleep.

It was queer how in those early days of her breakdown her thoughts were very little on the subject of Maurice and her marriage. On the whole she cared little what happened to her now. Neil was dead. He had died for his country. She felt that what happened to her now was of minor importance. She was like a numbed being. And she welcomed the numbness. It was unbearable when her feelings, her thoughts, became acute; when she pictured vividly the man she had loved with all her heart and soul. It hurt to remember La Marita and all their golden hours on the island. It hurt to remember that perilous adventure which they had shared together, returning to England. To recall every kiss he had laid on her lips and every word he had said. And, most of all, it hurt to visualise his end… That sudden, cruel annihilation of his youth and strength and all that was Neil. But life had to go on. The days had to be got through. The nights were worse. It was such agony to her to lie awake in the dark for hours with all those hurts accumulating into one blinding pain.

Doctor McKenzie tried to help her with sleeping draughts, but they only brought temporary relief and could not be taken regularly. And Alice Hanley, now the most beloved person in the world to Julie, often came into her room at night, fearing she was lying awake and grieving. She felt that she could never sufficiently repay *'Marraine'* for all the help and understanding she had given her.

The papers had been full of Neil. More hurts … those photographs of him in the illustrateds. The paragraphs about the bombing expedition which had ended in the loss of Flight-Lieutenant Richardson. The announcement of the D.F.C. which had been conferred upon him, and which in time would be given to his aunt.

He was a national hero. All England knew about the exploits of 'Devil Richardson'. It seemed to Julie that, from every paper she opened, that beloved handsome face smiled at her. And she knew that she should try to be glad that he had died such a glorious death (it was the way he would have chosen to die), but she could not be glad. She could only miss him intolerably and wish to God that he could have been spared a little longer.

And so the days went on and the war went on. The bombing, the torpedoing, the gigantic conflict. The determined struggle of the British nation against the evil forces of a ruthless enemy.

And then … for Julie, an August morning in the garden lying in the sunshine on a long chair, looking down into the Exe valley. And Maurice, whom Lady Hanley had left alone with her, breaking to her the astounding news that he wanted his freedom.

Maurice stated his feelings with a slight feeling of anxiety … mainly because Julie still looked so fragile. When she had come out of the house on his arm, she had seemed to him even thinner than before. Indeed she had laughingly showed him how much too big now was the belt of her linen slacks. The hollows in her cheeks, her throat, were deeper. Lying back against her cushions, she looked to him as though a breath of wind might blow her away. Yet the large brown eyes were tranquil and her lips smiled at him. There was a queer aura of resignation about her which he did not understand. She had suffered. That he could see. But he did not quite understand how or why she should have suffered so much. He wondered if it was brutal of him now to suggest a break with her. All the same, he had not altered his resolution to do so since he had seen Pat Wallis off on leave. And tomorrow she would be returning (the Matron had given her two weeks instead of one in order to be with her mother), and Maurice felt that he must have something definite to tell Pat when he saw her again.

Julie did not love him. She commanded all his pity and affection, but he could not feel that he was about to deliver a mortal blow at her when he told her the truth. She did not even seem to want his kisses or notice the lack of them. So gently but firmly he explained to her that things were not the same as they had been in France, and that he thought it would be better for both of them to wipe out their obligations towards one another.

When Julie, alternating between her surprise and relief, questioned him further, Maurice, somewhat red in the face, admitted his love for Pat Wallis.

'Do you think very badly of me, *chérie?*' he asked. 'You see it all happened in the hospital when I first came here and I had forgotten the existence of my Julie.'

She shook her head, her heart-beats quickening a little with emotion.

'I do not think badly of you at all, Maurice. Indeed, I only wish you had told me this before.'

'Then you have not wanted to marry me all the way along?'

She turned her gaze from him.

'No – to be honest – I haven't.'

He clicked his tongue against his cheek.

'What a pity we have been misunderstanding each other all this time.'

She stared at the green valley below Mulverton Court. It was like a blur before her eyes in the summer sunshine. She was still so weak that she was easily exhausted and that heart of hers would hammer on every provocation. She thought:

'What a pity! I would have said *what a tragedy!* For all this time I have been thinking that Maurice wanted me. I never dreamed about Pat. Neil never dreamed, either. And if we had known – we might have been together for a little while. I could have given him that happiness before he died. Oh, my darling, *my darling!*'

Maurice took her hand and held it gently.

'You are not going to be unhappy about it, are you, *ma petite?* You do not want to marry me? It will not make you sad if I marry Pat?'

She looked at him with her tragic eyes.

'No, I won't be sad. I shall be very happy for you both.'

Much cheered by this, Maurice added:

'You won't feel that I am deserting you? After all, it seems so poor of me when you came over here to find me and now … for me to let you down…'

'But you aren't letting me down,' she interrupted. 'I don't want to marry you, Maurice dear; I don't want to marry anybody.'

'Ah, no! One day you will think differently,

you will find somebody else.'

Her lips curved into the ghost of a smile. She thought: 'So even now he doesn't understand...'

But she said nothing. It was better so. Needless for Maurice to know about the wild struggle through which Neil and she had passed in order to keep faith with him.

Futile sacrifice! Oh, bitter, bitter indeed to realise that Neil need not have gone and that she need not have sent him away. Maurice had all the time been in love with Pat. Confusedly she recalled that day in the drawing-room when Maurice's memory had reawakened and he had knelt at her feet, babbling of his love. It had all been hysteria, reaction and nothing more. They might have told him the truth *then* and he would have fled straight to Pat's arms. And *she,* Julie, would have had all the following weeks with Neil; would have had the right to mourn him now; *might even have born his son.*

But that was a though too agonising to be borne. A regret too futile. In her weak condition it was all too much for Julie. The tears began to roll down her cheeks. Her whole body trembled with misery. Maurice bent over her, alarmed and dismayed.

'Julie, dearest, have I hurt you? Isn't it true that you wish our engagement to end?'

She cried:

'Yes! Yes, it is true. I swear it. It is just that I

am not well yet. You won't understand. But, believe me, dear Maurice, and don't worry.'

'But I do worry,' he said, his face puckered.

She smiled through the tears, wiping them away.

'Go to your Pat,' she whispered.

'She's not coming back till tomorrow.'

'Then tomorrow you will be happy. I envy you. And I like her so much. She will make you a far better wife than I would have done.'

'She is a wonderful girl,' he said, 'but you, too, are wonderful and beautiful. One day, I know, you, too, will find happiness.'

She did not answer. She lay back with her eyes shut, hoping that he would go away. He did so, thinking she might wish to sleep. But sleep was far from her. She just lay there with the sun on her face and grey twilight in her heart. It seemed so ironic and cruel that she should find herself released from her engagement ... free when it was no longer of any use. She murmured:

'Neel ... *Neel...*'

Then the sharpness of her pain gradually lessened. Courage returned, and it was as though she felt him there with her. Almost as though he was at her very side, and she could hear his voice telling her to be brave; saying to her as he had said once before in this very garden: *'I shall love you till I die...'*

Well, he had died. But just as her love had

gone with him beyond the grave, so his endured, and would remain with her always. A love that nothing could conquer. Not death itself.

It was another fortnight before Doctor McKenzie allowed Julie to attempt the work which she so much wanted to do. By that time the enforced rest, sunshine, and her own new philosophy of courage and endurance had done much to restore Julie's health. When she first went down to the local canteen to help Lady Hanley, she looked almost herself again, although she was still painfully thin and shadowy-eyed.

Alice Hanley was happier about her now. In her opinion the greatest tonic which Julie could have had was the release from her engagement. She would not easily recover from the wound which life had dealt her about Neil. But she could at least suffer the pain of that wound in peace since Maurice had so astonishingly confessed to his feelings for Pat.

Maurice and Pat were now officially engaged. It had all been a considerable surprise to Lady Hanley, but she was pleased. She liked Maurice. Pat seemed radiantly happy, and Julie was released. It all seemed very satisfactory. But she knew how bitterly poor little Julie must be regretting that Maurice had not made up his mind sooner ... before Neil was lost to her.

27

There were two people in the world, anyhow, who regretted nothing. And they were Pat Wallis and Maurice Dupont.

They were surprisingly happy and content with one another, this seemingly ill-assorted pair ... the voluble and sentimental Frenchman, the practical and more reserved English girl.

The day on which their engagement was announced in the papers, was also the day on which Pat was given a weekend's leave to take Maurice home to meet her parents.

It was typical of her parents, as she told Maurice on the way to Cheshire, that they should consent to the engagement before meeting him. They were like that ... they trusted to her taste, and they neither of them believed in ordering about the life of a girl of her age. She must make her own choice.

Maurice grew a little nervous as the train brought them near to their destination. He realised that he was going to be very much 'on approval' with Pat's large family, and it was a formidable prospect.

Pat teased him unmercifully.

'Daddy's the toughest colonel that ever

came out of the Indian Army, his liver's been ruined by countless curries, and he'll snap your head off. Mummy has the eye of an eagle and will pick out your bad points straight away, and my sisters will make fun of you from the moment we arrive to the moment we leave the old homestead.'

Maurice eyed his newly-made fiancée doubtfully.

'Is it that I am a dove that has walked into the eagle's nest?' he exclaimed.

'Dear little dove,' said Pat, and cooed at him.

He shrugged his shoulders in the way that she loved.

'You do not love me, you detest me,' he said gloomily.

They were sitting together in a railway carriage occupied by a Naval officer and his wife and two old ladies. Knowing her Maurice, Pat was horribly afraid that he would kiss her in front of them all, just to prove his mastery. Her English blood recoiled at the thought, and to prevent the catastrophe, she squeezed his hand and whispered:

'*Je t'adore.*'

'*Mon Dieu!*' muttered Maurice. 'What an accent.'

She grinned.

'You're improving, Maurice. Very soon you'll be as rude to me as I am to you.'

He grinned back, well pleased with her.

The village of Applethwaite, in which Pat had been born, was about eight miles' drive from Chester. It was Colonel Wallis, himself, who met the young couple when they arrived on the three o'clock train after a tiresome cross-country journey from Tiverton.

Maurice braced himself for the first meeting with his future father-in-law. He saw a tall lean man, in the well-cut grey flannel suit with which Maurice had learned to associate Englishmen, a club tie, a rose in his buttonhole (Pat exclaimed afterwards that her father was never without a buttonhole). A green felt hat of the pork-pie variety on an iron-grey head.

An exceedingly good-looking man, just in his fifties, with the lean brown face of one who has spent many years in the East. Maurice was most impressed. The Colonel shook him warmly by the hand, and said:

'So this is my Pat's future husband. You're very welcome. And I hope, my boy, you're feeling fit again.'

Maurice, once more in uniform, held himself proudly erect as he saluted Pat's father.

'I am much honoured to meet you, *Monsieur le Colonel.*'

And with his hand in the firm grasp of the elder man, the 'bogey' with which Pat had threatened Maurice vanished. Here was an easy-going and charming gentleman for all his years of India and curry! And a gentleman with tragedy in those blue eyes which were too touchingly like Pat's. Pat had explained to Maurice that the death of his only son, Francis, had been a stupendous blow to her father, and things were not made more easy for him by virtue of the fact that, despite his appearance of good health, he suffered from an incurable kidney complaint which prevented him from playing his part in this war. There was no more disappointed man in the county than Geoffrey Wallis, unable even to become a member of the Home Guard, let alone rejoin the regiment.

By the time they reached Applethwaite, to which they drove in the Wallis's ancient Morris shooting brake, the delightful September afternoon was fading a little, but Maurice had yet another pleasant vista of English countryside. Different entirely from the green deep valley of the Exe. Here were more gentle hills, villages less rustic and less 'picture post card'. Not so much the white-washed, thatched cottages with honeysuckle and creeping rose as the sturdily built brick and stone houses of the Queen Anne and Georgian age.

Applethwaite itself was a lovely little place with Georgian houses flanking a broad main road. It had the inevitable war memorial at one end, and there on the rough stone, Pat pointed out to Maurice, were engraven the names of two Wallis's, members of her family who had lived in Applethwaite and died for their country before she was born.

Pat's own home, which bore the quaint name of Gays House, was one of the most beautiful places Maurice had ever seen. It was reached by a long drive cut through a small wood, which remained wild and uncultivated, and which, Pat told Maurice, was purple with bluebells in the spring. Then suddenly one came upon the house, beautiful in its simplicity, its chaste design, half-hidden by flaming red Virginia creeper. Vivid clematis twined around the stone pillars of the portico. There were fanlights over the tall windows.

In front of the house stretched a smooth lawn, and a great cedar tree. The flower garden, the orchards were at the back.

Gays House had been in the family for three hundred years, and Pat's face glowed with pride as she showed it to her fiancé.

Reverently he looked about him.

'It is the Frenchman's idea of the English home,' he said, 'it makes me feel, what shall I say ... so small ... that I have so little to offer you, *ma petite* Pat. Almost as if I have no right to take you away from this to be the wife of a roving soldier. It may be years before I can show you my own home in

Provence which one day will be yours.'

Pat shrugged her shoulders. She was much too happy today to worry over any such problems. Home and gardens were not of such absorbing value these days as they used to be. One's dearest possessions were growing to mean less as time went on. Anyhow, nothing mattered to *her* now, except Maurice and her wish to belong to him entirely. As for Provence, and the day when she would accompany him there, and renounce her British passport, her nationality for his, that all seemed fantastic and a long way off.

Mrs Wallis came out of the house to meet them. Dark-haired and slender in type, she bore a strong resemblance to her sister Alice, which Maurice at once recognised, only she was shorter and more *petite* in every way, and Pat had her tip-tilted nose. She looked amazingly young to be the mother of a big family, and Maurice's susceptible heart was completely won over when she held out both hands and welcomed him.

'Well, my dear, so you are my future son-in-law, are you? I'm so glad you've come to us.'

He kissed both her hands in turn, and then her cheek.

'Please accept my homage, *Madame*. You have a delightful daughter and I am sure you and *Monsieur le Colonel* must dislike the thought that she marries a poor French-man.'

'Not at all,' said Angela Wallis briskly, and then turned to her daughter and hugged the young figure in the V.A.D. costume.

'Lovely to see you again, darling.'

Tea was waiting for them in the long white-panelled dining-room, full of gracious Chippendale furniture; the tall windows framed in green and white chintzes of Jacobean design.

Maurice sat down with his fiancée at the long mahogany table, which was spread with a white linen lace cloth, and opened his eyes wide at the tea which was waiting for them. Here was no sign of rationing. Great dishes of yellow butter and jugs of cream, home-made scones, sections of honey, and a variety of cakes.

'OOH,' said Pat, 'a real Gays House tea, Mummy; it isn't hardly patriotic! I don't know how you do it.'

'Only because we have our own farm, dear,' said her mother, 'and I make the butter myself. But it won't be so long before such teas will vanish from every table, so enjoy it while you can.'

Maurice watched his future mother-in-law pour out fragrant China tea from a silver Georgian pot and sighed.

'The people of my country today would like to see this food and these things,' he said sombrely.

Angela Wallis turned her soft eyes upon him. She liked the look of this young Frenchman. She liked his humorous mouth and his honest eyes. It was as big of a disappointment to her that Pat had not chosen one of her own countrymen. But Maurice was a soldier of de Gaulle, a citizen of Free France, a true ally, and she could not gainsay that fact. Nor begrudge Pat her obvious happiness. In the family Pat had never been considered one to easily fall in love, and as they adored her they were ready to take the man of her choice to their hearts.

Mrs Wallis said:

'Poor France, but never mind, Maurice. She'll come back into her own again.'

Colonel Wallis immediately launched into a political discussion with the young Frenchman, and was well satisfied with his intelligent and sensible replies.

Mother and daughter talked together; Mrs Wallis had domestic troubles. Cook was leaving to go into a munitions factory, and the parlourmaid was threatening to marry her young man. More evacuees had been sent to Gays House and they had only one elderly and incompetent gardener to tackle both the flower garden and the orchard. None of it was easy, but, of course, one had to expect these trials in the war, said Angela Wallis, cheerfully.

'Where are the kids?' asked Pat, and was told that her young sisters were helping in a canteen to which they cycled on Saturdays and Sundays when Pip and Peggy were not at school. During that week they attended a day school in Chester. They were due home any moment.

By the time they came, Maurice had melted in the homely and delightful atmosphere of Gays House, and was thoroughly at ease with his future in-laws.

When Peggy and Phillipa, otherwise 'Pip', first saw their future brother-in-law, he was sitting on a stool in front of the log fire which had just been lit in the library. Their elder and much respected sister lay on a rug at his feet, and both were nursing the golden cocker spaniel pups which had just arrived in this world a fortnight ago. Jill, their mother, sat somewhat anxiously regarding her brood, not yet sure of the stranger in the foreign uniform.

Pat kissed the two girls, then introduced them to Maurice.

'These are my two ugly sisters, Peggy and Pip. Urchins, this is Maurice.'

Maurice rose, bowed in approved style and (much to the delight of Peggy and Pip) kissed each of their grubby hands in turn.

'I am *enchanté*, my two little sisters-to-be,' he said.

They at once fell in love with him. They

decided that he was as good-looking and as fascinating as Maurice Chevalier himself. They could not imagine how 'old Pat' could have won the love of so glamorous a figure.

Maurice beamed at them both. Certainly they were not 'ugly' sisters as he thought. Peggy, aged fifteen, was long and leggy, very much in the awkward stage, and wore a gold band over her teeth, but she had Pat's radiant blue eyes, curly hair, and upturned nose, and one day would be exceedingly pretty. Pip was small, dark, and slight like her mother, and in the dreamy and some-what shy stage. Both wore grey flannel slacks and jerseys.

Peggy said, eagerly:

'I say, I thought your name was *"Jeudi"*. That's what Pat used to write and tell us.'

'That is what she called me when she did not know my real name,' he explained.

'I still call him *Jeudi* sometimes,' said Pat.

'It's rather silly calling him that, unless it's on a Thursday,' said little Pip, anxious to show that she knew the meaning of the word.

'Ah!' said Maurice. 'I see your point. To-day I should be *Samedi,* and tomorrow *Dimanche.*'

Pip thought that very humorous and giggled. Both the young girls stared frankly at the young Frenchman's glamorous uniform, asked what the ribbon was, on his

313

tunic, and were thrilled to learn that it was the Croix de Guerre. They gave him no peace until he had told them how and when he had won it. It was before he had become liaison officer in Neil Richardson's unit. At the mention of their cousin Neil, the girls looked sorrowful.

'Poor Cousin Neil is missing,' said Pip. 'We simply adored him.'

'It is much to be hoped that he will return,' said Maurice.

Mrs Wallis came into the library, left Maurice to chat with the younger girls, and bore her eldest daughter off to her own boudoir for a chat.

'You're tremendously happy, aren't you, dear?' she murmured, when they were comfortably seated together with their cigarettes.

'Tremendously, Mum,' said Pat, 'I've never thought it possible I'd love anybody like I do Maurice.'

'Your father and I think he's charming. Naturally we wish we knew a little more about him.'

'Poor Neil knows more than we do, as he met Maurice's former fiancée and people out in Provence.'

'Yes, of course, he was engaged before. You're quite sure, Pat, it wasn't, shall we say, a little *mean* to take him away from a French girl when they were both exiled over here?'

Pat's cheeks burned.

'That's absolutely all right, Mum. Maurice had it all out with Julie. She's a funny little thing ... frightfully attractive ... in fact I can never understand why Maurice didn't stay in love with her. But apparently *she* fell out of love with *him,* long before I came on the scene, which clears my conscience. And also you must remember that when Maurice and I first met, the past was a closed book to him and he didn't even know he was engaged.'

'Oh, well,' said Mrs Wallis, 'I suppose it's all right.'

'Quite all right, Mum, we haven't hurt anybody. But between you and me, although I haven't mentioned it to Maurice, I think Julie de Vallois fell for poor Neil. You know they had that thrilling escape from France together, and so forth, and you know how attractive Neil is, and no man could be blamed for falling in love with her. She's like something out of a Watteau painting. It's so tragic, now that Neil's lost.'

'We must pray that he'll turn up, my dear.'

Simultaneously, mother and daughter turned their gaze to the photograph on the little satinwood bureau by the window. A leather-framed photograph of Francis Wallis in his uniform. His mother and his sister felt afresh the tragedy of their loss. It seemed so hard to believe that he, who had been missing since Dunkirk, must now be presumed lost to them forever. Dear beloved Francis, with his engaging smile, his love of life, his idealism. Cruel and hard that one so young should die, and *why,* as the mother had asked herself a hundred times, must it always be the best, the most worthy, that are taken?

With eyes full of tears, Mrs Wallis pressed Pat's strong young hand. 'Daddy and I will do all we can to love your Maurice and be glad to have him as a son-in-law,' she said.

'You're an angel, Mum,' said Pat, huskily.

'You won't be married too soon, will you, darling?'

'No, darling. We've decided to wait till Christmas, anyhow. Maurice is off to London soon and no doubt he'll be posted to one of the Free French units, and no doubt it will be where I can't follow anyhow, so I shall stick to the hospital for a bit and we'll see how things develop.'

Mrs Wallis avoided looking at the photograph of her son again, and essayed a smile.

'Well, let's cheer up, my pet. We'll make this a good weekend. I heard Daddy say that there was still a bottle or two of champagne in the household, and we'll celebrate the great engagement tonight.'

Pat hugged her mother.

'Angel! And I can tell you, you've got an expert in Maurice where champagne is concerned. His people are in the wine business.

One day I shall be the *châtelaine* of a whole lot of vineyards, and I'll be able to keep you and Daddy in good wine for the rest of your lives. When the war ends.'

'*When!*' echoed Mrs Wallis.

28

Julie enjoyed her first afternoon's work at the canteen. There was a big aerodrome close by and it was a mass of R.A.F. lads who crowded to the counter for their meal.

Her feet, her legs ached, her arms grew weary carrying heavy trays. But spiritually she was satisfied. At last she was able to do some work for the country. And every one of those boys whom she served *was Neil.* Everyone who wore the uniform he had worn, and took the risks that he had taken. She felt that she could never do enough for any of them. And it was plain to Lady Hanley that Julie, with her silver cloud of hair, her slenderness wrapped in an apple-green overall, her lovely smile unfailing, would soon be a popular addition to the R.A.F. canteen.

The canteen itself was in a newly-erected hut, redolent of fresh wood and tar and cooking, but it was a good, appetising odour, evidently enjoyed by the men, and

Julie soon got used to it.

The kitchen was partitioned off by glass and wood from the long, wide room with its snack-counter. Julie took turns with the other helpers in washing up and serving the food. The men came in at irregular hours, as their work allowed. Sometimes there were few. Sometimes the room was crowded and a queue filled up waiting for a chance to sit on the high stools at the counter. The favourite choice of the day was a 'high tea' round about five o'clock. Bacon and eggs, sausages, cold meats and salads, sandwiches.

Officers came as well as men. There were urns of coffee or tea, according to choice.

At the furthermost end of the room stood a ping-pong table, and there was a darts board, a varied selection of books and comfortable chairs.

Julie was at first a little flustered by the babel of voices and in having to keep so many orders in mind. But she soon learned the routine:

'One egg and bacon ... two sausages ... one cold meat ... one tea and biscuits ... one coffee, cake, and an apple...' so it ran on.

And she learned to remember which of the hungry young men had given which particular order, and found it very satisfying to watch them sit down and eat a hearty meal.

A young pilot-officer was particularly attracted by her faintly foreign accent.

'You're not English, are you?' he asked as she handed him his tea.

'No, I'm half French, and I come from Provence,' she smiled.

'I say, do you really?' asked the boy eagerly. 'I spent the last holiday of the war at a place called Bandola.'

Julie forgot the other demands which were waiting. Her whole body quivered with interest at the idea that here was somebody who knew her beloved Provence.

'Oh!' she exclaimed. 'How well I know Bandola – it is so near La Marita where I was born. Did you go to La Marita?'

Yes, the young pilot-officer had been there, he said. They had taken an excursion from Bandola one day. He remembered the island. Julie grew more and more thrilled as he described his memories.

Her face was quite pale with intensity as his words conjured up to her the vision, which never really faded from her mind, of that adored and adorable island where she and Neil had loved. The young officer had been there in the spring. He knew all about the flowers; the exquisite clearness of the water, the radiance of the light. And as she talked with him in the thick, steamy, smoky atmosphere of the canteen, she felt as though a great weight were crushing her heart.

'Oh, shall I ever see Provence again?' she sighed.

The young airman felt a little troubled by the tragedy in the girl's great eyes. He leaned across the counter.

'Oh, I say,' he murmured, 'don't be depressed about things. Of course you'll see Provence again. We're going to win this war and chuck those damned Nazis out of France jolly soon. Don't you worry! You'll go back to La Marita and I shall spend my honeymoon in Bandola,' he grinned, ... 'not that I am engaged, but that's the place I've chosen already.'

Julie's misty eyes smiled at him now.

'You have cause. Provence is the right place for a honeymoon.'

'You going to spend yours there?'

It was as though a knife entered her heart, but she continued to smile.

'There ... in my dreams, if not in reality.'

One of the workers touched her arm.

'Three waiting for sausages. Lady Hanley's cooking them for you, if you'll fetch them with a tray.'

With a jolt, Julie returned to that grim reality which in these days threatened to obliterate those lovely dreams of hers altogether. She tore herself away from the young airman who could speak to her of Provence. She thrust the memory of Neil out of her mind. She went back to the monotonous job of serving food, carrying trays, collecting empty glasses, refilling milk jugs and sugar basins, cutting bread.

She saw the same pilot-officer again just before he left the canteen to go back on duty. He beckoned her and, when she went to him, somewhat shyly asked her if she would like to go out with him one evening.

'We've got something in common,' he said. 'Provence! You live round here, don't you? I don't know a soul. My home's in Bristol. It'd be awfully nice if you'd have dinner and do a flick with me?'

She was touched, but gently refused the invitation.

'It's so very kind of you ... but I really couldn't. As a matter of fact I live at Mulverton, and it would be much too far to come in the blackout.' (She was letting him down lightly. That wasn't the real reason. Blackouts held no particular terror for Julie. It as just that she had no interest in any man in the world except Neil. She would have felt it a flagrant disloyalty to his memory to spend an evening with anybody else.)

The boy looked disappointed, but said that 'he understood', saluted, and left her.

'Good luck,' she said.

'Good luck to you,' he answered, 'and a speedy return to Provence. Send me a bunch of flowers from that island if you get there before I do.'

She nodded, not trusting herself to speak. It was so awful, she felt, that the mere mention of that island should rouse such poignant emotion within her. That nice boy must have thought her very stupid and sentimental.

Back to the food and the countless orders.

At six o'clock there was a lull in the buzz of voices, when someone switched on the radio for the news.

Alice Hanley called Julie in from the counter and made her rest and have some coffee. She, herself, had been cheerfully cooking over a grilling fire for the last three hours. She was hot and flushed, but as serene as ever. She looked rather anxiously at Julie's pale little face, and the dark circles under those big eyes.

'Don't let your ardours run away with you, darling,' she said, 'you're not all that strong!'

Julie sat down, protesting.

'I'm loving it, *Marraine*.'

Their eyes met in secret understanding. And Alice Hanley knew that she could not have done better than bring Julie here to work amongst these airmen.

The news started with the usual grave accounts of aerial battles, of attempts to penetrate the defences of London, of the exploits of the Coastal Command, of warfare in the Mediterranean, the Middle East, the Colonies.

Then there was a pause. The announcer cleared his throat and began on a more cheerful note:

'News has come through of the miraculous return from death of a young Flight-Lieutenant of the Royal Air Force who, for the last fortnight, has been reported missing, believed killed, during an attempted night raid upon Holland...'

Julie's fair head shot up. The coffee cup, which she had been holding in her hand, dropped back on the saucer with a clatter. She drew in her breath with an inaudible sound, and her eyes sent a look of almost agonised inquiry at Lady Hanley.

'Oh, listen ... *Marraine,* did you hear?'

Alice Hanley felt her heart stir as it had rarely stirred before in her life. She held up a warning finger, hushing Julie, as the announcer continued:

'The British pilot, who has already distinguished himself in France, was given up for lost after his brother-officers had seen the bomber which he was piloting shot down into the sea. But a message has now come through that, after clinging to a portion of the fuselage for several hours, he was picked up at dawn, exhausted and half-frozen, by a Dutch merchant ship which was proceeding to Amsterdam. The captain, although under Nazi domination, had obvious sympathies for the British cause. For ten days or more he was forced to hide the young pilot until the chance came to hand him over, not into Nazi

323

hands, but to one of H.M. Armed Trawlers, which had sighted the Dutch vessel. The young pilot, now safely on English soil again, gives a thrilling description of the dramatic escape which he made with the help of the Dutch captain, rowing himself in the dark at dead of night to meet the British trawler. Soon after this he was landed at Harwich and immediately rejoined his squadron nearby.

'The B.B.C. is hoping that this pilot, who is well known to his brother-officers and to many of the public as "Devil Richardson", on account of his daring exploits in the air, will be able to broadcast his experiences shortly after the nine o'clock news tonight...'

The announcer's voice ended with the usual information that it was the end of the six o'clock news, and would be followed by the announcements.

Julie sat very still in her chair. She might have been a small graven image. Only her large shining eyes were alive. So intensely alive and filled with unutterable emotion that Alice Hanley could hardly bear to look into them. But then Lady Hanley for the first time in her life was openly weeping. The calm, controlled Englishwoman stood there in the canteen with a plate in one hand and a toasting-fork in the other, crying like a child.

Suddenly Julie ... the whole of Julie

sprang to life. She rushed at Lady Hanley and flung both her arms around her.

'Oh, Marraine, *Marraine,* did you hear, did you *hear?*'

Lady Hanley put the plate and the fork down on the kitchen-table and hugged the girl, still unable to speak. Julie added:

'He is alive! *He is alive,* my Neel, my beloved Neel!'

And then the two women were weeping and laughing in turns, their arms about each other.

During the next half-hour Julie's brain did not really register anything that she was doing. Somehow or other she had to carry on with her work, following Alice Hanley's example, until the end of the shift. Mechanically she handed the hungry lads their food and drink and mechanically answered their quips and jests. But there was only one thought in her mind, one burning, glorious thought. Neil was not dead. He had come back as from the very grave itself. He had been spared as though by a miracle and was at this very moment back on English soil ... with his unit at Ipswich.

Now and again, as Julie, carrying a pile of dirty dishes, passed Neil's aunt, she managed to shoot questions at her. Lady Hanley, busy with the cooking, answered as best she could.

Why hadn't Neil got in touch with them,

personally? Possibly he had done so, but the message had not yet come through, and his first duty would have been to report to his Squadron. And then the Air Ministry would have been informed of his escape and given the B.B.C. the thrilling story.

Would there be a message for them when they got back to Mulverton Court? Doubtless there would, either a phone call or a telegram.

Would Neil be given leave at once? More than probably after his hazardous adventure.

And of course, Julie said, he had still to learn of her broken engagement and Maurice's switch-over to Pat, and when he heard *that* she was sure that nothing would prevent him from coming straight down to Devonshire. She was sure enough of his feelings towards *her* to believe that.

In a daze, a haze of joy, of excitement such as she had never known before in her whole existence, Julie carried on with her work. One of the men sitting up at the counter stared at her curiously. He had noticed her from the first moment she had come into the canteen and thought how marvellously pretty she was. But she looked radiant ... as though she was glowing with some inner fire. Cheeks warm and pink, eyes brilliant, her whole expression that of a girl who has been through some terrific emotional experience. The man, in the Air Force for the duration of the war, but in private life an artist, could not take his eyes off Julie. He lamented the fact that he had not got paint, brushes, and canvas with him. Only, he thought, it would take a Master to catch that indescribably joyous expression of hers.

When she handed him the eggs and bacon he had ordered, he said:

'Do you know, you look as though you've just seen heaven. You might tell me where to look and then I might see it too.'

Julie gave a little laugh.

'It is true. I *have* seen heaven, but it is my own particular heaven which no one can share with me.'

'Lucky girl,' he said enviously.

'I *am* lucky,' she said, breathlessly, 'you don't know how lucky.'

She moved away from the counter and he followed the slender figure in the green overall with a puzzled gaze. He had never seen anything quite like Julie before, in any canteen.

That shift seemed to Julie intolerably long, but at last it came to an end and she found herself driving back to Mulverton Court with Lady Hanley, talking, talking, talking of Neil. Could there ever be anything else to talk about?

'It's too good to be true ... oh, it's too good!' she kept saying feverishly.

Lady Hanley pressed the girl's knee.

'Darling child, I'm so happy for you. Honestly, when I heard the news, I felt I was your age again and it was my Percy they were talking about. I've never made such a fool of myself in public before.'

Julie laughed.

'It is one of God's miracles! To have been picked up by a ship belonging to the Nazis and get sent back to us. What he must have been through, all those hours in the water! Oh, it's too thrilling to imagine.'

'It certainly is,' Lady Hanley agreed.

Then Julie, out of breath from so much talking, sat silent and let her thoughts run away with her. Oh, those bitter nights of weeping in the past ... those bitter tears that had been shed ... those wild prayers before her crucifix, which she had thought unanswered. But now all her faith was justified. She had prayed to Mary, Mother of God, to intercede for her, and this was the answer. Neil was not dead but alive, and soon she would be seeing him. She would be free and he could come to her without doubt or question. So sudden and so unexpected after the long days of grief and despair.

In a transport of happiness, Julie rushed into the house calling for Maurice. Maurice had not gone out today. He was expecting his Pat for dinner. He came into the hall to meet her and the moment she saw him she knew that he, too, had heard the news. His blue eyes were beaming.

He caught both her hands and pressed them hard.

'You heard on the radio that our friend is alive and back with us? *Mon Dieu, mais c'est merveilleux!* And not many minutes after that broadcast came a telephone call from Ipswich. Yes, from Richardson *le Diable* himself.'

Julie, clinging wildly to Maurice's fingers, cried:

'Oh, it's *too* good! What did he say?'

'That he is well and has suffered no harm beyond a few cuts and bruises. That he has leave which he will take from tomorrow. Tonight he has promised to broadcast his experiences.'

Julie drew in her breath, her brilliant eyes searching Maurice's.

'Did you tell him about us?'

Maurice gave a sheepish laugh.

'I had to. He asked after my wife. He thought we had been married.'

Then Julie burst into a ripple of laughter, laughter with a broken note in it. She said:

'Oh, but it's funny, it's *too* funny! And you told him that now you were going to marry his cousin Pat?'

'I did.'

'What did he say?'

'He seemed ... what you call "staggered".

He wished me luck. Then I said that you had been very ill and he sent you a message. I don't quite understand, but he said *you* would understand.'

Julie, hardly able to breathe in her excitement, hung on to Maurice's fingers with a grip that made him wince.

'Tell me, tell me, quickly.'

'He said: *"Tout pour toi."* I was just to tell you that, and that he would be down here tomorrow.'

Julie let go of Maurice's hands. For a second she looked wildly around her, almost as though expecting to see Neil's tall figure walking in at the very door.

Lady Hanley had gone up to her own room. Julie was alone with Maurice in the lounge. She heard him add:

'What is this? *"Tout pour toi."* What does it mean? It is so unlike an Englishman to say such a thing.'

Then, Julie, her whole face glowing, said:

'Maurice, Neil loves me and I love him.'

The young Frenchman stared at her. In bewilderment he stared, then ran his fingers through his thick fair hair. His underlip jutted out a little more than usual.

'What are you saying, crazy one?' he asked in his own language.

In French she answered him:

'Now you can know, now the whole world can know, and it doesn't matter. I love him, madly, madly, dear Maurice. And I think that is how he loves me.'

Maurice blinked. For a moment he thought that Julie was a little out of her mind. Yet he had never seen a human being so altered. The pale, sad-eyed girl, who had for so long been seriously ill, was glowing with health and strength. He had not see her look like this since those golden days in La Marita when they had laughed and danced together. And even then, never *quite* like this.

He spoke almost severely:

'Explain yourself, Julie, *ma petite.*'

She gave a low laugh of pure happiness. Taking his hand, she pulled him down on to the sofa.

'You shall hear my whole confession. And now that you have your Pat, you will be glad to learn of my happiness.'

'There is nothing that I want more than your happiness, Julie,' he said earnestly.

Then she told him the story of the island of La Marita, of that deep passionate love which had sprung up between Neil Richardson and herself during his convalescence in Provence, of their efforts to 'do the right thing' because of her engagement to him, Maurice. Of the long struggle since those days. And the rest, he knew well enough.

It seemed to Maurice Dupont, as he sat there listening to Julie, that he must have been a supreme fool not to have guessed all this before. It hurt him, not because his friend and his former fiancée had loved each other, but that they had suffered so on his account. That struck him as being the real tragedy. He was overcome with gratitude because they had endeavoured to maintain such loyalty. In a hushed voice he said:

'My poor, poor little Julie. My poor friend Richardson! But, of course, it was typical of both of you to do what the English call "playing the game". Only I wish you had told me. I wish you could have been spared all that terrible suffering.'

'It doesn't matter now, Maurice, it's all come right!'

'But how nearly you married me,' he said in a shocked voice.

'Yes.'

'It would have been a calamity. Almost a crime. No woman should marry just because she feels it her duty. *Mon Dieu,* Julie! Do you not realise that you would not only have wrecked your own life and mine, but Neil's and Pat's?'

She spread out both her hands.

'It was all such a tangle. I thought you loved me and *you* thought I loved you. But it does make me shudder now I can see how big a mistake we would all have made.'

He took one of her hands and carried it to his lips.

'I salute a very brave woman,' he said, 'and

I thank God you have no further need of such courage on my account.'

'Oh, Maurice, dear, it's so truly wonderful to think that Neel is alive and that he will be here tomorrow.'

'And tonight we will listen to him speak.'

'I shan't be able to bear it,' said Julie, pressing both hands to her burning cheeks.

Through the open door walked Pat in her Red Cross uniform, the usual cheerful smile on her face. Maurice and Julie rose to their feet. They both rushed at her.

'Have you heard the news?' exclaimed Julie.

'Do you know about your cousin being still alive?' asked Maurice.

Pat took off her cap and threw it on a chair.

'Yes, I heard on the wireless. We all did. It's marvellous.'

Maurice caught her round the waist.

'And do you know, *ma petite* Pat, something else of great importance. That all the time this bad girl, Julie here, has not been wanting to marry me, but your cousin, Neil. Yes. It is monstrous! They have been in love for weeks and months. This two!'

Then Pat gave one of her widest grins.

'I knew that ages ago. You're just a mutt, Lieutenant Dupont. Just a priceless old duffer, going around with your eyes and ears closed.'

He gave her a look of almost comical dismay.

'You mean *you* guessed it, *chérie?*'

'That's what I mean,' she laughed.

Julie just said:

'Oh, *Pat!*'

And then as though she could bear no more, with joy bubbling up inside her anew, she ran upstairs and shut herself in her room. And this time, when she knelt before her little crucifix, it was not to weep, but to give thanks, alone with her wild dreams of happiness.

29

On that bright September morning when Neil Richardson boarded a train at Paddington for the West Country, people looking at him saw what was a very ordinary sight in these days. Just a good-looking young officer in the R.A.F. wearing the familiar blue uniform; gas-mask slung over one shoulder, suit-case in his hand. The only thing that might have caused a passer-by to take a second look was a fresh-looking scar across this particular man's left eyebrow, a criss-cross of sticking plaster on one cheek. That might mean that he had been 'a casualty'. But there was nothing really about him to suggest the terrific adventure through which he had recently passed. And no one recognised him as Flight-Lieutenant 'Devil' Richardson who had so recently returned to life after having been reported lost, and who, last night, had broadcast his experiences for the benefit of millions of listeners.

Neil's personal reaction when he found a seat in that train was one of intense excitement and pleasure because he was going to meet Julie. His own narrow escape from death was of secondary importance in his mind. And to find himself hailed as a hero and dragged into the limelight had merely been an embarrassment. The fact that he had gained the Distinguished Flying Cross, and promotion ... he was now a Squadron-Leader ... was just pleasing news, and all in the day's work. But to know that Julie was free ... free and waiting for him ... *that* was of real, vital importance to Neil. What Maurice had told him yesterday had been the best news he had ever received in his life. He could scarcely believe it even now. When he had left Mulverton Court the whole affair had been a hopeless tangle from which none of them, he imagined, could extricate themselves. It had never once entered his head that Maurice could deviate from his affection towards Julie, and that it would be Maurice who would eventually open the door to happiness for Julie and himself.

It was a mentally satisfied but extremely impatient young man who waited for that train to draw out of Paddington station. Ruefully he reminded himself that there was a war on; the train was bound to be late getting away and late in arriving at Mulverton. Already he had missed one connection, because immediately upon his arrival in London from Ipswich the sirens had sounded and, greatly against his will, he had been forced by a dutiful warden to take cover. All the time he could think only of Julie and his immense desire to see her, to take her in his arms, to say all the things that he had wanted to say for so long; to arrange for their marriage; to see that beloved little face, which had been so grief-stricken when they were last together, transformed by happiness again. Once more they would be companions, lovers as they had been in La Marita. Only now it would all be so much better because they belonged rightfully to each other. There would be nobody to stand in their way. Together they could recapture that dream of love which at one time had seemed beyond their grasp.

It was Julie's face, Julie's great dark eyes, and her silver hair; her enchanting voice; the thrilling touch of her hands and lips which held him in a spell all during those hours while he was going to her. When he listened to the distant roar of 'planes, the sharp thunder of anti-aircraft guns, the distant boom of dropping bombs, he heard them all laconically. He was burningly impatient for the raid to be over; infuriated that enemy action should temporarily bar his progress towards his Julie. And when the 'all-clear' sounded, half-crazy with impatience, he had rushed out of the shelter and taken the first taxi to the station.

And now at last he was on the train. And the exquisite dream that was Julie, was growing nearer. Soon, he told himself, to become reality.

During the journey he tried to concentrate on papers and a 'thriller', but eventually he cast them aside. He could not read. He did not want to think of anything except Julie. And, now and then, he congratulated himself on being, surely, the luckiest man in England.

As he had told the world in his broadcast last night, he ought by right to be a corpse at the bottom of the sea. It had been a near shave all right. First the thrill of that dog-fight in the air against the German 'planes, the enormous excitement of an aerial battle which he always loved. Then, a momentary sensation of defeat when they got his engine; that breath-taking descent into the dark water. But by the grace of God he had managed to get his straps undone and extricate himself from the cockpit. The rest of his crew, poor devils, he had never seen again. They must have died, been caught by machine-gun fire before they could bale out. But he, miraculously unhurt except for a few cuts and bruises and the one deep gash in his forehead, had fought a duel with death itself, and conquered.

The hours of clinging to the fuselage in that ice-cold water were distinctly unpleasant to remember, but his final rescue by the Dutch steamer blotted out those more harrowing memories. There had followed days and nights of continued danger and suspense, but in the end, with the help of the sympathetic Dutch captain, he had reached the British trawler. And to Neil there had never been a sweeter moment in his life than when he set foot on a British ship again, heard English voices, and knew he was heading once more for Harwich – and home. For even then, when he had believed Julie to be Maurice's wife and utterly lost to him, life seemed precious. He was young and vital and there was work to be done. He was not giving up the good fight, yet!

Now the dark days were over. What he was facing seemed so brilliant and inspiring that he felt almost a sensation of guilt. With so much chaos and suffering going on around him, it seemed to him wrong that he should experience this intense happiness. But to make Julie equally happy was his main wish. It had been so since the first moment when that amazing tempest of love had swept them into each other's arms.

The train was, as he had anticipated, late in arriving at Mulverton. Twilight was wrapping the country-side in a purple mist when he stepped out at the familiar little station. By this time he was in such a fever of impatience to see Julie that ... as he afterwards told Julie ... he was sure that the two ladies and an old gentleman in his carriage must have thought him a victim of neurasthenia. He could not sit still. He had to pace up and down the corridor. He smoked every cigarette he had brought with him, and the journey had never seemed longer. Even in those remote days of his boyhood, when he used to travel down to Mulverton from school to spend some of his holidays with his aunt, he had rarely known such impatience and excitement.

He stood a moment on the platform, eagerly searching for the one face in the world he most wanted to see. But Julie was not here. In fact, nobody appeared to be meeting him, and for a moment the returning hero was conscious of disappointment.

Then he saw Andrews, Lady Hanley's chauffeur, who hurried to him and took his suit-case:

'Good evening, sir, good evening. I have a

message for you from her ladyship. She regretted not being able to meet you, but she thought you would be on the earlier train and she has to be at the canteen at this time, sir, and couldn't get away.'

'That's all right, Andrews,' said Neil. Then before he could question him, the old chauffeur added:

'The young lady, sir ... from France...' Andrews never could pronounce Julie's name ... 'is waiting for you in the car, sir. I've taken out Sir Percy's big car tonight, sir, as her ladyship has driven the little one to the canteen.'

Then Neil's heart seemed to slip a beat. So Julie was out there in the car. He knew at once that she had not wanted to meet him in public on the platform. He could appreciate her sentiments. For there was nothing in the world he wanted more than to be alone with her – quite alone.

He tried to speak casually to Andrews as they walked out into the station yard.

'Is Mr Dupont still here?'

'Yes, sir, but he's gone into Tiverton with her ladyship.'

Neil's heartbeats quickened still more. So Julie, all by herself, would be waiting for him in the car. That was very discreet of Maurice!

And then he saw her.

Dusk though it was, she was plainly

visible, framed by the open window of the big Daimler limousine. He felt his whole soul rushing out in an excess of emotion as he looked upon that flower-like face which had never been out of his thoughts, day and night, since their last meeting.

Andrews opened the door of the car and placed the suitcase inside. Then he took his seat at the wheel. The driver was separated by a partition from the passengers of this car, and through the sliding glass windows between them, they could not be seen in the darkness.

For an instant Neil stood speechlessly staring at Julie. He took in every detail of her appearance. She wore the black dinner dress which she had brought with her from La Marita, with its soft touches of white at the throat and rounded arms, and her jewelled cross. Over this a light camel's hair coat. The cloud of fair hair, just as he remembered and loved it, floated about her neck, unconfined. How ill she had been was not apparent to him in this moment. For there was a brilliant flush on the high cheekbones and a light in her eyes which he had never seen before in the eyes of any human being. It held him spellbound.

Then he heard her voice, with its faint attractive accent:

'*Neel.*'

'Julie!' he said.

She gave a low laugh of sheer delight.

'Aren't you going to get in, or shall I drive away without you?'

'God forbid!' he said.

And the next moment he was beside her, and had slammed the door. Andrews switched on the engine. The big car began to move slowly and sedately out of the little station yard.

For Neil there was an instant's immobility. He was still drinking in the sight of her. He caught the intoxicating fragrance of red roses, *Etoile d'Hollande,* which she had pinned to her coat. In the dusk of the big car, her two small hands came fluttering like white moths towards him and touched his cheeks, his hair. She said:

'Is it really, *really* you? Oh, *mon amour … mon amour!*'

He drew her into his arms. Under the coat his hands caught and pressed the slenderness and sweetness of her so close to him that he could feel her heart beating beneath his heart. Her small hands locked about his neck. Then with a gesture he swept off his cap, and kissed her mouth. Held it in a kiss to which there seemed no ending. A kiss which, for both of them, was but a continuation of that first passionate union of their lips in their first embrace at La Marita.

For both of them, all the old wild thrill and rapture was here renewed and intensified. The car moved on through the quiet village and out on to the winding road which led through the valley and up towards Mulverton Court.

But for Julie and Neil there was no place, no time. That passionate embrace was an enchantment, a culmination of all that they had endured apart from each other, a fulfilment of the desire which had never for an instant diminished since the first hour they had loved each other.

There was no car, no Devon valley. They were back on their island in the sun-warmed grass under the benison of the crucifix ... the Christ who had answered their prayer.

They could hear the echoing cry of the seagulls sweeping over La Marita, their wet wings flashing in the sunlight. They could hear the faint lapping of the sea against the shell-strewn shore. They could smell the wild thyme and lavender. The salt tang of the sea. The pungent odour of Hortense's coffee, of freshly-baked rolls, of fruit with the sun on it. *That* was La Marita. That was Provence. And in Provence their love had been born, and had followed them here.

When Neil raised his head it was only to draw Julie closer yet in his hungry embrace, and to whisper against her cloudy hair:

'Darling, my sweet ... heart of my heart. You're more beautiful and lovely than ever. Julie, sweetest, I can taste those cherries on your lips. Do you remember the cherries on your island. Do you?'

'I remember everything,' she said and her voice was broken with love, she was experiencing the supreme satisfaction of reunion with the man who meant life itself to her, and who, at one time, she had believed to be dead.

'Are you really and truly mine now?' he went on, 'or is it just a fantastic dream?'

'It is true. Maurice is going to marry Pat.'

'I can't believe it yet.'

'I could not believe it either when Maurice first told me.'

'It doesn't make sense,' said Neil, 'but I don't care. Nothing in the world matters except the fact that you *are* free and that I can ask you to marry me at once.'

She nodded dumbly, her cheek pressed against his cheek. Nothing was left of sorrow and of the black despair which had so often eaten into her very soul. The weeks of anguish, of frantic grieving for Neil had vanished, just as nightmares vanish when you wake up, she told herself. He was here beside her, safe and well. She was in his arms and they were going to be married. Could anything be more glorious?

'I've got a week's leave,' he said. 'With a special licence, my darling, we can be married at Mulverton Church the day after tomorrow. And then I'll take you down to

Cornwall. I know a little place there on the coast, with an island which will remind you just a bit of La Marita. Julie, my beloved, they're bombing London, they're threatening invasion, and we don't know what's in store for us. But it doesn't seem to matter tonight, does it?'

'Nothing, nothing matters but you and me,' she agreed ardently.

He smoothed a strand of the fair silky hair back from her forehead, and looked deeply into her eyes.

'Are you quite well again? You've been very ill, Maurice told me.'

'But I'm not any more, my darleeng. I'm well and strong. It was just when you were reported missing after that raid ... it broke my heart. I believe now that people can die of a broken heart, Neel. Only I tried to get better and to be brave because I knew you would want me to.'

'Oh, my little darling!' he said, and covered her face with kisses.

'It is such a miracle that you are back,' she whispered; 'when I thought you were dead, my life seemed to end too. It was terrible.'

'Don't think about it any more.'

'When I heard your voice on the wireless last night, I nearly died of happiness...' she smiled up at him, 'it was so thrilling, listening to you and hearing of your experiences.'

'It wasn't a thrill for me,' he laughed. 'I

was scared to death of that broadcast. But they wouldn't give me any peace till I'd made it.'

'You did well! So very well! And we are all proud of your decoration.'

'And what about my promotion?'

'Have you really been promoted?'

'To Squadron-Leader, darling. Do you like the sound of it?'

'Oh, I like the sound of anything you say,' she exclaimed, and clung tightly to him, both her arms around him.

He looked out of the window.

'I can just see the house through the trees. The moon is coming out. We're nearly home.'

'It is indeed home, now that you are back,' said Julie.

'Can you imagine what it means to me?'

She gave a breathless sigh.

'What a night this one will be! Maurice will bring Pat back for dinner from the hospital, and there will be a special celebration for your return. We will all be so happy.'

'And then, my darling, it will be followed by the celebration of our wedding.'

'Oh, Neel.'

He took her hand, and carried it to his lips.

'I found time between two raids in London to slip into a jeweller's shop and buy the ring for this little finger.'

'Oh, Neel!' she repeated.

'There wasn't time to have it inscribed,' he added, 'I wanted to have those words *"Tout pour toi"* put inside for you.'

'They are in my heart, darleeng. They've been written there ever since you said them to me.'

'I love you very much, my Julie. And this week will belong to us. Every day, every night of it. What happens afterwards is in the lap of the gods.'

She leaned her head against his shoulder.

'I know that.'

'We may have to separate. I can't always take you with me, but you'll know that every moment I'm free, will be spent with my wife. And one day when this war is over, we will go back as man and wife to La Marita. It's my firm belief that that day will come, and perhaps not as far ahead as we think.'

'It will be another dream come true ... but I'm not going to think too much about it,' she whispered. 'I'm going to be thankful for *this* moment and ask for nothing more.'

A moment's silence. The car was climbing up the hill to the house. Julie, in the circle of Neil's arm, considered to herself the amazing change in her fortunes. How many times had she come up this same hill, either walking, or in *Marraine's* car, during the past few days, believing that she would never see Neil again. How utterly dead she, herself, had felt then, living in a nightmare which she thought would never end. But tonight she was with *him* and soon, very soon, she would be his wife. Whatever she had to face in the future she would be *his,* and these few days together would be an immortal memory which nothing could destroy.

Tenderly, regretfully, she thought of her father in Provence, her dear country which seemed so tragically far away. She would have given much to be able to speak to him tonight, to have him here with her now in this great moment of her life; to tell him of her coming marriage with the young Englishman whom he had always liked so much.

She pictured Papa at this hour in their villa. Hortense would have lit a little wood fire in the *salon.* Perhaps he would be sitting there with one of his friends, or alone, reading his paper. A paper issued under German authority, alas! But he would know that everything in it was a tissue of lies. He would believe that she was in safe hands in England.

Neil pressed the palm of her hand against his lips.

'Are you going to sing to me tonight, my little darling?'

'If you want me to.'

'I do. I want to hear this…' he whistled the first two bars of a tune which drew a long sigh from her:

'"*Parlez-moi d'amour*…"' she murmured.

'Yes, indeed I could "speak to you of love" all night, my darleeng. I shall not want to go to bed. I shall just want to sit and look, and look at you in order to reassure myself that you are really here.'

He laughed and kissed her hand again.

'I'm here all right. I promise I won't fade away into nothingness.' Then he added: 'Shall I show you something which was in my tunic pocket when I was shot down, and which has never left me?'

He handed her a small snapshot. She lifted it up to the window of the car so that she could see it. Very faded was that picture and stained with salt water, but it was clearly herself, in the gardens of Villa Vertige, with the two pigeons on her shoulders, pecking at her cheeks.

She gave a little cry.

'Oh, my darling Co-co and Ton-ton!'

'Yes, that was always my favourite picture of you, Julie. So adorable! I think one of my wedding presents will have to be a pair of tame pigeons to take the place of poor Co-co and Ton-ton.'

She handed him back the snapshot.

'I do love you so,' she said irrelevantly.

Their lips met again with a passionate urgency, as the big car drew up outside Mulverton Court. The lovely old house, in spite of its darkened shutters and that air of mystery which seems to wrap around all houses

349

which are blacked out from the enemy, had also a welcome waiting for the lovers.

Inside, they knew there would be lights, and a big log fire, Alice Hanley's exquisite flowers, and many friendly faces waiting to greet them.

Neil was the first to get out of the car. Andrews waited at a respectful distance to take the suit-case.

Neil opened his arms and Julie stepped into them. He picked her right up, crushing the roses on her breast. He paused an instant holding her like that.

She caught a brief glimpse of the first bright evening star in the western sky and of the deep content in Neil's eyes as he carried her into the house.

The publishers hope that this book has given you enjoyable reading. Large Print Books are especially designed to be as easy to see and hold as possible. If you wish a complete list of our books please ask at your local library or write directly to:

Dales Large Print Books
Magna House, Long Preston,
Skipton, North Yorkshire.
BD23 4ND

This Large Print Book, for people
who cannot read normal print,
is published under the auspices of

THE ULVERSCROFT FOUNDATION

... we hope you have enjoyed this book.
Please think for a moment about those
who have worse eyesight than you ...
and are unable to even read or enjoy
Large Print without great difficulty.

You can help them by sending a
donation, large or small, to:

**The Ulverscroft Foundation,
1, The Green, Bradgate Road,
Anstey, Leicestershire, LE7 7FU,
England.**
or request a copy of our brochure for
more details.

The Foundation will use all donations
to assist those people who are visually
impaired and need special attention
with medical research, diagnosis
and treatment.

Thank you very much for your help.